A
LIFE'S AMBITION

BEING THE ADVENTURES AND
TRIBULATIONS OF AN ACTOR

AND

MY ODYSSEY

BY

ALEXANDRE DUMAS

A First Translation into English.

With an Introduction

BY

R. S. GARNETT

PHILADELPHIA
DAVID McKAY COMPANY

PRINTED IN GREAT BRITAIN BY
WILLIAM CLOWES AND SONS, LIMITED, LONDON AND BECCLES.

CONTENTS

CONTENTS

MY ODYSSEY

EDITOR'S INTRODUCTION

ONE of the most beautifully produced French modern books known to me is the edition of

UNE VIE D'ARTISTE

which Calmann-Lévy published in 1902 with exquisite illustrations in colour by Gaston Mélingue. The book, however, contains not a word beyond the original text. The reader is left to conjecture whether it had been printed before or not, and to guess as to the relationship between Gaston Mélingue and the celebrated " Artiste " of that name whose life Dumas narrates. I must suppose that neither publishers nor illustrator knew the circumstances in which the author wrote and published the book in 1854, for had they known it is impossible to believe that they would have refrained from recording them.

Let me do what I can for English readers, after stating that Gaston was the second son of the famous actor.

" You are going to publish a paper ? "

" Yes."

" A literary or a political one ? "

" Literary."

" Ah ! "

" What ? "

" It won't do."

" That is what they always say to me when I undertake anything."

" But it does not prevent you from going on nevertheless ? "

" Certainly not."

" And do the results never make you repent ? "

" Sometimes, when I have done good."

" And when you have done harm ? "

" I have never done any consciously."

" And what will your paper be called ? "

" *Le Mousquetaire.*"

" It won't do."

" Why not ? "

" It is a provocative title."

" It is essentially a French title ; it has become popular owing to the success, whether deserved or not, of a modern romance ; at any rate, it is the title I have chosen ; and you come too late for it to be changed."

" But why are you founding a paper ? "

" For several reasons."

" What are they ? "

" First, because I am tired of being attacked by my enemies and badly defended by my friends in other papers ; also because I have still forty or fifty volumes of my Memoirs to publish ; and because as these volumes become more and more compromising as they approach the present day, I wish to take the responsibility not only as author but as publisher."

" You are continuing your Memoirs ? "

" Yes."

" It won't do."

" And why not ? "

" Because they reveal all sorts of things which you would do better to leave in obscurity."

" To my mind nothing should remain in obscurity, the good should emerge from the shade to be praised or applauded ; the bad should be dragged into daylight to be blamed and hated."

" But in your Memoirs you not merely attack events but men."

" Men are the fathers of events, and fathers have to answer for their children."

" You will find yourself attacked on all sides."

" We call ourselves d'Artagnan, and our friends are Athos, Porthos, and Aramis."

Such are the opening sentences of the characteristic

dialogue headed " Artistic Programme between Alexandre Dumas and the first comer," which on Saturday the 12th November, 1853, challenged the eye on the first page of the specimen number of

LE MOUSQUETAIRE

JOURNAL DE M. ALEXANDRE DUMAS.

Paris welcomed that number warmly. Paris was glum, Paris was moody, Paris was still quivering from the bloody scenes enacted in her streets following the *coup d'état* of 2nd December, 1851. A new daily paper conducted by the most popular of her men of letters—was it not a hopeful sign ? Though Lamartine was silent, Hugo exiled, Michelet dismissed from his post, Sue interned somewhere, here was Dumas returned from Brussels and without a sou in his pocket but as lively as ever. A queue of subscribers speedily lined up at the bureaux of *Le Mousquetaire* at the Maison d'Or in the rue Laffitte, and Dumas' friends of the pen streamed along to enlist under his banner. Very soon the new paper had a considerable following and every prospect of making a big hit. The following letter was received from Lamartine, and, of course, printed at the top of the first page.

"Saint-Point.
" 20 December, 1853.

" MY DEAR DUMAS,
" You have heard that I am your subscriber and you ask my opinion of your journal.
" I have one on things human ;
" I have none on *miracles.*
" You are superhuman. My opinion of you is a mark of exclamation !
" Some men have tried to solve the problem of Perpetual Motion ; you have done better.
" You have created *perpetual astonishment.*
" Adieu, live that is to say write. I am here to read.
" LAMARTINE."

Next came this letter :

"Piémont-Nervi, near Genoa.
"26 December, 1853.

"VERY DEAR FRIEND,
      "I arrived here in a very weak condition, and
for a moment I thought that my poor remains would
have to be interred among the orange trees of Nervi.
The place is attractive.   Imagine a marble circle
one hundred and twenty-five miles in circumference
from Nice to Spezzia.   Genoa is placed in the centre.
It is on this shore that Byron burnt *à l'antique* the
body of poor Shelley, the author of *Queen Mab*, in
pursuance of his last wishes.   The atmosphere bright
and bracing, the soil somewhat barren, the sea transparent, lifeless, without fish, upon a bed of marble
all seems ready and disposed greedily to absorb life,
or to favour transformations.

      "Well, I resist these seductions and I live.   I live
on air and light.   Latterly nothing else, except I have
a glass of milk every day.   Yesterday only I lapsed
from the noble and spiritual existence.   Shall I tell
you ?   I eat !   I fall again.

      "What was I doing during that dreamy condition
in which I existed so lately—the result of my abstinence
—in this air so new to me, in this climate so different
from ours ?   Before this vast sea the real ' dead sea '
of Homer, I lost myself in my thoughts : the Infinite,
Nature, the Future !

      "All this was sharply interrupted by the thought of
France, of friendships left there, left for ever as I
sometimes believed.   I should have been very sorry,
believe me, and should never have ceased to regret
not knowing what had become of your great undertaking, your perilous enterprise.   Oh ! yes, perilous
in these days.   I am with you in spirit at your battles
of every kind ; and if I am impressed by your indomit-
able talent, bending under so many absurd necessities,
I am no less impressed by your heroic perseverance.

"My dear Alexandre, I shake your hand and love you sincerely.

"MICHELET."

And then this letter :

" Jersey.
"1st January, 1854.

"DEAR DUMAS,

" I read your paper.

" You restore us Voltaire.

" Supreme consolation for gagged and humiliated France.

" *Vale et me aima.*

"VICTOR HUGO."

To print this last letter would be to publish the last number of that journal ; for the Emperor Louis Napoleon (Dumas called him *le sacré Hollandais*) would have instantly suppressed it. So sorely against his will Dumas showed it only to his intimate friends, who were vastly impressed.

Gagged France, as things were, fully expected *Le Mousquetaire* any day to share the fate of a hundred other journals which had offended. In the meantime, it was good to read every day an instalment of Dumas' Memoirs, some twenty volumes of which only had appeared in *La Presse*. The Memoirs ! what a feast of good things was served up in them ! They had every fault as " *MES Mémoires*," for they were, in fact, the history of everybody whom Dumas had met or heard of and cared to write about, but it was impossible to put an instalment down unfinished. What wit ! What vivacity ! What crowds of thrilling incidents ! What enthusiasm for the author's epoch, for his rivals in art, and for himself ! Forty or fifty further volumes seemed all too few for such a writer. *Le sacré Hollandais*' fingers may have itched to release the knife of the guillotine ; if so, Dumas' lucky star saved his crowing infant *Le Mousquetaire ;* or perhaps the military Emperor had a kindness for Athos, Porthos, Aramis, and d'Artagnan—soldiers all.

The Memoirs then being in full career, with accounts

of suppers with Georges the great actress, of unsuspected revelations about Chateaubriand and Béranger, Meyerbeer, Véron, Horace Vernet, Delacroix, Grandville, the Johannots, of the ball given by the author which was talked of in Paris more than twenty years after—and one must turn to those chapters to gain a just idea of their charm—in the midst, I say, of the great success of his Memoirs Dumas one day began a new chapter of them in the following words :

" Towards this period—permit me not to give a precise date to the visit I am going to narrate for I fear to commit an error of some days and perhaps of some months. Towards this period, my servant entered my room, and as it was still early delivered himself of these portentous words : . . . "

And the public read, still under the title " Mémoires de M. Alexandre Dumas," the history of M. Gustave—otherwise Mélingue—which I, in my turn, am printing in the present volume.

No, gentle reader, Dumas is not indulging in a mystification to relate a chapter of his own experience that he was unwilling publicly to own. So marvellous is the vivacity and truth of the narrative that it is necessary to warn you, for surely, one thinks as one reads, this cannot be a second-hand story ; these are the very words of impetuous youth chafing against the narrow life of a provincial town, and of one who has trudged these weary miles with an empty pocket and himself found a lodging in the ruined cellar of an empty house. But no, I assure you ; Dumas' life, with all its adventures, never included these particular ones. It was only in spirit that he shared Étienne's boyhood under the loving but stern father who had forgotten how to smile ; and wandered with old Dumanoir's band of strolling actors from town to town. But how completely he had identified himself with his hero ! Stage-struck youth, and the trials of the obscure, unbefriended actor, are preserved for all time, fresh and vivid as life, in this little work.

And yet it was only a stop-gap thrown off without premeditation to fill the daily ravening maw of the *Mousquetaire*, each number of which contained seventy thousand letters. Nothing gives one such an idea of the marvellous talent of Dumas as the spirit, the power, the charm of his lesser works. It is possible to debate over his romances and dramas their exact places in the Valhalla of Art ; but no man of taste could possibly take up such a work as this without feeling it to be a little gem, perfect of its kind ; the colour bright, delicate, fresh ; the feeling deep and tender ; the incidents true to life, vivid, and moving ; the whole sparkling with wit and with that much deeper charm, humour.* Such was the work Dumas threw off when he was at a loss for a subject !

How was it done ? Is it possible that Dumas, as he avers in his first chapter, wrote the book from his recollection of a talk with Mélingue twenty years before ? Impossible ! Here is his explanation in the *Mousquetaire*, always under the same heading, "Mémoires de M. Alexandre Dumas" :

"Here we are again, dear readers, after a separation of more than two months ; for these Memoirs—permit me to tell you, if you have not yourselves perceived it, are nothing else than an immense and interminable chat.

"Well, this chat was interrupted, and we are continuing it.

"How was it interrupted ? I am going to tell you.

"I had reached the time in which I had made acquaintance with Mélingue. I knew that in his life there were episodes which would have made the author of the *Roman Comique* jealous.

"I wrote to him and asked him to call.

"Mélingue came ; we conversed : he had no very clear recollections of his life, and what he did recollect seemed to him unworthy of publicity.

"I had to convince him.

"At first we thought there was material enough for three or four numbers. It proved sufficient for forty or fifty.

"It made a 'hunch' on my Memoirs which I had to take out.

* Rather curiously, a book exists which if it were necessary to prove the truth of the general tenor of Dumas' narration would go far to do so. The comedian Bouffé, a contemporary of Mélingue, lived to write in his eightieth year his Souvenirs. Many having read it will say, "Bouffé and Mélingue might well have been twins, their adventures as comedians were so similar."

" It was my publisher's affair. Cadot will give you the ' hunch ' in two volumes."

Had Dumas when Mélingue—an unknown man—came to his door for assistance turned him empty away very possibly the French stage would have lost one of its great actors, and Dumas' countless admirers would have seen his *Tour de Nesle* without Mélingue as Buridan; *Les Mousquetaires* and *La Jeunesse des Mousquetaires* without Mélingue as d'Artagnan; *Monte-Cristo* without Mélingue in the title rôle; *La Dame de Monsoreau* without Mélingue as Chicot; and *La Reine Margot* without Mélingue as Henri de Navarre   But, indeed, there was not the slightest chance of such a disaster. Dumas was never known to neglect an opportunity of doing a kindness—it was one of his few luxuries.   Did a friend fall ill on the other side of Paris, he would arrive with his arms full of food, of linen, of anything he had or could get which he thought would be of use, and he would nurse that friend like a woman. But of obligations imposed on him by law he was neglectful, and if suspicion entered his soul *le bon Dumas* would disappear and give place to a volcano in eruption which it was dangerous to approach until the lava had cooled.

Naturally a man who responds to every appeal makes many mistakes, and Dumas made them every day if his major-domo at the Maison d'Or is to be believed.   In that establishment Dumas had rooms on the third floor to which the hubbub created in the office of the journal on the ground floor ascended in great volume. This he enjoyed, noise and movement being necessary to his existence.   At times, when all the members of the staff of the *Mousquetaire* seemed from the racket to be having a free fight, he would suspend his pen in the air for a moment with the remark :

" This newspaper office is a nest of serpents ! which is precisely the reason why they do not swallow one another ! "

Well, on one occasion when three of the said staff were leaving the office they met in the courtyard the major-domo, a small, elderly, meagre Italian named Rusconi. He was hurrying along apparently in great excitement.

" Well, Rusconi, what has happened ? what is the matter ? "

" I am distracted, completely distracted."

" How is that ? "

" It is another of M. A. Dumas' incredible follies. Not a day passes but he commits one."

" Tell us about this."

" Oh, I'll tell you. About half an hour ago appeared at the Maison d'Or a tall, pale, fair man, an utter stranger. He inquired at the office for M. Alexandre Dumas. Michel, who is only a gardener, did not recognize that this was a leech who wanted to suck our blood ; he stupidly said, ' To the right, on the third story.' The man rushed up, taking four steps at a stride as you may suppose.

" He rang ; I opened the door."

" ' Who are you ? '

" ' A German.'

" ' So much the worse for you.'

" ' My name is Egel.'

" ' What is that to me ? '

" ' I want to speak to M. Alexandre Dumas.'

" ' He is at work.'

" ' I have something very interesting to tell him.'

" ' So I suppose, but I tell you he is busy.'

" And I slammed the door. The man went and sat on the staircase. In five minutes he rang again. I jumped up.

" ' What—you again ! What do you want this time ? '

" ' I want to speak to M. Alexandre Dumas.'

" ' But I tell you again, he is at work.'

" ' Not on my account.'

" ' Not on your account ! I'm only too afraid it is on your account and that of a set of *tudesques* of your kidney.'

" I shut the door again. At the end of another five minutes another ring of the bell !

" ' *Nombril du pape*, you again ? '

" ' Yes, again ! I want to speak to M. Alexandre Dumas.'

" ' Must I expire in telling you that he is working ? '

" I was mistaken, gentlemen ; he had left off working. He was coming to us, pen in hand, and saying :

" ' Rusconi, let this poor man come in.'

" This *poor man*, this infernal German, saw his chance in a flash, the wily fox, he paid a thousand compliments to Alexandre Dumas, said to him in a tearful voice :

" 'Monsieur Dumas, I have not enough to pay for my lodgings.'

" 'Neither have I,' answered M. Dumas.

" 'Monsieur Dumas, I am to be turned out of doors to-night.'

" 'What do you want me to do for you ? '

" 'Monsieur Dumas, if you do not help me, a strolling artist, a musician with a future, and the greatest admirer of your works, I shall have to throw myself into the Seine this very night.' "

Dumas never in his life found an answer to this argument. He went at once to his desk, and gave all the money he found in it—fifty francs—to the German.

" He gave all he had," repeated Rusconi. " I would have willingly offered him ' something else,' " and he made an expressive gesture.

The journalists laughed.

" Do not laugh, gentlemen," went on the distressed major-domo. " There's another side to the picture. The German departed with the fifty francs—God knows what he will do with them—and night closes in. M. Alexandre Dumas calls me.

" ' Rusconi, get my dinner ! '

" 'Your dinner, Monsieur Alexandre père! Get it, but how ? '

" I had two francs. Here they are, gentlemen, and it is with them that I am hurrying to buy eggs, parsley, and butter for M. Dumas to make an omelette ; you know that he is the best cook in the world. But it is too bad when one had fifty francs to be obliged to dine two on an omelette ; it is a hard case for any one like me who has been with Napoleon Bonaparte, the Duchesse de Berry and is the major-domo of the great writer who has earned three millions with his pen. Ah ! those Germans ! "

I think it is Medwin who records a conversation with Byron in which the poet makes it clear why he never staged one of his plays—he dreaded the endless *tracasseries* of the theatre. Now the theatre was to Dumas what the ocean is to a whale, it was as his natural element. His first, boyish, dramatic attempt was to make a melodrama of " Ivanhoe," and he produced nothing of importance until he was twenty-four, when an English company came to Paris, and he saw *Hamlet, Romeo and Juliet,* and *Othello* capably played. He says that he then " saw light " and was strengthened by the confidence which never afterwards failed him. During the forty years following scarce a day can have passed without there being question of one or other of his plays. Dumas, and more Dumas, and again more Dumas! To-day, his creations are reappearing : the *Mousquetaires* in opera ; *Chicot, Monte-Cristo,* and *Kean* at the cinema. What is the secret of this ever-green popularity ?

The secret is not undiscoverable, and may be looked for in " Ma Odyssey à la Comédie Française,"* the first translation of which into English I offer in this volume, so that as it contains the life and adventures of an actor, it may give also the experiences of a dramatic author.

Successful as is Dumas when relating the adventures of others, it must be admitted that he is at his very best when those in which he had a share are in question. In France, his " Odyssey " is celebrated for its revelations about himself and certain of his plays, for its portraits of so many actors and actresses, and for its curious information about the Comédie Française green-rooms. French critics recognize in particular that Dumas' portrait of the great Mars— that " autocrat in petticoats " as some one has described her—is perfect. But, indeed, the whole " Odyssey " is a marvellous record. " How was it made ? "

R. S. GARNETT.

---

* " Souvenirs Dramatiques," par Alexandre Dumas. 2 vols. Paris, 1868.

A LIFE'S AMBITION

CHAPTER I

WHICH INTRODUCES OUR HERO

ONE October day in the year 1832 my servant came into my room and, as it was still very early, made use of these portentous words :

" Are you at home, sir ? "

I looked at him.

" Well, that depends," I replied.

" That's what I said to myself, sir."

" Who is it ? "

" He's very good-looking, sir."

"Well, that's something. I like handsome faces about me. But it isn't enough."

" That's what I said to myself, sir."

This phrase, " That's what I said to myself, sir," was a characteristic saying of my new servant. I had lately engaged him and his name was Louis.

" If you said that to yourself, Louis, I suppose you asked him his name ? "

" Yes, sir. Certainly, sir."

" And what is his name ? "

" He hasn't got a name, sir."

" He hasn't got a name ? "

" Well, sir, it isn't what you'd call a NAME. M. Gustave—— "

" M. Gustave what ? "

" That's what I said to myself, sir."

" It would have been wiser to say it to him than to say it to yourself."

" I said it to him too. Oh, I didn't make any bones about it."

" And what did he reply ? "

" He said : ' Tell M. Dumas that I've come from Rouen and that I bring a letter from Mme. Dorval.' "

" A letter from Dorval ? You fool, why didn't you tell me that before ? "

With this I ran to the door.

" Pray forgive me, sir," I cried to the visitor standing in the hall, " but I've a new servant and he doesn't yet know the names of my old friends. I hope you'll be one of them one day since you bring a letter of introduction from dear Mme. Dorval."

I held out my hand to the young man whom I could now faintly distinguish in the half light.

The young man seized my hand and pressed it cordially.

" I must confess, sir," said he, " that, kind as your welcome is, I am not surprised at it. Mme. Dorval told me you would receive me as you have."

" Is she still at Rouen ? "

" Yes."

" Is she making money ? "

" She has had quite a success."

" That isn't exactly what I asked you."

" These aren't good times for the theatrical world."

" Anyway, you are her friend. Has she written to me ?

" Here is her letter."

The young man handed me a letter which he did not hold between his finger and thumb as a clerk or a shopman would have done, but between his first and second fingers.

When I see a man for the first time I keep my eyes open and the least thing attracts my notice.

The hand which offered me the letter was well-shaped, refined, and tapering ; the thumb was a little long, which is always a sign of an artistic temperament ; the phalanges were delicate, which indicates distinction in artistic achievement.

The hand came from the folds of a cloak which fell about its wearer with the gracious lines of drapery on a statue.

The young man had not left his cloak in the lobby ; beneath his careless demeanour he was evidently timid ;

uncertain of himself, with little self-importance, since, in
spite of his letter of introduction from Mme. Dorval, he
did not expect to stay more than a few moments.

He saw that I was looking at him, and, with a little
movement of his shoulder, he readjusted two folds of his
cloak that had become disturbed.

This young man seemed to me like a living statue.
Whilst he was kept waiting in the lobby he had rolled a
cigarette between his fingers ; he held this cigarette as
one would hold a pencil.

Since it seemed to offer the best chance of finding out
his profession, I opened the letter and read it. I need
not say that as I read, I glanced over the top of the page.

This is what Dorval wrote :

" MY DEAR DUMAS,
          " I am sending M. Gustave to you. He has been
playing with me here, in Rouen. . . . "

So he was an actor, or I should say a tragedian, since
he stood there posed and draped, as if modelled on a
statue. And yet I felt about this youth an atmosphere
rather mediæval than antique. He belonged more to the
century of Leo X. than to that of Pericles.

I went on reading the letter :

" He is, as you will see, a good leading man, as in-
experienced as he is zealous, obviously cut out for the
Porte Saint-Martin. . . . "

He was, indeed, a fine cavalier as the word would have
been understood in the time of Louis XIII., with his long
hair, his magnificent eyes, his straight nose, his well-pro-
portioned figure. His hair was black and thick and his
complexion a clear ivory. The only fault of his very
handsome face was, perhaps, the too marked line of his
lower jaw ; but this defect was hidden by a fine black
beard, shot with chestnut lights, such as you see in the
beards painted by Titian. Moreover he was tall, carrying
his head with pride, and visibly lissome and athletic.

As I looked at him, I noticed in his hand a wide-brimmed
felt hat, and as I glanced from his felt hat to his face and
from his face to his carriage, I was conscious of surprise

at not seeing the hilt of a sword emerging from the elegant folds of his cloak.

"Whatever you may do for him, I believe he will repay you some day by playing the leading parts in your plays as no one has ever played them before."

"The devil!" said I to myself. "It's true that with that face and that carriage if he has a grain of talent he ought to go far!"

"At any rate have a talk with him. Get him to tell you his life and you will see that you have to do with a true artist.

"Your affectionate friend,
"MARIE DORVAL.

"P.S.—If there is no vacancy for him at the moment at the Porte Saint-Martin, do try to be of service to him by getting him work as a sculptor or painter."

"Why, M. Gustave," said I, laughing, "you are an artist of all trades!"

"I have tried my hand at pretty well everything," replied he, with that movement of the shoulders characteristic of a man accustomed to look on life with a certain degree of philosophy; as if it were, in fact, something in the nature of a dance on the tight-rope.

"You've been a mountebank?"

"Why not? Kean was a mountebank."

"Have you seen Kean?"

"Unfortunately, no; but, God willing, I'll see him one day. The Channel isn't as wide as the Atlantic nor London as far as Guadeloupe."

"You've been to the Antilles?"

"I've just come from there."

"I am beginning to think that Dorval was right when she advised me to beg you to tell me the story of your life."

"Oh, it isn't very interesting. Any Bohemian could tell you as much as I."

"Please don't make any mistake. I should have no desire to hear the life of 'any Bohemian' as told by himself!"

" But it would take so long ! "

" Are you due at rehearsal at eleven, for a quarter past ? " asked I, laughing.

" Unfortunately, no."

" Well, then, we've both time. We'll breakfast to-gether, and after breakfast you shall tell me all about it. I can't give you as good coffee as you must have got in Martinique ; but I'll give you better tea than you can get anywhere, tea which is sent me specially from St. Peters-burg, by a pretty woman. If you go to Russia, I'll intro-duce you to her, as Dorval has introduced you to me. That's settled then. We breakfast together, don't we ? "

" Oh, I'm agreeable ! "

I rang for Louis.

He came.

" Lay for two, please, Louis. M. Gustave will break-fast with me."

" That's what I said to myself, sir, that M. Gustave would breakfast with you."

" All the better. Then I suppose you have laid the table and put plenty to eat on it."

" Oh no, sir. I should never take a liberty like that."

" Then you were ill-advised. Hurry up, Louis. I've a rehearsal this morning."

Louis left the room.

" Wouldn't it be as well," said the young man, " if I got some of it over before breakfast ? "

" By all means."

" Am I to tell you everything ? "

" Everything."

" Even the silly things ? "

" The silly things above all ! What most people call folly I am apt to think picturesque."

" Well, that is the sort of thing I meant."

The story I am now about to tell was told to me twenty years ago ; do not be surprised, dear reader, if I substitute myself for the narrator and write " he " instead of " I."

Since that morning M. Gustave has become one of the most distinguished of Parisian actors. I hope, therefore, that the following story will not be without interest for you.

CHAPTER II

M. GUSTAVE—HIS STAGE NAME—HIS TRUE NAME—HIS
BIRTH, HIS MOTHER AND FATHER AND EARLY YOUTH

M. GUSTAVE only called himself Gustave to his fellow men.
It was his stage name.   His real name was Étienne
Marin Mélingue.

He was born at Caen, rue des Carmes, 1808 ; therefore
in 1832, when I first made his acquaintance, he was between
twenty-four and twenty-five years old.   The reader already
knows what he was like in appearance and there is no
need for me to paint his portrait again.

When he looked back into his memory, he first saw
himself in the arms of a good sort of woman, with his little
brother Adolphe.   This good woman and the two children
were standing beside a bed of sickness and pain.   In that
bed was a dying woman, her eyes lit with the delirium of
fever, her teeth chattering, her lips white.   She was holding
a bunch of grapes out of reach of the group whom she did
not recognize, crying in a voice raucous and dry with fever :

" These are for my children ! These are for my
children ! "

A man in uniform resembling that of a soldier was seated
on a bench by the fire, his head in his hands.   That poor
woman was the mother of our little Étienne and his small
brother Adolphe ; the man was their father.

We will speak of the child by the name of Étienne until
he relinquishes it himself to take that of Gustave.   The
child had no other memory of his mother except this
night of agony as he recalled it dimly twenty years after ;
yet this memory haunted him so persistently that he said
he could have painted the scene even after a lapse of twenty
years and made a perfect likeness of his mother.   Nevertheless he remembered nothing else, neither the taking of
the Last Sacrament nor the death nor the funeral ; either
because they had sent him away that he might not see
these piteous events or that his memory had proved too
weak to retain them, letting them slip as one's hand lets
slip water gathered from a brook, into the palm, and escap-
ing drop by drop through the crevices of the fingers.

His father, who was never called by his family name, but simply " Father," was at this time a man of about forty or forty-five ; he had volunteered in '92, been one of the soldiers of the " Camp de la lune " and played his part in our first victories. He had left the service in 1806, and married the young bride who died so prematurely ; he had two children by her, one of whom was destined to follow his mother without long delay, and the other is our hero. He was tall ; his voice resonant, his glance piercing and stern.   His hair was already white but his eyebrows and beard, jet black, showed that he was still in the prime of life. Never once did his children hear him laugh.

When he left the service he had obtained a post as customs-house officer with a salary of six hundred francs a year.   At this date, customs-house officers ranked as a kind of soldier ; they wore a green coat and three-cornered hat, with a sword at their side and a carbine on their shoulder, a brace of pistols in their waistbelt. They had to be ready for instant service, especially on the coast of Normandy, having to sally forth against corsairs and English smugglers, always trying to seize a chance of landing on our shores.

His service, which was a hard one—for he often had to be absent from home for a week or a fortnight or even a month at a time—this arduous service he scrupulously performed, whilst keeping up a perpetual chant.   Though he never smiled he was always singing.   It is true that the air he hummed, for one cannot really call it singing, was a terrible one ; an air which struck the chill of death into those who heard it at Valmy and Jemmapes.   It was the Marseillaise.

" Father " continued to sing the same song even after the Bourbons had succeeded to the throne, but by then people were so accustomed to hear him humming that particular air that no one took any notice.

After 1815, when peace was declared with England, the customs service became much less severe ; when he was not on duty he took care of his children himself, and no nurse or governess of high position ever gave more care to the children of a royal prince.   They were always dressed in uniform fashion ; in a costume that had a military style about it ; it consisted of jerseys with two rows of round buttons, similar to those of the Hussars, dark pantaloons, and sabots in the winter and white pantaloons and shoes in the summer.

But the sabots had a touch of coquetry that delighted the children, since it distinguished them from their comrades; the upper part of the front was covered with leather taken from the tops of old boots and polished with English wax. There is no need to say that the old grenadier made this wax himself, mixing it from ingredients known to him, beneficial to leather, helping to preserve and soften it.

Every year, at Eastertide, the children left off their old sabots and donned instead a pair of new shoes. These shoes had to last till the next winter.

But what care " Father " took of those tunics with their leather buttons, of the leather-covered sabots and of the shoes, new at Eastertide, and, though worn, yet still carefully polished when All Saints' Day came round! He rose each morning before daybreak; coats and pantaloons, sabots or shoes, he took them all out of the house; the shoes or sabots were polished, the pantaloons and coats well brushed and their buttons rubbed up with infinite patience. All these things shone in the rays of the rising sun. Then there were the children to wake and dress. Summer or winter they had to wash in cold water, and with their skins red with cold in winter or pearly white in summer, they put on the well-brushed garments.

And now it is time for us to pass from the master to the house.

That house is well worth special description.

CHAPTER III

The Paternal Home

The home consisted of one large room and a cupboard.

The room was warmed by a huge fireplace; the mantelpiece ornamented by a clock of papier-maché which had a large pendulum; on each side of it crouched two wooden lions with their eyes fixed on its face, their manes stiff

with curls and their tails ending in little tufts. They gave
forth an agreeable odour of resin. A little further off—
the clock being always strictly in the centre—stood two
brass candlesticks, shining as mirrors, and in these
candlesticks were two candles that the child only once
remembered to have seen alight ; we will explain under
what circumstances. The decoration of the mantelpiece
was finished off with a small bottle and a little china vase.

The fireirons and the dogs were of steel and shone
like " Father's " carbine and pistols. The fireguard was
an iron hoop that had once encompassed a wheel ; the
blacksmith had laid it on his forge and closed up the holes
with his hammer. He then polished it, but preserved its
circular shape so that it would stand up of itself.

A huge oak bedstead which one saw in the distance
as one stood on the threshold was outlined, with its green
curtains, against a wall which had never been papered but
roughly coloured with sand and lime. From time to time
a little shell, once an inhabitant of that now extinct world
from which the sand had come, caught the children's eyes,
and they amused themselves detaching it with the point
of a knife and crushing it against the wall. In the other
corner, parallel with this large bedstead, was the small
bed in which the children slept together. This was shorter
and narrower than the big bed.

A large and heavy mahogany table stood in the centre
of the room ; it was surrounded by chairs with straw seats,
the wooden frames being painted a greyish blue. There
were a dozen chairs arranged thus : three round the table
and seven along the walls, one in front of a desk at which
" Father " wrote his reports, and one near the fire, facing a
small wooden bench of the type usually known as a settle.
If these articles of furniture were disarranged for any cause
whatever, such as a visit, breakfast, or dinner, or even for
simple refreshment, the moment the cause of this dis-
arrangement was over the chairs were invariably put
back into their accustomed places and one might almost
say that, as in a fairy story, they returned to their places
of themselves.

Four black wooden frames, enclosing four engravings of
the Four Seasons, formed the artistic ornamentation of
the four walls. The military ornamentation consisted of

"Father's" carbine, pistols, and sword arranged crosswise, in a group. A large oak cupboard completed the furniture of the room.

After the mother's death—she died in 1811 or thereabouts—after her death, when their father was on duty at the coast, the house was shut up and the children sent to board with two maiden ladies who had a school at Caen ; they were known as Mlle. Meulan and Mlle. Poupinette.

But, as we have already said, "Father's" absences from home came to an end with the Empire. The Coasts of France managed to guard themselves after peace was declared, or at any rate, the ordinary coastguard sufficed, and so "Father's" periods of duty seldom exceeded twenty-four or forty-eight hours—or at most three days. During these times the children went every day to their school kept by the two old maids, but they were brought home every evening and went to bed in the big bed, which was quite an exciting event for them.

Their father often came home during the night ; but thanks to that deep slumber which is the recuperating gift of childhood, and thanks, too, to the care taken by the old soldier, with a mother's tenderness, not to awaken his little sons, they would not know that he had returned until they saw, next morning, the customs officer's muddy tunic lying on the ground. On the mahogany table would be lying his sword, carbine, and pistols, and in the children's little bed would be reposing the officer himself, his legs, too long by a foot and a half for the bedstead, would be resting on a chair, so that their father seemed to them bigger than ever by comparison with the bed. And then the children would rise, half dressed, and climbing down from the big oak bedstead noiselessly creep towards the little one and stare with their great round eyes at the tall republican, as astonished as Virgil's peasants at the giant bones that the ploughshare turned up in those fertile fields that had once been fields of battle.

Their father was a freethinker himself ; he called priests " old women " and the mysteries of religion he characterized as " tomfoolery." But he always attended military Mass and sent his children regularly to High Mass. The youngsters always managed to bring back a bit of the consecrated bread. Their father would then lay his pipe down

on the mahogany table or on the desk and take the consecrated bread delicately between the thumb and first
finger of his right hand. With his left hand he would then
lift his cap or hat and make the sign of the cross with the
consecrated bread, putting it in his mouth and swallowing
it with as little noise as possible. All this exactly to time
in military fashion.

But the children had now grown older and passed from
the care of the two old ladies into that of a retired sergeant,
who had started a school. He had married the daughter
of a professor and his father-in-law taught Latin and
French at this school whilst the son-in-law gave lessons in
geography and mathematics.

On those nights when their father was not on duty, both
he and his children went to bed at eight o'clock in winter
and nine in summer, and there they stayed till daybreak,
when the rising sun, as a rule, caused them all to open their
eyes. On the days—or we should say the nights—when
the father was keeping watch the children went off, just
before nightfall, to visit him at the guard-room which was
built on the river-bank. Then they were sent home to
bed, at ten o'clock, or sometimes at eleven, or even, if the
customs officers, their father's comrades, were amused by
the children's chatter, by special favour, at midnight ;
being given the key of the house on condition that they lit
neither fire nor candle. The youngsters took their leave
but under protest, being visibly reluctant to go ; they
wanted to remain in the guard-room and sleep on the camp
bedstead, but their request was always sternly refused.
Their father himself escorted them to the door and said,
" Off with you ! " The youngsters went without daring
to resist longer and their father shut the door behind
them.

Then they walked off, quietly at first, whispering together, and when the nights were dark and foggy they
searched the skies for a shadowy form which outlined itself
against the heavens. On moonlight nights they had no
need of a landmark, but when they did require one this
shape showed up either pale or as a dark mass, according
to whether it was against a clear or darkened sky, clean-
cut on the blue star-spangled vault above them. It was
the form of a high tower. Sometimes it seêmed as if the

two windows at its summit, lit up by the red light of a fire, were the two red eyes of an ogre !

The two children were compelled to pass by the foot of this tower. When they were only about twenty steps from the granite giant, which loomed up in the darkness with the majesty of rigid forms, they took each other's hands, and, without a word, in dead silence except for their rapid breathing, they ran as fast as they could till they reached their home. Not till then did they halt ; the one who held the key thrust it into the keyhole with a trembling hand ; the key turned grating against the bolt ; the door opened and the children ran in, the bravest of the two, that is to say the elder, stopping to shut the door. Then they undressed as rapidly as possible, flew into bed, whispered together for a moment ; but the whispering soon ceased and was followed by the deep breathing of two sleeping children, sweet and pure as that of two slumbering doves.

Now why did that tower hold such terror for the children ? What was there more terrifying about it than about any other building ? Why did those two children, who were not timid by nature, tremble so and run so fast when they had to pass by the foot of that turret ?

That is what we are going to hear.

It was because that tower was known as the Tower of the Amphitheatre ; in that tower all the medical students from the hospital at Caen were in the habit of assembling to dissect dead bodies ; and tradition would have it that these ardent disciples of science brought to their studies a ghoulish avidity. It was also said that evil men who profaned the cemeteries brought to them the bodies of dead men who had died from more aristocratic diseases than those that usually killed the poor people who went to the hospital.

Those two brilliant eyes glowing in the tower were lit by the lights that shone upon the work of the sawbones.

Those black croaking crows that, from morning to night, flew round the summit of the tower like a sinister whirlwind, what were they seeking up there ? What were they demanding with hoarse cries when they were kept waiting ? Morsels of human flesh, their abundant feast, which was served to them at the top of the tower so that they had no need to go elsewhere seeking food.

That is what terrified the children when they had to pass the foot of the tower ; that is why they turned so pale, that is why perspiration bedewed their foreheads so freely, especially when they happened to meet on their way some belated traveller carrying a burden ; for they took this traveller for a despoiler of the churchyard ! They thought his burden was a corpse !

Moreover a local ditty sung about the port—a ballad as grisly and foul as its subject—preserved the tradition and raised it to legendary rank. Here is the song :

> " At the Amphitheatre
> You'll find our jolly knackers,
> Whackers !
> They flay pretty ladies
> And fine gentlemen, by Bacchus,
> Crackers ! "

Even as their father hummed the Marseillaise from morning to night so this wretched doggerel sprang into the minds of his children with the light of the first stars. If they did not hum it, it kept ringing always in their thoughts.

However, the elder of the two had just reached the age of twelve and the younger was ten years old when he complained one evening of a violent pain in the head and went to bed earlier than usual. They thought this pain in the head was a trifling matter and of no consequence, and so took little notice of it. The next day Adolphe wanted to get up, and they let him have his way, but he could only remain up about an hour. At the end of that time he went back to bed, scarcely able to stand. Five minutes after his teeth began to chatter ; he was feverish. The following night he began singing the song of the Knackers. He was delirious. They sent for the doctor. The child had brain fever.

The care and attention of the man of science were in vain. It was too late. On the fifth day of the illness the doctor told the boy's father that there was no hope of saving the child.

Beneath this blow the poor father bowed his head : that head that he had never stooped before the hail of bullet. He brushed away a tear, the only one that Étienne had ever seen him shed. He then turned to the woman who had brought the two children to the deathbed of their mother, on that sad night when that mother, too, had died delirious.

" Fetch a priest," he said.

The woman left the house. A quarter of an hour afterwards the bell tolling Extreme Unction sounded through the street, the door of the big room opened and the children's little bed showed white in its black depths, lit as it was by the two candles from the chimneypiece, which were burning one at the head the other at the foot of the bed, standing each upon a chair in its great brass candlestick.

It was nine o'clock at night, the fever had left the child, who, however, seemed exhausted.

The priest came in followed by two choir boys carrying candles and by the beadle carrying the cross. Behind them walked those pious neighbours who were always ready to offer up their prayers at the bedside of the dying. The children's father uncapped when he saw the priest, the choir boys, and the beadle. He knelt down and made Étienne kneel by his side.

The holy ceremony was soon over ; the feet and forehead of the dying boy were anointed with the sacred oil ; then the priest went out again as he had entered, followed by the choir boys and by the dozen or fifteen faithful who had come with him to pray that the child might have a peaceful and painless passing from this world to the next.

The door closed behind the last of these assistants. The father and elder brother remained alone with the dying.

At last his father rose, put out the two candles, and kissed his child on the forehead ; he then turned to replace the candles in their accustomed positions on the mantelpiece. This done, he took his seat on the settle before the fire which now gave the only light in the room.

Little Étienne sat near his father.

The older man supported his elbows on his knees and buried his head in his hands ; his face was veiled as that of Timanthes' Agamemnon. His child, however, sat with his two hands spread out upon his knees.

The dancing flames from the fire lit up these two figures, immobile as statues, and then played tremblingly upon the wall behind them, but they did not carry far enough to dissipate the gloom that overshadowed the corner where stood the sick child's bed.

Silence reigned in that room where a double sorrow mourned.

Cold and solemn, this silence lasted for some moments. One could feel that death was near.

Suddenly, the funereal stillness was broken by the sound of a voice, soft, clear, and entreating, from the little bed.

"Father," cried the child with a note of unspeakable terror in his voice, "do the knackers of the Amphitheatre who flay pretty ladies and fine gentlemen cut up little children, like me?"

Étienne shivered and began to pray.

His father rose and, putting one hand to his throat as if to throw off the clutch of invisible fingers, he bent over the child's bed, saying:

"No, my dear boy, no. Don't be afraid. Besides, I will watch over you."

"Thanks, father," replied the child in his sweet clear voice.

These were the last words that Étienne heard his brother say.

Only an hour after, the death rattle sounded in the throat of the dying child.

"Go to your aunt's," said his father to Étienne, for he did not wish the boy to witness his brother's dying agony. The child obeyed in silence.

Luckily on his way to his aunt's it was not necessary to pass the foot of the tower. After what he had just heard his brother say he would rather have passed the night on the doorstep than encountered the granite giant with his red and flaming eyes. He reached his aunt's house at a run, and there he told all that had just happened.

His father, however, remained with the dying boy. God alone was witness of his agony.

The next day, about twelve o'clock, the aunt's door opened and the boy's father appeared on the threshold. He stood there, pale and silent. Gently he shut the door behind him and then, still in silence, took a seat in a corner of the room.

No one dared to speak to him or ask a question. Yet, a moment later, little Étienne turned to him.

" Father," said he, " how is my brother ? "

" Better," replied the old soldier, and the tone of his voice was indescribable.

The child was dead !

Next day the funeral was held in a little cemetery out on the countryside, which seemed to belong more to the environs of Caen than to the town itself. Few were present. Just the father and brother and the aunt and those three or four compassionate souls whose prayers belong to all who need them ; these and the customs officers, the father's comrades. The same priest, choir boys, and beadle who had appeared forty-eight hours before bringing Extreme Unction to the child, walked at the head of the mourners.

Every one knows how quickly prayers are said over the graves of the poor. The priest gabbled through those prayers, and with a sprinkler sprinkled a few drops of holy water over the bier, handed the sprinkler to one of the mourners, and went away again with his choir boys and his beadle. The mourners, standing along the entire length of the grave, passed the sprinkler to one another, each shaking it in turn.

In defiance of custom, the child's father was the last to leave the grave. Little Étienne wanted to stay with him ; but his father spoke a few words in a low voice to one of the customs officers and this man took the boy away with him.

In the cemetery there was no one now except the father and the gravedigger, one each side of the grave and the dead body in its coffin lying in its narrow trench.

The gravedigger was getting ready to throw the first spadeful of earth upon the coffin. The father stopped him.

" What is it now ? " asked the gravedigger.

" There is one last precaution to be taken," replied the father.

" What is that ? "

" Descend into the grave and lift the lid of the coffin."

" But, sir—— "

" Do as I say ! "

The gravedigger thought that the father bereaved now of both wife and son wished to see his dead boy once more.

He climbed down into the grave, lifted the lid of the

coffin and removed the shroud. The child was white as alabaster.

" And now," said the father, " open the child's breast with your knife."

The gravedigger, frightened, lifted his head.

" Do as I tell you," said the father, his voice growing more and more imperative.

The gravedigger obeyed. A long wound soon showed from the sternum to the navel.

" What now ? " asked the gravedigger.

" Now," said the father, taking a bottle from each of his pockets, "empty into the child's breast these two bottles of vitriol. I do not want the Resurrection men to steal my child's body to sell to the surgeons."

The gravedigger took the two bottles and emptied them into the child's body ; then, leaving the corrosive liquid to do its work of destruction, he reclosed the coffin and began to climb out of the grave.

But the father held the spade ready in his hand, and dismissing the gravedigger with a wave of his hand :

" That's my affair," said he.

And he filled in the trench, stamping the earth down after till it was as flat as the surrounding ground.

Then he went off without another word, his arms crossed and his head sunk on his breast.

For a whole month the customs officers of his brigade kept watch, each in turn, in the cemetery for fear the body-snatchers should come to steal the child's corpse to sell to the surgeons.

CHAPTER IV

LITTLE ÉTIENNE'S EDUCATION—THE DRAWING CLASS-
THE SCHOOL OF SCULPTURE—A FIRST PRIZE—PATERNAL
RECOMPENSE.—CIRCUS RIDERS AND MOUNTEBANKS

THOUGH his father uttered no complaint, though he did not even shed a tear or change the even tenor of his ways, yet his grief was so profound that little Étienne began to fancy that he might take his own life, and stuck close to his heels without a word, following him everywhere he went like a shadow, never leaving him. He did not know that a father will not take his own life when he still has a child who depends on him for his.

It was not till six weeks or two months had gone by that the child began to be a little reassured. Not that his father ever spoke of the absent. One would have said that he had never had but the one son, if, from time to time, he had not fixed his brooding eyes in grief upon the bed on which little Adolphe had drawn his last breath. Yet, little by little, the life of the household took again its accustomed train and little Étienne fancied that his father was beginning to forget because his own remembrance was becoming dulled.

By the following year grass had grown over the grave. And what eye but that of a mother or father knows what is beneath the grass of a grave ?

Étienne was now alone, it is true, but with solitude he developed a taste for reading. During the long winter evenings of 1821 and 1822 he stayed at home reading either those blue-covered stories that we all enjoy in our early youth or the books of travels that might be made quite interesting with only half the talent that their authors employ in making them tedious. These narratives of journeys to the four corners of the world it was that first gave him the idea of becoming a sailor ; but as the first condition which Nature imposes on sailors is that they shall be able to sail the sea without sickness, it was decided that Étienne had better accompany his father on the first voyage he took on the packet boat.

From the moment that the boat left the river till it returned again the future sailor never ceased to vomit.

His father, who would have been glad enough to see his son a sailor, would not accept defeat. They tried again ; but this second attempt was even more disastrous than the first one. That first time the child merely vomited bile, but the second time he vomited blood. This time they decided that some other choice must be made. But, unfortunately, it was difficult to think of anything else.

His father's stories, though concise ; the tales of distant

voyages related by M. Laharpe, though dull, had instilled into the child's brain an absolute passion for roaming. He proposed that he should become a soldier.

His father shook his head. He agreed that one might become a soldier when one's country was at war ; the only attractive feature of a soldier's life, according to him, was the risk of being killed ; but, in times of peace, the life of a soldier was deplorable.

There was one profession that had for the child a fascination greater even than that of sailor or soldier ; it was that of a mountebank. Alas, we must confess that when Étienne was fourteen years old, his sole ambition was to beat a drum at the door of a booth, dressed in a suit of scarlet, or dance the tight rope and turn " cartwheels " inside. The position of circus rider tempted him greatly. It was entrancing to stand upright on the bare back of your steed, throwing kisses to the ladies, or to leap through paper hoops, returning gracefully to your saddle on your knees. But, more than anything else, the boy would have loved to be an actor in a real theatre. This ambition, however, seemed to him altogether beyond the reach of man.

It need scarcely be said that he did not think well to breathe these secret desires to his father. Besides, our hero had already commenced a sort of career for which he certainly felt no repugnance, though it halted in his judgment far behind that of mountebank, circus rider, or actor. He had begun to study drawing at the drawing school in town.

And this is what had put into his father's head the idea of sending his son to this school.

The year following the death of little Adolphe they had gone to spend the summer in some barracks on the bank of the river. The lieutenant of this excise station had a large snuffbox on the cover of which was a small lithograph of " The Soldier of Waterloo." Every one of my age will remember to have seen at every picture shop during the years from 1820 to 1825, a lithograph of a grenadier holding his banner against his breast and defending with outstretched sword a wounded comrade who clung to him with both arms. That was the picture called " The Soldier of Waterloo."

The lieutenant was quite proud of having a repro-
duction of this picture on his snuffbox.

Little Étienne already drew so well, either with pencil
or pen, that he succeeded in achieving something which
resembled a copy of " The Soldier of Waterloo."

" You ought to send that boy of yours to the drawing
school in town," said the lieutenant ; " he has talent ! "

And, when they returned to the house in the rue des
Carmes, the boy's father followed this advice. Yet, in spite
of the lieutenant's prophecy and in spite of the student's
good will, he made but little progress. He bent for hours
at a time over noses, ears, and eyes many times larger
than nature ; and his noses were always the most hooked,
his ears the most deformed, his eyes the most squinting of
the whole class.

The children worked in the evenings, for they must
not be taken from the studies which they pursued during
the daytime ; they were seated in two long lines, and
light was thrown on their work from two double-branched
lamps, hung over their heads. Besides this, each had a
candle with its flame shielded by a shade, similar to that
used on the orange stalls in the street. After half an hour
had been spent in blackening their paper with their pencils
and rubbing it white again with bread crumb, the professor
would enter the room. His name was Elouis. He would
come in with great dignity, candlestick in hand, spectacles
on nose, and stop at each pupil's desk, criticizing his work
aloud. But for poor Étienne, whose hands were always
the dirtiest and his paper the most greasy, he had only
three exclamations, always the same, ascending the scale
from grief to absolute despair.

" Oh, sir ! Oh, sir ! ! Oh, sir ! ! ! "

And he passed on.

These three remarks were scarcely encouraging to the
pupil ; nevertheless he stayed in the drawing class till
the end of the year.

To make use of his daytime and to teach him a profession, he had been sent to a wood-carver. This man
used to make for the furniture dealers those large wooden
cupboards, with wings, which the Norman shopkeepers
and better class of peasant give to their children when they
marry as tokens of affection and union.

Our boy took a fancy to carving. The result was that
as there were two courses, one of drawing and the other
of sculpture, Étienne, on New Year's Day, passed from the
drawing class to that of sculpture.

This sculpture class had for instructor an Italian, a
man of from forty to forty-five years of age, good-looking,
and, above all, full of the dignity of his art. He held his
head high, from time to time shaking his magnificent locks.
There was something grand and poetic in his manhood,
as in that of François Arago. He was sculptor, black-and-
white artist, architect and composer at one and the same
time. His name was Odelli. He had come to Caen to
build a chapel to the Virgin in the Church of St. Peter.
The chapel finished, the municipal council had suggested
that he should remain at Caen as Professor of Sculpture
and Architecture in the Municipal Schools. He accepted.
M. Odelli, therefore, was teacher to the class for sculpture
even as M. Elouis was teacher to the drawing class. The
two classrooms, indeed, were parallel to one another.

On the 1st of October, 1823, little Étienne made his
first appearance at M. Odelli's class.

" Where have you come from ? " asked the professor.

" From home, sir."

The Italian smiled.

" I wasn't asking that. I wanted to know if you had
studied elsewhere."

" I belonged to M. Elouis's drawing class for eight
months."

" Come with me."

The Italian took him to a cupboard where the models
were hanging up, and giving him an engraving of a fragment
of the capital of an antique pillar :

" Do you think you can copy that ? " he asked.

" Yes, sir," the child replied, resolutely.

" Then come to-morrow and take your place here."

And the professor showed the child his table and chair.
No doubt he wished his new pupil to work in solitude,
so that as no one was by to help him with pencil or advice
he could better judge the value of his composition.

On the next day little Étienne arrived before the stated
time ; but, once face to face with the drawing, once actually
at grips with its difficulty, he felt the perspiration stand

on his forehead ; he was utterly unable to do the work. Luckily, he was alone. As he could not copy the design, he took a tracing of it. He had scarcely finished this and was occupied in putting in some shading when he heard the door open and shut. He dared not turn his head. A step approached him. He remained immovable.

A hand rested on his shoulder. He sat waiting.

" That's very good, my boy," said the voice of M. Odelli ; " you have caught the feeling exactly. Come with me and I'll give you something else."

Then at last the boy began to breathe again.

From this time onwards, M. Odelli gave particular attention to Étienne, and in spite of his frequent lapses, in spite of his visits to the circus when the Fair was held at Easter-time, he was in the running for the first prize.

The distribution of prizes for drawing and sculpture in a large provincial town is an important ceremony. The mayor and municipal council attend and there is a band and the beating of the big drum. His father was there too.

They called for Étienne.

He advanced, almost ready to cry, for all this solemn ceremony seemed to affect the beating of his heart. The mayor proclaimed him winner of the first prize and embraced him ; every one applauded ; the band played " See the Conquering Hero Comes," and the drums rolled.

The boy returned to his home with his laurel branch in one hand and his silver medal in the other, walking beside his father. Suddenly his father stopped, and cried :

" Why, I forgot to thank M. Odelli ! "

" Oh, father ! So you did ! "

" Go on home and wait for me."

The boy continued on his way to the rue des Carmes and his father went back to the Town Hall.

His father's sudden thought was one of evil consequences for Étienne. M. Odelli was grateful for the courteous intention but he confessed frankly to Étienne's father that his son had only received the first prize because none of the other students were any better than he was, and he added :

" If the little wretch would only work ! "

" What ! " cried the father ; " doesn't he work ? "

" Oh, he works ; yes, in a way !   Every one has to work here ; but he might work harder ! "

" Then what does he do ? "

" Ah !   Ask the circus riders and mountebanks in the booths on the common for whom he is always designing costumes."

" So that's it, is it ?   I've been told something of that before.   Well, he shall pay for it ! "

" But surely, sir—not to-day . . . "

" Oh, one day's as good as another.   Luckily, I know where to find him.   Make your mind easy about that ! "

With this, the boy's father set out at a run for the rue des Carmes.

The boy himself was busy twining his wreath of laurels in and out of his father's carbine and pistols.

When his father entered the room, he saw the object of his search perched on a sort of scaffolding that he had made for himself by placing a chair on the mahogony table.   He took a ruler and hid it behind his back, then he approached the table.   But his son had seen him take up the ruler, not without some anxiety.

" Look, father," said he.   " Look where I've put my laurel wreath ! "

" Come down ! "

" What for ? "

" You'll know when you've come down."

" But, father . . . "

" Come down ! "

" But, father . . . "

" Will you come down ? "

" Here I am, father."

His father seized him by the collar of his jacket and beat him with the ruler in the accustomed place.

" You rogue, you . . . "

" But, father, I won the first prize ! . . . Ah ! "

" You lazy dog ! "

" But, father, I won the first prize ! . . . Ah ! Oh ! . . . "

" I'll teach you to waste your time with circus riders ! "

" But, father, as I won the first prize ! . . . Ah !   Oh ! Ah ! . . . "

" Designing costumes for mountebanks ! "

" Oh ! . . . Ah ! Oh ! . . . "

And at this moment, as a fit accompaniment for his shrill cries, he heard the roll of a drum.

Then a bass voice cried :

" That's a salutation in honour of M. Étienne, winner of the first prize for drawing and sculpture in the town of Caen ! "

Rataplan !   Rataplan !   Rataplan !

The young laureate never forgot that Roll-call of Honour nor the strange position in which he happened to be when he received the tribute.

However, he bore no grudge against M. Odelli.

As for his father, it was his habit when administering correction of the type that our laureate had just received from him, to repeat at each stroke of the ruler : " It's for your good. It's for your good. It's for your good." His son had acquired a habit of repeating the same words and he had such confidence in the stern justice of his father that when the goodwives of the district said to him : " So your father's been beating you again, Étienne ? " he contented himself with replying : " It's for my good."

The thrashing bore fruit ; the boy worked with doubled ardour. But Eastertide was coming round again and with it the Easter Fair. It was held every year and lasted for fifteen days, officially, but for fifteen more unofficially. Unhappily, our hero's father happened to be called away on special duty. What an opportunity to make his debut as a circus rider or as a mountebank !

Our young man began with a trial of horsemanship.

But Étienne was now nearly sixteen ; he was as tall as his father and mother had been and too tall altogether to ride standing ; so they let him try vaulting. Now, in trying to jump over a horse his foot struck its haunch and he fell flat on the other side.

This one fall sufficed to cool our young rider's zeal for equitation ; even as one voyage in the cutter had cured him of his desire to be a sailor.

He went on to the neighbouring booth, which was managed by the great Gringalet of Rouen, one of the provincial celebrities of those times. Three days following he appeared in a pantomime as best man at a wedding. He hung up the decorations in the home of the bride.

All this distracted his attention a little from the school of sculpture.

" What the devil have you been doing with your time ? " demanded M. Odelli.

" Why, sir," replied the actor-apprentice, " my master has been keeping me busy carrying home completed work."

" Ah ! "

One day, however, when M. Odelli had repeated his question for the tenth time and for the tenth time received the same answer, he began to suspect.

" Well," said he, for he felt sorry that a pupil so talented should stay away from him. " Well, the next time you are sent to take back completed work, bring it along here for me to see, so that I can judge for myself the sort of work you do when I'm not there to help you."

There was no way of getting out of this, but the Fair was over and the circus people and mountebanks had gone.

The next time that the young man—for time was passing and little Étienne was now young Étienne—the next time the young man was sent out with a cupboard top carved to represent two doves beak to beak in a crown of myrtle, he brought it along to M. Odelli.

The professor looked attentively at the two doves and then said, simply :

" Vile ! "

" Do you think so ? " asked his pupil.

" You mustn't go on doing that sort of thing a day longer."

" But what am I to do ? "

" Leave."

" But my father likes me to be there."

" Then get yourself dismissed by your employer."

" But if my master dismisses me my father will beat me."

" Well, let him ! "

The young man thought this reply heroic ; it reminded him of the historic " Strike but listen " of the Athenian General. Only Themistocles himself was the one who was to be struck and not his pupil ; this fact, perhaps, made the remark even more heroic.

None the less, our youth thought the advice over ; it chimed in with his mood.

One day, he appeared before his master, prepared for the worst.

But perhaps we had better tell what had happened the day before and why it was that he had now the courage to brave the paternal switch.

CHAPTER V

ÉTIENNE'S BAPTISM AND CONSECRATION

THIS is what had happened the day before.

Whilst loafing—we have confessed that young Étienne did loaf—whilst loafing along the Place de la Comédie, gazing at the monument from a respectful distance and studying the theatre bills as closely as possible, M. Odelli's pupil had found himself facing a muddy little lane which ran between the side of the theatre and a block of houses.

He turned up this lane—simply, as you will understand, to be able to rub against stones which were privileged to hear plays being performed.

You know the proverb, " Walls have ears."

On his left Étienne found a door as dark and gloomy as that of Ali Baba's cave. Slippery stone passage, damp walls, rivulets of water tracing glistening trails all down those walls—the likeness with Ali Baba's cavern was complete. As for the stage doorkeeper, he was conspicuous by his absence. The black throat of this cave-like place seemed to have devoured him.

Our young man ventured to descend three steps. He then went up twenty more, leaving the light of day behind him, plunging with each step deeper and deeper into the gloom. At the top of the staircase he pushed open a door ; this door led right into the entrails of the monster.

Never did Jonah in the belly of the whale throw a more astonished glance at the dorsal bone, the ribs, the bladder, as big as one of Godard's balloons, the five hundred feet of lank intestines, or on the trapdoor that, far in the distance, led out to sea, than that which was cast by our youth at the rake, the flies with their iron stairways, the innumerable ropes hanging from the roof, and the gigantic door through which the flats were brought on to the stage.

He advanced step by step into the obscurity and solitude of the stage, moving as lightly as he could upon the boards so as not to make the slightest noise, when suddenly he felt a large and powerful hand upon his shoulder. He thought for a moment he had fallen into the hands of a giant. Terrified, he turned ; then he gave a cry of surprise and delight.

" Why," cried he, " it's M. Aubin aîné ! "

That was how people usually referred to the elder son of a sculptor who had a studio in the Place de la Comédie to distinguish him from his younger brother.

" Yes, it's I," replied Aubin. " It's I. What then ? "

" What then ? Why, I'm very glad it is you."

" Why ? "

" Because you won't turn me out."

" Turn you out of where ? "

" Out of this theatre."

" Were you afraid they'd turn you out ? "

" Yes."

" Do you take such an interest in looking at a stage ? "

" Rather ! I've long wanted to get the chance."

" Do you want to be an actor, then ? "

" Oh, M. Aubin, I should think I did ! "

" What prevents your being one ? "

" My father. If you knew how he beat me when he heard that I'd appeared in the pantomime that Gringalet of Rouen put on."

" And in spite of his blows you still want to be an actor ? "

" More than ever ! I really think I should go mad if I couldn't be an actor, some day."

" Then come here."

" Here I am, M. Aubin."

" Kneel down."

" What for ? "

" Kneel down."

" I'm kneeling."

D

" Wait."

He took up a can full of oil, and said :

" In the name of Talma, Garrick, and Roscius I baptize you Actor ! "

With this, he sprinkled oil on his forehead.

" What are you doing, M. Aubin ? "

" You can't get out of it now. You've been baptized in the sacred name of the Art. You'll have to be an actor whether you like it or not."

He was more than baptized ; he was consecrated.

This is what had been happening the day before ; it was this sybilline prediction that gave M. Odelli's pupil courage to get himself dismissed by his master.

The next day, about nine in the morning, he was sent to deliver two carved pigeons at the furniture dealer's. It should have taken a quarter of an hour, at most, to go there and back. Heroically, Étienne managed to take three hours and a half over it. He got back at a quarter to one.

" Where have you been, you idle vagabond ? " asked his master.

" Where have I been ? "

" That's what I asked."

" I've been where I pleased."

" Where you pleased ? "

" That's about it."

" So that's how you answer me, is it ? "

" You shouldn't have asked, then I wouldn't have answered."

If his master had been standing in front of a glass he would have looked at his reflection in it to see if he were really awake.

" Do you want to be shown the door ? "

" Oh, you needn't trouble to show me the door. I can find it for myself."

" Wait a bit, you rogue ! "

" Don't call me rogue. My name's Étienne Marin."

" You dare to speak to me like that ? "

The master wood-carver snatched up two rough-cast doves to throw at his apprentice's head.

The boy sprang over a bench and was out of the door in an instant.

" Your father shall hear about this. You just wait ! "

The wood-carver took off his apron, seized his cap, put on his coat, and set off with long strides for the rue des Carmes.

There was now no doubt about it. Retribution was sure ; it was now merely a question of how heavy it would be.

However stoical M. Odelli's pupil might be it was obvious that if a choice were possible he would choose the less rather than the greater. For one moment he had an idea that perhaps he might escape even the lighter punishment.

His father was to be on night duty. Usually in this case he left the house about seven o'clock in the evening, leaving the key under the door, so that his son could get in after he had finished his work with M. Odelli. It was therefore just a question of not returning till eight o'clock. His father would have left an hour before and the late-comer would have the whole night before him.

Étienne went for a walk till eight o'clock. Then he took his way to the rue des Carmes.

At the very moment that, gliding along the wall, he reached the door, it opened and his father appeared, carbine on shoulder, pistols in his belt, his sword at his side, humming the Marseillaise.

The youth stopped, astounded, glued to the wall.

Scarcely had he taken two steps when his father saw him, and turning and drawing his sword, he cried :

" You wretch, is that you ? "

The boy rushed down the lane, but his father rushed after him. As his son reached the staircase his father came up to him and struck him a heavy blow with the flat of his sword. He followed him in this way, with continual blows, to the third floor. That was as far as the boy could go ; the staircase went no further. There was a floor less than in the popular song, " My Lodging is on the Fourth Floor." The poor youth had to stop and receive his punishment. It was long and severe.

The next day, at eight in the morning, Étienne turned up at M. Odelli's, very pale and bruised all over.

M. Odelli had merely to glance at him to see what had happened.

" Oh," said he.   " So you've got it over ? "

" Yes, sir," said his pupil, piteously.

And it was not referred to again.

For another whole year Étienne remained with M.
Odelli, studying sculpture, but continually playing truant
to go to theatres, circuses, or penny gaffs. This brought
upon him such innumerable rebukes from his father that
he resolved that, come what would, he would go to the
capital in pursuit of art.

When men have their place marked out for them and
a future before them, there is always a providence which
at the right moment borrows the name of some man, takes
the elect by the hand, and leads him whither he would
go. The providence guiding our youth took the name of
M. Lair.

M. Pierre-Aimée Lair was counsellor to the prefecture.
He was one of those men who are invaluable to second-rate
provincial towns because they put themselves at the head
of all schemes of progress and lend a hand to every
improvement.

Let us describe M. Pierre-Aimée Lair, physically and
morally. The town of Caen had the misfortune to lose
him some two years ago. Physically, he was a man
of medium height, spare and bronzed, somewhat pock-
marked, always well shaven, so that the lower part of his
face was a sort of cobalt blue ; he dressed with somewhat
old-fashioned provincial style, but that did not lessen his
air of distinction, both natural and acquired. He usually
wore a blue coat, white waistcoat, and, in summer, trousers
of nankeen, giving place to cloth ones in winter. He
seldom wore boots, and when he did not, no matter what
colour his trousers might be, his stockings were blue.

Morally he was a man of so perfect a courtesy and so
affable in manner that he suggested a prelate. This
supreme politeness served to mask a potent energy.

One day, dressed in his counsellor's coat of dark blue
braided in a lighter shade of the same colour, nankeen
trousers and blue stockings, his chin freshly shaved and
shrouded in a white cravat, he was assisting at the drawing
of names for the conscription when a poor lad from Normandy drew No. 1. The poor fellow had no claim to
remission and there was every probability, therefore, that

he would have to go. His mother, who was waiting in a
corner of the great hall at the mayoralty, began to sob
loudly. These sobs struck disagreeably on the ear of the
general who was superintending the drawing.

"Turn out that noisy woman!" he cried roughly.

Such brutality revolted M. Lair, and in his softest and
most caressing tones he said:

"Oh, general, consider the sorrow of a poor mother!"

A murmur of approval followed his words, contrasting
forcibly with the icy silence that had followed the general's
remark.

M. Lair had given him a courteous lesson, but the public
made it a severe one.

As the general could not resent the action of the
public he took offence at the speech of M. Lair.

He threw back his head till it rested on the back of his
armchair, so that he could speak to his aide-de-camp,
standing behind him, and, loud enough to be heard by
all around, and also, therefore, by M. Lair himself, he
said:

"Tell me, do you know the name of that man with a
blue chin, dressed in a blue coat braided with blue and
blue stockings?"

The aide-de-camp laughed complacently at this sally
of the general.

M. Lair did not move an eyelash. Every one turned
to look at him, but he and he alone seemed not to have
heard.

But when the drawing was at an end he went up to
the general.

"Sir," he said with that courtesy of which it seemed
as if he could not have divested himself even had he wished
to do so, "you seem to wish to know my name. You
asked your aide-de-camp what it was, and he, it seems,
could not tell you. I will tell you myself. My name
is Pierre-Aimée Lair."

"I am glad to know it," said the general.

"Then as to the description you gave of my dress and
person, it was accurate enough, except on one point."

"What was that, sir?"

"You forgot the sword I wear at my side, the point
of which I shall be happy to introduce to you where and

when you please, general, so as to prevent any chance of your forgetting it in future."

Gently as he spoke, his provocative intention was clear ; the others standing by interposed. It would be setting a bad example for a general to fight a counsellor of the prefecture. The duel did not take place.

Ten years later, when fifty years of age, M. Lair was seized with the idea of making a tour of France. He was one of the most distinguished members of the Society of Antiquaries of Normandy, and the travels he proposed had for their principal object archæological study. One fine morning he set out on foot, walking six, eight and even ten leagues a day, and holding in his hand his stick with its gold knob, he travelled in this way for a year or eighteen months.

But, luckily for M. Odelli's pupil, he had not started on his travels in the year of grace 1826.

He often visited the drawing school, talking affection-ately with the pupils, especially with those who showed promise, and for this reason he had several times halted by young Étienne, putting various questions to him on the subject of his wishes and hopes.

The youth told him that his hopes and wishes united in the single resolve : to go to Paris.

M. Lair suspected that one of the principal obstacles to the journey to Paris was a lack of the money necessary to the young traveller.

One day he said to him :

" Before you leave us, my boy, I should like to buy one or two of your sketches."

The next day he came to the rue des Carmes ; he chose a time when the boy's father was sure to be there. He talked at length about the youth's talent and how necessary it was that he should go to Paris at some time or other to pursue his studies. He bought a head of Seneca and a head of Cicero, paying twenty francs for each ; also a huge hand and foot which he priced at ten francs each.

Our youth found himself with sixty francs pocket money.

Since an authority like M. Lair advised Paris, the boy's father dared risk no objection. He bought a trunk, had made for the youth a complete suit of fustian—we use his own expression—laid this suit on top of two dozen shirts which were packed at the bottom of the trunk, brought the sixty francs up to a hundred, paid the coach fare, and, stoic as a Spartan, escorted his son himself to the vehicle.

Étienne cried bitterly. Directly it came to leaving his father he forgot the numerous and severe punishments which he had received, or, rather, looking into his conscience he felt that these punishments were not undeserved.

His father appeared firm as a rock.

The postilion cracked his whip ; the coach rocked and the heavy vehicle set off at a good pace, keeping this up whilst passing through the town. Our young man, half sad, half joyous—yet, to tell the truth, more joyous than sad—had made his first step towards posterity.

Since we have set out with him, let us arrive at the same time.

Who can say that the future Talma, Garrick, and Roscius—you will remember that our young man had been baptized under this triple patronage—did not find an education both in art and philosophy lurking in the vagabond life that we are now about to describe ?

CHAPTER VI

THE ARRIVAL IN PARIS—THE PORTE ST.-MARTIN THEATRE
—MME. CARRÉ AND HER HOUSE—THE OTHER LODGERS
—HIS BED-FELLOW—HIPPOLYTE—THE SCULPTORS OF
THE MADELEINE—AN AMATEUR PERFORMANCE—THE
POLONAISE OVERCOAT—PROVINCIAL ENGAGEMENT—
OLD DUMANOIR—HIS BOX—FERDINAND THE COSSACK

OUR hero entered Paris about five o'clock one evening, and got off the coach at 6 rue Nôtre-Dame des Victoires, left his trunk at the office there, and, anxious to see what Paris was like, went off at a trot, without knowing where. After about ten minutes of a madly rapid run—his head being almost turned with the noise and traffic, he found himself brought up short in front of a sort of monument.

" Why, it's a theatre ! " cried he.

He stopped, resolved to go no further, at any rate that evening.

He had not dined ; he bought a dumpling and devoured every crumb of it ; then he went into the theatre. Can't you fancy his delight ? He was in Paris—the Paris of his ambitions ; he was in a real theatre and need not fear a beating—nor even a scolding when he went back home after the play was done. Alas, poor boy, he had no home to go to and he had only a hundred francs in his pocket.

A hundred francs ! Why, it would build a mill on the banks of Pactolus or a castle in Eldorado !

The play finished at a quarter to twelve.

Our hero left the theatre with the rest of the audience, but he was the only one among them who did not know where he would sleep that night.

He decided to be guided by chance ; chance had taken him to the Porte St.-Martin and chance would now take him to some inn.

He took the first turning to the right.

At a distance of some three hundred paces he found himself at the end of the little rue St. Jean, and saw a card on which was written :

" HOTEL CARRÉ.
Lodgings for the night."

Étienne entered the house and asked for a room and a bed. Luckily he had his passport on him ; had it not been for that the fact that he had neither trunk, portmanteau, nor even a knapsack would have made a bad impression.

The passport was read and seen to be correct ; the traveller clinked the coins in his pocket—he had already spent a twentieth of his capital since his arrival in Paris— and they instantly gave him the room he asked for with obsequious civility. They were not accustomed to travellers who asked for a room and a bed to themselves.

The hotel was used by sculptors, carvers, and painters ; as a rule Mme. Carré's guests—for, though there was a M. Carré it was usual to speak of Mme. Carré's hotel—as a rule, her guests pushed economy to the point of sleeping two in a bed, under pretext of fraternity.

The next day, as our sculptor-student complained of

the exorbitant sum of fifteen sous that they charged for his bedroom, they told him the usual custom of their lodgers ; he was free to get a comrade to share his room and bed if he liked ; if he did, then his share for the half of the bed and room would be seven francs ten sous per month.

That day at dinner they introduced to the newcomer a companion who was in the same boat as himself, that is to say, he wanted to find some one to share a bedroom with him. His name was Hippolyte, and he was a painter on porcelain. The two atoms drew together and are friends to this day.

Étienne didn't want to waste time loafing about ; he went in search of his luggage, put on the suit his father had given him, and began at once to call on various contractors.

The first he went to was a M. Bochard.

M. Bochard had the contract for the carvings at the Madeleine. He chatted for a moment with our young artist, and as he liked his manner and address, he asked :

" From what province do you come ? "

" I am from Normandy."

" From what town ? "

" Caen."

" I thought so."

" Why, sir ? "

" You have the Norman hand ; Normans are usually adroit. Take your tools to-morrow to the Madeleine ; you'll find yourself on familiar ground."

At eight o'clock next morning our youth was at the Madeleine. The decorators were hard at work.

" Hullo ! " cried one of them ; " here is my godson."

" Your godson ? "

" Yes. I baptized this boy on the stage of the Caen theatre with lamp oil. Come along here, Talma ! "

Étienne approached the speaker and recognized Aubin ainé.

Near him was his brother.

The two Aubins rank to-day among the finest wood-carvers in Paris.

" A speech ! A speech ! " called out the sculptors.

The newcomer laid down his tools, put his left fist on his hip, stretched out his right arm, and began :

" Burrhus, doubt not, no matter how unjust . . . "

The entrance of Nero was received with applause. Talma was dead and his successor seemed to them most promising.

But while waiting for theatrical laurels he had to content himself with hammer and chisel. The future Star of the Théâtre-Français put on a pair of huge glasses to shield his eyes from the bits of stone that might otherwise fly into them and blind him, and, thus arrayed, started to work on the capital of a pillar.

Here he worked, day after day, but at the hospitable hotel run by Mme. Carré he took his recreation. Every one of her lodgers spouted poetry : painters, sculptors, wood-carvers. Hippolyte, Étienne's comrade, was absolutely mad about the theatre. They decided to get up a play at any price ; and with considerable pains a company was got together. What should they play ?

Their choice fell on *A Simple Story*, by M. Eugene Scribe.

Étienne studied the lead ; Hippolyte was the jeune premier, and they rehearsed on the stage of the theatre in the rue Lesdiguières.

The day of the performance arrived ; the two youngsters, Étienne and Hippolyte, took the honours.

At all amateur performances of this sort a certain number of agents are always to be found. One of these agents now proposed that our amateurs should give a performance or performances to the general public. This sort of amateur production has the advantage of helping an actor after a few successes to get a professional engagement. Only a provincial one, of course ; but when a man can slap his breast pocket and say, " I've got my contract," he is legitimately proud of himself and looked up to by his friends. Besides, he need not tell them what town his contract is for.

These avocations, however, did not exactly assist the progress of work as a sculptor of marble or a painter on porcelain ; but it did represent a step forward towards the stage ! One can't hope for progress in every art at one and the same time.

At this epoch—that is to say, in 1827—actors coming back from tour used to meet at the cafe des Comédiennes, rue des Vielles-Etuves. The managers went there to engage their companies. Every one wore a polonaise at that time.

There wasn't a Trial or a Martin or an Eleviou who wasn't wearing a polonaise. The great ambition of our two youths was to possess a polonaise. Not two, you understand ; two polonaises would cost the ransom of a king ! But one polonaise for the two of them, even as they had one room between them and one bed which they shared in common. They would go to the café in turns and it would look as if each had a polonaise.

The suit bought by his father had only been worn three or four times, so Étienne carried it off to a wardrobe dealer and bartered it for a polonaise that had only been worn some eight or ten times—or so the dealer said ! Anyway the polonaise, which was of royal blue with black brandenbourg knots, and collar and cuffs of astrakhan, was still quite presentable. It made quite a sensation when Étienne wore it on the first day and again when Hippolyte donned it the next day. The fact was that both our friends had concluded an engagement with M. Dumanoir, manager of a Number Three Company for Number One towns, among which were reckoned those in French Flanders.

It is obvious that during this time the Madeleine had to get along by itself.

The manager was late, so of course he hustled his company. They set out on foot ; a waggonette followed or went in front of the company with the women and baggage.

Let us cast a friendly eye on this caravan which twined so joyously along the Amiens road, in the warm sun of that May day. We too, like Scarron, must write our chapter of comic romance.

The manager, veritable and privileged—we say veritable and privileged because by and by we shall have to speak of the usurpation of the stage manager—the real and privileged manager was, as we have already told you, M. Dumanoir.

M. Dumanoir was the type of the old beau, a marquis, as one might say, or dandy of the Directoire, who had pirouetted at the Tuileries and Luxembourg with his nankeen knee breeches gartered with ribbons, striped stockings, buckled shoes, double watchchain, apple-green coat, and dimity waistcoat, a high white cravat, his hair lifted by a comb on the top of his head, hat perched on the back of that head, and his light cane under his arm.

At the time of which we write, when he had reached the dignity of being manager of the Number Three Company for the Number One towns, as he now made his triumphal exit from Paris he was sixty years old, tall, spare, dry, the angles of his bony body showing through the folds of his coat which was too large for him, and we should have said too long as well if it had not been the fashion to wear the garment in those days flapping against one's heels. Of the costume in fashion in 1798, he had only retained the most characteristic portion, that is, the chignon. His former head of hair, which had been the admiration of the fair sex in those days, had disappeared beneath the breath of time, leaving the ex-maccaroni merely a crown, or, as one may say, a hemicircle of hair, thick at the nape of the neck, but thinner over the temples. But one knows what an illusion can be created by a few hairs cleverly disposed ; those at the nape of the neck were collected into a tress, somewhat like the tail of a lobster, which was brushed up from the neck to the bump of reverence, embraced the whole contour of the brain, and ended by spreading itself flat upon the top of the forehead.

Let us add that to this tress was joined the hair from the temples and from the intermediary territory between the temples and the nape of the neck. The cranium showed through their thin thatch. Moreover, at the extremity of the aforesaid tress, much as the badger hair appears at the extremity of that flattened type of brush we call a codfish-tail—at the extremity of the tress appeared a capillary tuft which, showing as it did about half an inch beneath the brim of a hat, simulated well enough the absent chevelure.

M. Dumanoir was the politest man in the world. No matter who stopped to speak to him, he took off his hat, though he had the best reasons in the world to remain covered ; he placed the hat between his knees, then with both hands he smoothed a wide parting in his hair, rising to his full height, but still retaining the hat between his knees.

" And what can I do for you, my friend ? " he would ask.

En route, it was his habit to stop at every cutlery shop he passed, whether right or left of their road, remaining before the shop in a way that caused his company considerable anxiety, for they thought they were about to be abandoned by him, and turning their heads in his direction, they stopped from time to time for him to catch them up ; then they would see him take a peep at the dusty horizon under his long legs.

He always carried under his arm a little box, very heavy, fashioned after the manner of a portmanteau ; this box he would never be parted from ; indeed, like the cash-box of Molière's miser, one would have thought that the box had eyes and that old Dumanoir was enamoured of those bright eyes.

One day, contrary to his usual custom, he forgot this box for one second, leaving it on the ground. One of his company lifted it up carefully, and giving it to him, cut a caper, crying :

"It weighs over sixty pounds, my boys. Over sixty pounds ! "

On this every one clapped their hands and showed for M. Dumanoir an increased respect.

Why were they so pleased at the news and why did it increase their consideration for their manager ?

Because the whole company believed that that little box contained M. Dumanoir's capital, the funds to run the tour, and that that was why he would not let the box out of his sight. Now, if that box represented the treasury, even if it merely held sixty pounds weight of silver, it meant that there must be 5900 francs in the box ; but if it held gold, then it gave promise of 92,000 francs. Old Dumanoir, then, was a Midas, a Crœsus, a Rothschild !

After old Dumanoir—or we might even say before him—comes the stage manager—M. Ferdinand.

He was usually known as Ferdinand the Cossack, because he declared that he had served with the French Army and exterminated in 1814 and 1815 entire hordes of those subjects of the Emperor Alexander who were born on the banks of the Don and the Tanais. But why, if he had exterminated Cossacks, should he be called Ferdinand the Cossack ? He couldn't explain this very well ; indeed he didn't explain it at all. But it was the fact, and though you may doubt a fact, or discuss a fact, or be sorry for a fact, you can't explain it. It was so because it wasn't otherwise ; that's all.

Ferdinand the Cossack—if you don't count M. Dumanoir's little box, of which no one really knew the contents—was the only member of the company who had any real baggage. This baggage consisted of a wardrobe, sufficiently well supplied for a provincial actor. Therefore he was down, in all future receipts, for the lion's share.

The touring company intended to exploit French Flanders.

These are the conditions that Ferdinand the Cossack had wrung out of M. Dumanoir :

1. A share and a half for his own personal work.
2. A share for his wife.
3. A share for his daughter.
4. A share for his stage management.
5. And a share for the use of his costumes.

Therefore M. Dumanoir was obliged to take merely a single share for himself, and all the rest of the company had only half shares. Nevertheless this did not prevent Étienne, Hippolyte, and the rest of the half-sharers, men and women, being as happy as was the cobbler in the story before he made his fortune.

Unfortunately it was not fortune that was destined to take from them the youthful gaiety which made their hearts bound as they ran from side to side of the great North Road, beneath the rays of that Mayday sun, reaching the open country with songs and tripping steps, some crying like jays and others singing like thrushes ; some with swelling throats, like turkey cocks, and others cooing as softly as turtle doves !

CHAPTER VII

Dumanoir's Company open at Valenciennes—The
Company of M. Bertrand, called the Zozo of the
North—Étienne transfers to this last Company
under the Name of M. Gustave—Pros and Showmen—Bohemian Domesticity—Gustave goes back
to the Dumanoir Company—Belgian Campaign—
Retreat—Disaster.

IN this way they travelled to Valenciennes, the whole
careless caravan, striking the earth, as Horace says, with
the soles of their free feet ; all laughing, singing and—
except old Dumanoir who was sixty and Ferdinand the
Cossack who was forty—all as young as the springtime in
which they were now making their first flight.

At Valenciennes they stopped. They wanted to feel
their ground ; so they announced a performance, and on
the next day they gave it.

Once when Mme. Dorval was playing at Anvers, to
give me some idea of the impression she made on the
compatriots of Jacques Philip Arteveldt, she sent me a
drawing of the front of the house with a crowd of rats
playing about at the entrances, as if to say that there
was no cat in the house. Étienne, who had taken a first
prize for drawing and sculpture, might have sent his father
a drawing of the front of the house at Valenciennes in the
same style as that which Dorval sent to me.

No receipts !

That same night they left the town. There wasn't a
moment to be lost ; they must at once reach a town of
more literary tastes than Valenciennes. Yet Valenciennes
was the birthplace of Mlle. Duchenois and of a poor child
who died at the age of nineteen and whose history I shall
recount by and by.

The next day they reached St. Amand. There was a
parish fair on ; they reckoned on this.

They played *Palmerin, or the Last of the Gauls*, and
took 105 francs.

Ferdinand the Cossack divided the spoil ; his five and
a half shares came to thirty francs. Old Dumanoir took

ten francs for his share. The others had five francs each
as their half-shares.

Ferdinand, his wife and daughter ate well. Old
Dumanoir fed fairly well. The others had light meals.
They had to make up with patience.

However, as they expected to give a performance
every day there ought to be a livelihood of some sort, and
for the first three days they did manage to live.

But the fourth day another company arrived ; the
troupe of M. Bertrand, known as the Zozo of the North, the
finest acrobat in France. This troupe, having joined forces
with that of M. Colombier, was a formidable rival, and the
Dumanoir and Ferdinand Company could not fight against
them. They had to close down.

They talked of splitting up, drawing lots as to which
should take the turning to the right, which that to the left,
each making the best use he could of his talents. But
that did not suit Ferdinand.

While they remained a company he drew five and a
half shares. Alone with his wife and daughter he would
only get three shares. And what shares !

He lost his temper, drew his sword, and swore he would
run through the first who spoke of separating.

Étienne ventured to doubt the power of Ferdinand's
sword and announced boldly that, having received an
offer from Zozo of the North to appear as Coriolanus he
was passing over to the enemy. That same evening,
Étienne found himself seated at the hearth of the Volsci,
under the victorious name of Gustave.

Since Scarron wrote his *Comic Romance* every one
knows more or less what a wandering troupe of actors is
like ; but we are, on the whole, much less well-informed
about the picturesque existence of circus folk. Here is
a description of the people forming the troupe of Bertrand,
called Zozo of the North, the first acrobat of France, joined,
as it now was, to that of M. Colombier.

The company consisted of :

1. Colombier's grandfather, conductor of the band,
props, producer. He played the clarinet when they went
in procession round the towns and first violin in the
orchestra.

2. Bertrand himself, called Zozo of the North, top of

the pyramid on parade and Pierrot in the dumb-show plays.

3. Mme. Bertrand, who hung head downwards from the trapeze and supported the column.

4. Mlle. Bertrand, the elder of the two girls, playing Columbine and dancing the gavotte and graceful dances on the tight-rope.

5. The younger Mlle. Bertrand, playing the statue in *Pygmalion*.

6. M. Mustapha, known as the Little Devil, who leapt through the air and did all sorts of dangerous things on the tight-rope.

7. M. Flageolet, who did, under the tight-rope, all the tricks that M. Mustapha accomplished upon it.

It was in the midst of this new and strange company that M. Gustave went into voluntary exile after his quarrel with Ferdinand the Cossack.

His contract—verbal, of course—assured him food and promised him fifty francs a month. Zozo of the North had added, wittily, that he would also have the privilege of travelling on foot.

In exchange for these advantageous terms M. Gustave undertook to make the flags, decorations, and transparencies in calico, reproducing the principal scenes and *tours de force ;* to play the leading parts in the melodramas and vaudevilles ; to play the magicians in the pantomimes ; to ride in procession through the towns on horseback.

Zozo of the North intended to make use of his new recruit without delay.

The bills that evening announced that on the morrow there would be a wonderful spectacle, particulars of which would be announced during the morning's procession through the town.

The next morning, at eleven o'clock, M. Gustave, in the uniform of a general, mounted on a horse whose harness was completely covered with spangles, preceded by a lame drummer and followed by the rest of the band, started off on his journey, stopping at all the squares, at every cross-road in the middle of every important street, and crying in his loudest tones :

" With the permission of his Worship the Mayor " (here he raised his hat), " inhabitants of the town of St.

E

Amand, we have the honour to inform you that the grand troupe of M. Bertrand, known as Zozo of the North, in partnership with that of M. Colombier, will give this evening, in the large booth on the market-place, a sensational performance. The spectacle will consist of : Mme. Bertrand, France's leading acrobat, will hang for five minutes from a chandelier with no other support than a coin. The Mlles. Bertrand will dance on the tight-rope, the elder a gavotte and the younger gracefully, while M. Mustapha, called the Little Devil, will do a turn on a tight-rope, without a balancing stick, and will finish with a dangerous leap head first and then backwards. M. Flageolet will perform the same feats without the cord that M. Mustapha performs on it. M. Gustave will play in *Pygmalion*, a lyric scene by Jean Jacques Rousseau ; the part of the statue will be taken by the elder Mlle. Bertrand. After *Pygmalion* we shall have the honour of presenting *Harlequin Bulldog*, pantomime with grand spectacular effects with costumes and scenes suited to the subject. And to conclude, the performance will terminate with the *Carnival of Venice*, in which the entire company will appear."

Such an announcement was sure to pique curiosity, and the receipts were satisfactory.

Now we will invite the curious reader to enter the booth of Bertrand, called Zozo of the North, rhapsodize over the splendid spectacle, and gain some hint of the mysteries of this, as one may say, freemasonry of the barnstormers, mystery into which M. Étienne, *alias* Gustave, has kindly initiated us.

One may use the word " mountebank " of any one who is a unit of the great Bohemian family of strolling players ; but a distinction must be made between the " pro," or " artiste," and the showman. The circus riders, tight-rope dancers, barnstormers, in short, any one with some sort of talent, are artistes. The animal tamers, or people travelling with a two-headed child or eight-footed calf, or talking seals, saying " Papa " and " Mama," are merely showmen. The artistes are the aristocracy ; the showmen merely the common folk. Every one with some sort of talent is respected. The showmen speak of the " pros " with their hats in their hands.

Now nothing could be more paternal than the authority

of the manager ; nothing more exemplary than these Bohemian families ; no time better employed than the intervals between the rehearsals and the performances.

The women wash the linen, dye the tights, cut out and make the dresses. The men set to work to put up the tent, prepare the fireworks, and make the props. Others make what they call " illusions."

How do you make " illusions " ? and what are they ? the reader will ask. That's what we are going to tell you.

Dip into tin and iron fused together a stone of the size of a large pea, cut and fixed to the end of a stick ; at the end of the stick will come away a spangle of metal ; this spangle is lifted out and pierced at once to be sewn on to costumes or round helmets.

Others look after the horses. Those who know how to read teach those who don't their lines. All, besides, practise playing some instrument or other, and when they have learnt to play one they pass on to another. All are drummers from their birth.

If ruin comes, after a bad season, when they have been forced to sell their chariots, pawn their horses, and send away the staff ; when, in short, the only remaining members of the company are the family of the manager, they " rest "; that is to say, they scatter about the country. Then each turns to his own specialty. One will make cleansing soap ; another a pomade to make hair grow ; another powder to whiten the teeth ; and another a special polish to get a good shine on boots. The children, with little strips of carpet, go into the cafés, where they walk on their hands, do the three " attitudes," front and back, and then dance the egg dance. Then, every day or every other day or every third day, according to the distance he has travelled, each Bohemian returns religiously to his father or mother to give them what he has earned.

For three months M. Gustave had been leading this picturesque and adventurous life, sufficiently well fed, but not receiving a halfpenny of the promised fifty francs, when he received a letter from Hippolyte, couched in these words :

" Come back, the Cossack has departed."

M. Gustave said nothing ; but as he did not think his honour engaged to Zozo of the North, who had only kept half of his engagement to him, he set out one night after a performance of *Pygmalion* and the *Charcoal Burners of the Black Forest*. He went off hot foot, without saying good-bye to any one, and took the road to Audenarde, where old Dumanoir and his company were camped for the moment.

And now let us say what became of the principal members of this troupe, whom we are leaving for good.

The leader, Mlle. Bertrand, became Mme. Thomassin ; she was killed some two years ago performing on the tight-rope at Batignolles. M. Flageolet, who was a medical student, took his degree and became a surgeon-dentist in a large town in France. Last, but not least, M. Mustapha, who was known among his comrades by the less pretentious name of Fafiou, is the brother of Bastien Franconi, and appeared at the opening of the Franconi Circus with Lalanne, the famous riding-master from the rue des Fosses-du-Temple.

M. Gustave found old Dumanoir's company badly disorganized ; it had, indeed, greater need of him than he of it. That very same evening they held a council. Ferdinand the Cossack, when he took away his wardrobe, had taken all the resources of the company. Old Dumanoir, whether his box held gold or silver, did not seem disposed to open it except in the last extremity. The company, therefore, had to get out of the hole as best they could by means of their own resources ; and it must be confessed that the resources of that company were mediocre.

Gustave and Hippolyte set to work to invent a repertory of military plays. It was not a big repertory, but they only gave two performances in each town. It consisted of : *Michael and Christine ; My Uncle's Château ; No Drum, No Trumpet ; A Marriage of Reason ;* and *Adolphe and Clara*. They played all these pieces arrayed in the uniforms of the garrison of whatever town they found themselves in, sometimes as cuirassiers, sometimes as lancers, and sometimes as chasseurs ; and, as they happened to be Belgian towns, the uniforms were Belgian.

When three months had gone by, they had, in theatrical parlance, just managed to " get out of " every town, and yet they had enough zeal remaining to glean in the villages, showing a courage and persistence worthy of a better cause.

At last, however, they had to agree to a retreat. The winter weather, which was rigorous to a degree, gave this retreat a real resemblance to the retreat from Moscow.

Their clothes were in a deplorable state, old Dumanoir's as well as those of the rest of the company ; yet he never breathed a word about opening his box over which he watched with a paternal care as active as ever. M. Gustave had arrived at his last shirt, and one fine day even this proved to be so worn and torn and, above all, so dirty that, as he did not dare to hang it up in the Church of —— as Isabella did hers in the Mosque of Granada, he threw it between the furrows of a ploughed field. A paper collar took the place of his linen one ; an overcoat buttoned from top to toe hid the deficiencies of his wardrobe. In short, they had reached such a state of poverty that one day the whole company had nothing to eat beyond the turnips that they pulled out of a field.

Old Dumanoir, his box under his arm, pastured with the rest, and as he pulled up a turnip that was half frozen he said what Charles XII. said of the ration of bread that was half putrid :

" It isn't good, but it's eatable."

They were beginning to believe that he had neither gold nor silver in that box !

But, if not, what was in it ?

CHAPTER VIII

DISAPPEARANCE OF OLD DUMANOIR—GUSTAVE AND HIPPOLYTE HUNT FOR HIM—GUSTAVE'S COSTUME—A SHORT CUT—FORCED MARCH THROUGH THE SNOW—STARVATION—THE LONELY COTTAGE—A GOOD WIFE BUT AN INHOSPITABLE HUSBAND—BREAD

ONE morning they found that old Dumanoir had disappeared, leaving a letter behind him. He bade his company meet him at the town of Armentières, situated, with regard to the spot they were then in, about three leagues the other side of Lille.

When this news, quickly spreading, woke Gustave and Hippolyte from their uneasy slumbers they had had no food since noon of the previous day. As usually happens when there is need for quick decision to avert calamity, two hours passed in exclamations of astonishment, in discussion, and in making, debating, and rejecting proposed projects. In the end it was decided that at the risk of not finding old Dumanoir there when they arrived, the remainder of the company would make their way to Armentières, each taking the road he preferred and making use of what resources he had the sense to muster.

Gustave and Hippolyte, or, as we may say, Orestes and Pylades, resolved to stick together and endure whatever fresh deceptions and, we may add, disasters Fate might have in store for them.

They began by waiting for midday to give time for the ravens to arrive who might be charged by a beneficent Providence with the task of bringing them their breakfast; but Providence did not think it well to re-enact for the benefit of two pagans like M. Gustave and Hippolyte the miracle it had permitted for the good Prophet Elijah.

At twelve o'clock they set out on their journey.

It was now exactly twenty-four hours since their last meal.

As each moment was now precious they would go straight to Lille; at Lille, they would sell the only thing they had left to sell—and, indeed, when we go into details of their costume, our readers will see that this is no exaggeration—a pair of stocking hose; they meant to sup and sleep on these, then to start off, as early as possible the next day, for Armentières.

Now, as our readers, less familiar perhaps than ourselves with theatrical slang, may ask what we mean by stocking hose, we will reply that stocking hose are half tights, blue, white, yellow, green, red, grey, chocolate, striped or parti-coloured, with which one can appear as any or every heroic personage, from Achilles to the Marshal de Saxe.

About twelve or half-past they set out, on a grey, cloudy day, with a foot of snow under their feet and a snowy sky above them, behind them, and around them.

And now let us go into detail as to the costume of M. Gustave, engaged to appear as juvenile lead, and play the lovers and fine gentlemen of vaudeville by M. Dumanoir and to play *Pygmalion* by M. Bertrand, or Zozo of the North.

A big, all-enwrapping overcoat, flapping at his heels, and carefully closed behind by a row of black pins so that it could not possibly blow open. Shoes trodden down at heel, but neither stockings nor socks. A hat that one had to take carefully by the front of the crown when saluting for fear the brim came off in one's hand ; the lower part of a pair of pantaloons making a sort of slack gaiter attached at the sides to the two pockets of the overcoat by black pins. No waistcoat ! No shirt !

Having described Gustave's costume we may dispense with a description of Hippolyte's.

Both were walking along the highway towards Lille, heads down, when Gustave had an unlucky idea, as he measured with his eyes a sidepath opening into their road.

" Surely there must be a short cut from here to Lille which perhaps might take an hour and a half from our journey."

" Oh, of course," said Hippolyte. " There are always short cuts."

" Then suppose we ask the first peasant we meet ? "

A peasant appeared on the instant as in the fairy tales.

(It need not be explained that that peasant was the devil.)

" Here, you there ? " cried Hippolyte.

Gustave advanced, and giving a military salute out of consideration for the fragile brim of his hat :

" Hullo, my friend ! " said he. " Do you know a short cut that will save us part of this long road to Lille ? "

" Oh yes, sir," replied the peasant. " There's one that cuts off a good two leagues."

Gustave looked at Hippolyte as if to say, " You see ! That wasn't a bad idea of mine ! "

" And where is this road, friend ? " he asked, turning to the peasant.

" It's the first you come to on the right."

" We can't mistake it ? "

" No. Plenty of carts go along there."

" You see, in all this snow . . . "

" You've only to follow my footsteps. I've just come from Lille myself."

" Then all is for the best. Thanks, friend."

And the two youngsters went on their way again with one idea in their minds ; to take the road to the right.

About a hundred and fifty paces farther along they found the road.

M. Gustave turned to wave a hand to the peasant, but he had disappeared.

They turned without hesitation into the short cut. The footmarks were distinct ; you could even see the marks of the nails in the soles. There could be no mistake.

They walked on for an hour, guided by these welcome landmarks ; but as the snow had begun to fall again since they had turned out of the main road the marks disappeared under the woolly covering. It was clear that in a short time there would be no marks to guide them. Never mind. They must get there ; and so they went on walking.

Then came the moment when the footmarks entirely disappeared. They were now walking haphazard.

When they had gone about a quarter of a league they felt by the unevenness of the ground that they had left the main track, and were walking over ground that had been turned up.

They took off their shoes, which were dreadfully trodden down at heel and therefore more fatiguing than helpful ; but as they could not enter the town barefooted they put their shoes in their pockets. Those pockets then began to hit against their sides.

Now began a time of absolute discouragement for our two youngsters, for they saw that the daylight was fading, the horizon disappearing from view, and the snow falling with redoubled vigour. As far as they could see the country was deserted ; one might have fancied one's self on the Siberian Steppes.

Our two travellers stumbled on in silence, bent double with hunger, the bitter cold freezing the tears upon their cheeks as quickly as they fell from their eyes. They dared not look at one another for fear of seeing despair on a comrade's face.

They kept up their courage by thinking each of the other. Hippolyte saw Gustave walking, Gustave saw Hippolyte walking ; so they both continued to walk on ; but had one of them fallen the other would have fallen too.

Night came on.

Until then they had been keeping a possible direction ; but, night fallen, they wandered on at a venture.

At last Hippolyte stopped. " I can go no further ! " he cried.

" What's the matter ? " asked Gustave.

" I'm dying of hunger."

More than thirty hours had now gone by since our youngsters had had any food.

" Take my arm and let's get on."

Hippolyte took Gustave's arm, but he soon found that the rough state of the ground made this an extra fatigue to them both instead of a help. He dropped Gustave's arm and went on walking by him ; or, rather, he did not walk ; he dragged himself along. The snow was not falling quite so thickly, but it was black night.

Suddenly, like little Poucet, Gustave cried : " I see a light ! "

" Is that true or are you only saying it to keep me from dropping ? " asked Hippolyte.

" Look for yourself."

" Where ? "

" There."

" I can't see it."

" There ! There ! "

" Yes . . . I do think . . ."

" I tell you it's a light ! "

" All right ; let's get on, then.'

And the two unhappy travellers made straight for the light. In ten minutes they stood before a lonely cottage.

" At last ! " cried Hippolyte. " We're here."

" Yes, we're here ; but . . ."

" But what ? "

" But what are we going to ask for ? " asked Gustave.

" Some bread, of course," said Hippolyte.

" Will you ask ? "

" Me ? "

" Yes."

" Oh, damn," said Hippolyte.

" Well ? "

" I wouldn't have thought it would be so difficult to ask—to beg for a bit of bread."

" Ah ! " said Gustave, his voice strangled. " When it's the first time one's ever done such a thing . . . "

" Well," said Hippolyte, " if you haven't the courage to do it, I shall lie down here, and in the morning they'll find me dead."

" Oh, that's absurd ! " cried Gustave.

And he advanced resolutely to the door.

The door was in two halves, as is often the case in villages, so that you can open the top half while the lower half remains shut.

The light that filtered through the hinge made a square frame.

After a last moment of hesitation, Gustave knocked at the door.

" Come in ! " said a woman's voice.

" Good !   There's a woman here," said Gustave.   " We are saved ! "

The upper part of the door looked right into the room and our youth could see the whole interior of the place at a glance.

Facing the door the woman who had said " Come in ! " was sitting at a spinning wheel, spinning.

Near her, a lamp was alight on a table.   At the back of the room, to the right, was a bed with a green serge coverlet.   Behind the woman, against the wall, a big sideboard, forming a bin at the bottom, and displaying on the shelves above crockery patterned with birds and flowers. Moreover, in the middle of the wall, to the left of the door, there was an immense fireplace where a wood fire was burning, before which a vague and formless object was dimly to be discerned.

The sight of the woman reassured our two youngsters a little.   It is possible that the sight of them had not exactly the same effect on the woman.   Their two heads, though handsome and young, appearing in the frame of the open doorway, against a background of snow, took on through their drawn pallor something of the sinister. Moreover the dress of the two travellers was not exactly in their favour. Nevertheless, at the very first words they said, the woman was reassured.

Both began to speak together ; but the voice of Hippolyte died away at the fourth or fifth word and Gustave finished the sentence alone.

" Madame," they said, " forgive us . . ."

This was where Hippolyte's voice ceased and Gustave continued by himself.

" We two poor fellows have lost our way . . . we are dying of hunger, and if you only . . . if you would be so kind . . . if you would have the charity . . ."

Then, with an effort :

" To give us a little bread . . ."

He couldn't continue ; his voice seemed to be muffled in his throat, and died away even as Hippolyte's had done.

At this, the formless mass that they had observed by the fireplace without being able to see what it was, appeared to come to life and a brutal voice cried :

" We've got nothing for you ; get off with you ! We aren't rich folk, and as for bread we have hardly enough for ourselves."

But the woman, for her part, had seen the pallor of the two young men and had been touched by their frank appearance. She now rose, and paying no attention to what her husband said, she went to the drawer, took from it half a loaf—a twelve-pound loaf, as large as a little hayrick—and cutting a slice the full length of the loaf and an inch thick, she said :

" Nonsense, husband. It's two poor boys, and they look honest. We shan't miss this mouthful of bread that I'm giving them. There you are, children, and may God bless you ! "

And she gave them the slice of bread which might have weighed a pound.

Then, as if she were afraid her husband might try to take it from them again :

" Off with you," she said. " You're not more than a league from Lille."

So she shut the door in their faces ; but it was evident that she did so more from kindness than hostility.

The youngsters understood this, and far from bearing her any grudge for it, they stammered :

"Good woman! Kind creature!" Their voices broken by emotion. "A woman after God's own heart. Yes, we'll come back, and if we are ever rich, don't worry, my good woman. You shan't have to work for your living."

Still murmuring blessings on the giver, Gustave divided the bread in half, giving one part to Hippolyte and keeping the other for himself.

But when they put the food to their mouths they could not eat it. It was charity bread, and both burst into tears.

CHAPTER IX

ARRIVAL AT THE GATES OF LILLE—CUSTOMS—THEIR POCKETS SEARCHED—THE GATES SHUT—INGENIOUS ENTRY INTO THE TOWN—GUSTAVE WITHIN, HIPPOLYTE WITHOUT—EXIT OF GUSTAVE—A FRESH ATTEMPT—SAME RESULT—DESPAIR OF HIPPOLYTE—DIALOGUE IN AN ABANDONED SENTRY-BOX—BREAKFAST IN HOPE—ENTRANCE INTO THE TOWN.

OH, Dante, Dante! Great poet who has given us an inspired verse on every human grief!

Our two poor boys were not even exiled; they were merely hungry. They did not mount the "hard stairway of the stranger"; they were walking barefoot over the ground of their own country. And yet both were crying, their bit of bread in their hand.

Neither of them could bring himself to take a bite. But this emotion, half sweet, half painful, brought back their strength. It seemed to them that the good woman when she said that Lille was only a league away had pointed towards a little wood that they saw about five hundred paces in front of them. They walked towards that wood, turning from time to time and crying:

"The good woman! The kind woman!"

At last, about eleven at night, or possibly later—our readers will surmise that our Bohemians had no watches

—at last, about eleven at night, they saw the walls of the town.

At this sight they gave great sighs of relief.

Before the gates of Lille they came in contact with the officials of the customs.

" Where are you going ? "

" To Lille."

" Have you anything to declare ? "

" Have you anything to declare ? " Gustave asked Hippolyte, half crying, half laughing.

" I have to declare that I'm dying of hunger."

" And I that, if you delay us, we shan't be able to get into the town."

" Come here," cried the rough voice of the customs officer.

And he passed his hand under Gustave's overcoat, touching his bare skin ; the boy shivered from head to foot when he felt that hand on his flesh.

" Have you any lace or jewels ? " asked the officer as a matter of habit.

" If we had jewels we should have pawned them ; and if we had lace we should have made ourselves some shirts."

" But what have you got in your pockets ? "

They felt in the travellers' pockets, in which were, first of all, their downtrodden shoes, and also the famous stocking hose, besides this each had put in his pocket the bread he had not eaten.

The search took a good quarter of an hour.

At last, realizing that they were not carrying contraband goods, the customs officers authorized the young men to pursue their journey.

So they had arrived ! The hospitable gates were shut, it is true, but no doubt they would be opened.

Confident of this, Gustave knocked.

They heard the guardian open the door of his lodge, approach the gates of the town, turn the key gratingly in the keyhole, and undo the bars.

Then the gates opened just sufficient to allow of a nose, red with cold, being poked through.

" Who are you ? " asked the porter.

" Who are we ? That's good ! " cried Gustave, affecting the utmost self-assurance. " We are young men from the town, of course."

" Your cards ? "

" Our cards ? What cards ? "

" Haven't you any cards ? "

" No."

" Then good night. You can't come in."

And before the two youths had had time to make any remark the gates were shut again.

Gustave and Hippolyte looked at one another in consternation. They had managed to find strength to reach the town; but at the gates this fictitious strength abandoned them.

What were they to do ? What would become of them ?

Could they pass the night outside ? Poor wretches ! they were already half frozen and that would mean that they would be completely frozen.

Gustave naturally thought of the guard-room, the warm firelight of which was to be seen dancing through the cracked window-panes.

As a child he had so often passed a night in the guard-room of the customs officers of Caen, why shouldn't they pass a night in the guard-room of the customs officers of Lille ?

Their feet in the snow were frozen ; it was painful to detach them from the ground. Then every one knows, when greatly fatigued, how difficult it is to start off again after a halt.

The two youths, dragging along their feet, which had gone to sleep and were bleeding from the rough road, reached the guard-room, and addressing the sentinel, their last resource, they said :

" Please, sir, we have forgotten our cards and the porter refuses to let us enter. Will you let us pass the night in the guard-room ? "

" It isn't allowed," said the sentinel.

The youths groaned.

The tone in which the sentinel had made that reply showed plainly enough that it would be useless to insist.

At this moment they heard along the road the peculiar noise made by a coach, the noise of chains and bells, accompanied by the cracking of a whip.

Gustave, when he heard this distant thunder, roused himself :

" Hippolyte, I've an idea ! "

" Is it any good ? "

" I think so. We shall get into the town."

" How ? "

" You'll see."

" But tell me how ! "

" I haven't time. Do as I do."

The heavy vehicle, indeed, had now come up to them and was stopping before the guard-room to allow a customs officer to mount the coach, since the inspection was always made in the town itself.

Gustave approached. " Conductor," said he, " we've left our cards behind us. We can't get into the town. Let us jump on the box ; we are dying of hunger."

" Phew ! " was all the conductor said in reply.

And the horses set off again at a gallop.

" Quick, Hippolyte ! " cried Gustave. " Let's get up, you one side and I the other. Hang on to the handle of the door, and we'll get in with the coach."

This manœuvre was executed instantly.

They ran the fifty paces that separated the guard-room from the gates without feeling their fatigue, their wounds, or their hunger. Hope caused everything else to be forgotten.

At the noise made by the coach, as by enchantment the gates opened, the vehicle went through, the gates closed again—and Gustave was in !

He turned and looked round him. Where was Hippolyte ? What had happened to him ?

This is what had happened.

The gate opened in two halves, the porter handling one and his wife the other.

Gustave was on the side of the porter ; he may have seen him, but at any rate he didn't stop him.

Hippolyte was on the side of the porter's wife. She had seized him by the front of his coat. Hippolyte, who knew the respectable maturity of that garment, had not dared to risk tearing it from her hands. He let himself be pushed out of the gate.

Let us declare to the honour of Gustave that he had

not for one moment a thought of remaining in the town while his friend stayed outside.

He approached the porter.

" Please," said he, " please let my friend come in."

" Oh, nonsense," said the porter. " Why is he such a fool ? He had only to do as you did. You're in, eh ? You're in, aren't you ? Let him remain out there and you stay here."

" Oh, sir, I beg you to have pity on him and open the gate."

" Impossible."

" Then let me rejoin him ! "

" Oh, as for that, with pleasure. Out you go ! "

And taking the young man by the shoulders while his wife held the gate open, he threw him out as soon as the opening was wide enough to let him pass.

Then both porter and wife, for fear of being taken by surprise, set to together to shut the gates.

The youngsters had not even a thought of fighting for it ; they were too exhausted.

The snow began to fall again.

Hippolyte leant against the parapet, his arms hanging listlessly by his sides, his head bent on his breast.

Gustave moved, not to sit but to lean by his side.

In a few minutes both lifted their heads at the same time.

A vehicle was approaching, and was even nearer than one would have thought, for the carpet of snow which covered the road had dulled the noise of its wheels.

It looked like a great black spot, approaching and growing rapidly larger.

" Now will you be quicker this time than you were last ? " asked Gustave.

" I'll try," said Hippolyte, but his manner was discouraged.

Gustave cast a glance at the vehicle.

" It's a travelling carriage," said he. " Now listen," he added. " This time I'll take the side of the porter's wife, and you take the other side. The man is the less hard-hearted of the two."

The same manœuvre was put in practice with this difference, that instead of running to the right, Gustave ran to the left, and that instead of running to the left Hippolyte ran to the right.

The gates opened. There was a moment's struggle ; a cry of pain was heard. As before, Gustave got past.

He looked round him ; total eclipse of Hippolyte.

The woman had seized Gustave by the overcoat ; but she had torn her flesh on the black pins.

It was she who had given the cry that was heard.

Gustave, then, had got in.

As to Hippolyte, he had let himself be caught and put outside the gates by the porter.

Gustave put up the same petition and met with the same refusal from the porter ; he was thrust out again into the country, being given this time a vigorous kick.

In his annoyance Gustave had but one word for Hippolyte :

" Fool ! "

" I'm going to throw myself into the moat," said Hippolyte.

" There's two feet of water in it ; you'll break your legs ; and you won't drown. If you would drown, if I could be rid of you for good, I wouldn't mind."

" Gustave ! " cried Hippolyte in a voice of lament.

" Well, it's enough to make a man mad. I'm furious ! Oh, suppose we have a fight. That would warm us."

" I haven't even courage enough to fight."

" Well, are we to remain here and go to pieces like a couple of lost dogs ? "

" Let's walk on."

It was the last resource for these two poor wretches who had been walking for a dozen hours on end.

" Yes, let's walk on."

" Where shall we go ? "

" I don't know. But let's go somewhere."

And in despair, the two youths began to run along the high road.

" Hullo ! " cried Gustave. " Here's a sentry-box."

" Where ? "

" Look there."

And he pointed out an empty sentry-box, silhouetted in black against the carpet of stainless white. Both ran

F

to the sentry-box. At any rate their bare feet were now on wood.

" I'm hungry," said Hippolyte.

" Well, we've got some bread."

" Of course we have. The bread that woman gave us."

The bread had frozen in their pockets and cracked between their teeth. Nevertheless they devoured it to the last crumb.

Even after it was finished, their jaws continued to work, only the movement was more hasty ; their teeth chattered.

The two friends huddled closely together, trying to get a little warmer in an embrace that one can only compare to that of shivering monkeys in the Jardin des Plantes, when autumn days are cold.

" Try and sleep," said Gustave.

" Sleep if you can. I can't. I'm too cold. I'm dying."

" Nonsense, you fool ! One doesn't die of cold."

" Why, my dear chap, in Russia—— "

" Oh, in Russia—but we're in France. Why, a night soon passes."

And Gustave began to sing Stanislas' refrain :

" In silence must an old soldier suffer
Without complaint."

Hippolyte replied with a sigh ; if the narrow sentry-box hadn't forced him to remain upright he would have fallen.

" My poor mother ! " he murmured.

" Egoist," cried Gustave. " I've been crying on my father's name for an hour past, but at least I've said it to myself."

" Ah ! " sighed Hippolyte.

" Why don't you go to sleep ? "

" I can't."

" Well, then, let's talk. Talk of what we're going to do to-morrow. To-morrow—— Do you hear ? "

" I'm trying to listen."

" To-morrow we'll sell our stocking hose. It will bring us in twenty sous."

" Do you think so ? "

" It'd be the devil if it doesn't."

Twenty sous. That was the goal of their ambition.

" If we had twenty sous what could we do with it ? "

" With twenty sous—damn it all, we could go boldly into a café and get a good warm."

" Yes, we could get warm first."

" Then we could each have a good hot cup of coffee."

" Boiling ! "

" And a good thick piece of bread and butter."

" Toast ! "

" Yes."

" Good ! "

" Then we should be refreshed—— "

" We're refrigerated now ! "

" Ah, he's joking. We're saved ; and I've been spend ing the last ounce of my vitality to make this creature smile. You old humbug, you ! "

" Oh, how cold it is ! " murmured the shivering Hippolyte.

As a matter of fact it was now that hour of the night which precedes the morning, an hour which, fresh even in summer-time, is glacial in winter.

" To-morrow," stammered Hippolyte, " we shan't be able to move a foot."

" Nonsense. We'll imagine we're going to play at night. The thought of playing gives me not feet but wings."

" Oh, the cold ! " sighed Hippolyte in such heart-rending tones that Gustave had not the courage to go on talking.

The youths shut their eyes, not in the hope of falling asleep, but just to try and deceive themselves.

After a bit, Gustave opened his.

" Why, I believe that's the dawn ! " cried he.

" It's the last one we shall see."

" Well, give it a cheerful greeting, anyway."

Hippolyte then opened his eyes.

" If that's daylight," said he, " the gates must be open."

" Why, of course ! "

" Let's get into the town, anyway."

" I must move my feet first. Aah ! Aah ! "

The two young fellows left the hospitable sentry-box. The gates of the town were open. They made a triumphal entry, hurling curses at the porter who was currishly warming himself over his stove.

CHAPTER X

Two Cups of Coffee—An Idea at the Bottom of the
Cup—Sale of the Stocking Hose—Old Dumanoir
at the Crown and Monkey—Round the Town
—Lent sends down the Receipts—General Fast—
Gustave thinks of returning to his Father—The
Frog Wheeze

Only twenty paces the other side of the gates was a tavern.

" Let us go in," said Hippolyte.

" One moment ; let's put on our shoes."

" You are right."

They took their shoes from their pockets and put them on.

Only a very great respect for Mrs. Grundy could have induced them to force their frozen and bleeding feet into leather, hard as iron, cutting as a razor. However, they put on their shoes ; and as soon as they were shod, went into the tavern.

" Oh, there's a stove," cried Hippolyte ; and he ran to the stove, clasping its chimney fraternally to his bosom.

" Coffee ! " cried Gustave, in the accents of a millionaire. " And hot, please ; really hot. Boiling ! Hm ! Hm ! "

In ten minutes they were served with two cups of coffee. The two cups were emptied at a draught.

Gustave looked at Hippolyte.

" Well, sybarite," said he, " anything to complain of now ? "

" What about money ? "

" What about the stocking hose ? "

" Yes, of course."

" Listen. Your shoes are not so trodden down as mine."

" Don't you think they are ? "

" You are more adroit than I am."

" Am I ? "

" Do listen ; this is what I want you to do."

" Well, I'm listening ! "

" In the company that was with Zozo of the North there's a little dancer called Mlle. Mine."

" Mlle. Mine ? "

" Yes. We played together at Lille."

" Well ? "

" Mlle. Mine had a sister, a charming girl, who used to come and see her."

" What's all this long story got to do with me ? "

" Wait a bit and you'll see, you donkey. Mlle. Mine had a sister, a charming girl, who lived at the fish market."

" The fish market is a fair size."

" You can't mistake the place. She lived at a corner house and there are only four corners."

" What floor ? I warn you if there are many stairs to go up—— "

" You don't go up. You go down."

" Oh, then she lives—— "

" In the basement below the street. In a cellar."

" Good."

" You'll go and take her a message from me."

" All right."

" You won't tell her I'm here."

" Won't I ? "

" You'll only tell her you are my friend."

" And then ? "

" Then you'll ask her to sell the stocking hose for us ; she'll get a much better price for them than we should."

" That is an idea ! "

" And do you consider me lacking in ideas ? "

" Not when you're near a stove."

" Well, I like that ! Whose idea was it to take that short cut ? "

" Are you going to boast of that ? "

" Oh, get along with you and find Mlle. Mine. Bring back a hundred francs if you can ; but, in any case, don't take less than ten sous."

" I'll do my best."

" Off with you, you have my blessing."

Three-quarters of an hour later, Hippolyte returned, his eyes sparkling.

He had sold the stocking hose to Mlle. Mine for forty sous.

When they had paid their bill they still had twenty-four sous left. They lunched on a bit of bread and cheese and a glass of beer.

"Waiter! Two small absinthes, please, and the bill! We must be off," said Hippolyte.

"And this is the fellow who declared he couldn't walk another step. Is your father waiting to kill the fatted calf for you, you prodigal, that you rush into these extravagances?"

They drank their absinthe and set out, each with a crust of bread in his pocket and with a reserve fund of twenty sous. It is true they no longer had the stocking hose ; but one can't have everything.

Two hours later they entered Armentières.

"Have you seen any actors go by?" asked Gustave of the first townsman he encountered.

"Yes, they've gone to the Crown and Monkey to the left of the square."

"Where is the square, if you please?"

"Keep to your right."

"Thanks.—Well, you see, old Dumanoir is an honest man."

"You know the old proverb : 'He who loses steals.'"

"But that box of his? That's an honest box, I'll swear."

"Now is the moment to find out what it contains."

"I gave it a shake one day ; it sounded like nuts inside—— By the by, I could do with a few nuts now!"

"Waiter! Dessert for this gentleman! Gluttony is one of the seven deadly sins."

The two youths hurried to the square.

The townsman had not deceived them ; old Dumanoir and the rest of his company were at the Crown and Monkey, busy making out tickets which they were going to take round from house to house.

When he saw our two youths, old Dumanoir took off his hat, thrust it between his knees, combed his locks, and standing as straight as he could, said :

"My dear friends, you are a little late."

"We lost the way," said Hippolyte.

"Sit down there and help us write these out."

" Write what ? Tickets ? That's not a good way to advertise," said Gustave.

" My dear friend, can you suggest any other ? " replied old Dumanoir.

" Why not go round the town with a drum ? "

" We thought of that, but the drummer wants twenty sous."

" I'll advance the twenty sous to the company on condition that I am paid back out of the receipts."

" Agreed ! " they all cried unanimously.

" But, my dear friends, what can we play without costumes ? " asked old Dumanoir.

" Why, military pieces : *No Drum, No Trumpet, Michael and Christine, Adolphe and Clara.*"

" All right."

He put on his hat again.

They went in search of the drummer, who demanded payment in advance. M. Gustave, with dignity, offered him his twenty sous. The drummer took them.

" Now," said he, " I want passes for my wife and two children."

" Are you in the Garde National ? "

" Yes."

" You shall have four passes if you'll lend us your uniform."

" All right."

" Start off, then ! "

The tour of the town began.

They dressed that evening's play with two uniforms belonging to gendarmes, the drummer's tunic, and the cast-off clothes of a keeper.

They took sixty francs net profit ; and as Ferdinand the Cossack was there no longer to run off with five and a half shares after Gustave had been repaid his twenty sous, each took a whole share.

Five francs sixty centimes !

Had this magic stream but flowed every day it would have been another Pactolus !

But, instead of rising like the Nile, Pactolus dried up.

Every one has failed to assign a scientific explanation of the rising of the Nile ; but, without fear of contravention, we can tell the cause of the drying up of Pactolus.

Lent began—time of fast for all true Christians, but above
all for actors, and particularly for touring actors.

One night, when they had only taken ten francs—less
than the actual expenses—Gustave said to Hippolyte :

" Hippolyte, I give in."

" What do you mean by ' I give in ' ? "

" I mean I'm beat."

" And what then ? "

" I shall have to find another profession."

" Which ? "

" I shall have to join the repentant sons ; making my
debut as the Prodigal. I'm off to Caen to-morrow ; I'll
fall at my father's feet and agree to anything he wishes, even
if he decrees that I am never to act again."

" You renegade ! "

" Can't be helped. There is a limit to human
endurance."

" But how are you going to get there ? "

" I've enough for my journey, nine francs ; four
francs for a new pair of shoes and five francs for the walk
from here to Paris."

" Do you know that Paris is fifty-five leagues from
Lille ? "

" Fifty-five ? That's twenty sous a stage, doing eleven
leagues a day."

" And from Paris to Caen ; how many leagues is that ? "

" Fifty-three."

" A hundred and eight in all ! "

" Yes, it's a good mouthful."

" A hundred and eight leagues to be covered with a
hundred sous in your pocket. It isn't a sou a league ;
you'll have your work cut out."

" I shall find some friend or other in Paris to lend me
a trifle."

" Then you've made up your mind ? "

" Irrevocably."

" Well, good luck to you ! "

" Won't you shake hands ? "

" To-morrow."

" To-morrow I shall start before you're awake."

" Then . . ."

The two youths said farewell.

" Oh, by the by—— " cried Gustave.

" What is it ? "

" You don't know in what position you may be——"

" That's true enough."

" You may even be obliged to seek your dinner in the fields again and may not find any turnips this time."

" We have found ourselves in that situation before."

" Then I'll give you a parting present."

" Do ! "

Hippolyte held out his hand.

" You material creature, be off with you ! "

" But—— "

" I'm speaking metaphorically—— "

" Oh, I'd rather you were speaking literally."

" Perhaps I'll pass from one to the other. You know I told you that all of us, whether we belong to the higher or lower branch of our profession, we all have our wheezes ? "

" Yes, you always say that."

" I've told you other people's wheezes but never my own."

" Have you a wheeze ? "

" I go frog-fishing."

" Whatever for ? "

" Why, to eat them of course."

" Ugh ! "

" You're wrong ; they're delicious food, something between duck and fowl."

" Oh, you horror ! "

" Why ? "

" You make my mouth water."

" Oh, so you don't despise frogs ? "

" You know the confidence I have in you."

" Now listen—— But it's no good if it's freezing."

" It must end by thawing."

" Let's hope so. You choose a bit of land where it's marshy."

" I don't have to choose ; I'm in that bit of land now ; this place is all marshy."

" You set out at night, take five hundred paces or so into a field, and listen to ascertain in which direction you hear the loudest croaks."

" Go ahead."

" Next day you go in that direction. By the by, there should be three of you—— "

" Like the Fates—— "

" Or the Graces. I always went out with Fafiou and Flageolet. When you come across a marsh you examine the surface of the water; you will see ten, fifteen, or twenty frogs' snouts sticking out of the water. They look like green leaves resting on their spread-out toes and snapping their golden eyes. You'll say ' Good ! ' Then you'll cut two sticks, one twelve or fifteen feet long, the other eighteen or twenty inches. On each of these you'll leave the beginning of a branch, forming a hook, but this hook ought to be at the finest end of the long twig of twelve or fifteen feet and at the thickest end of the short twig of twelve or fifteen inches. You follow me, of course ? "

" Yes."

" You give the short stick to your friends ; but you keep the long one yourself. Armed with it, you approach the edge of the pond. You pick out the frog you want to catch first and touch it lightly with the end of your stick. Lightly, you understand ? If you touch it at all heavily it will dive, and good-bye to your frog."

" Lightly ? "

" Lightly—like a caress ; then with the end of the switch you'll draw it towards you, very gently, with every pre- caution. If you work too quickly, it will give you warning. It will say ' Crroa ' ! "

" How well you imitate the croak of a frog."

" I've had some practice. Then, as I say, you'll draw it gently towards you, until it is just within your grasp ; then you'll slip your hand under its tummy—there's no fear that it will get away if you take the precautions I've recommended ; and then, with one twist, you'll kill it and throw it some fifteen paces on to the grass. Your two friends will run to the spot ; one will seize its hind paws and one its front paws ; the one who holds the front paws will cut it in two just where the two bones jut out, the springing bones ; the one who holds the hind paws will take them off, tie them together, and string them on the twig that you have given them. Meanwhile you will have picked out another frog whom you'll treat as you treated the first ; then you'll choose a third, then a fourth,

and so on, till they're all gone. When that happens, you'll
go to another pool and continue. When you've got three,
four, five, six dozen frogs—according to whether you really
like them and whether you and your comrades are really
hungry—you'll bring your fishing to an end."

"But it isn't enough merely to get the frogs. One
wants something to season them with and something to
eat with them."

"Wait a bit ! This is how we managed. We went
along to some cottage ; Flageolet played an air on his
cornet, Fafiou turned three difficult tumbles forwards and
three backwards, and the cottager would give us either a
bit of butter or lard or a little cream. Then we went to
a second cottage ; Flageolet repeated his cornet solo,
Fafiou did his three dangerous tumbles forwards and backwards, and this cottager would give us a bit of bread. Then
we went on to a third cottage ; Flageolet and Fafiou gave
a third performance and the third peasant would let us use
his fire and saucepan. You are clever enough to guess
the rest for yourself. One man alone might do the same
thing ; it would take longer, that's all ; as he would have
to fish for the frogs, to run after them, catch them, cut them
in two, and pull off the legs without help ; but in that case
he would only have to fish for two dozen instead of six, so it
would come to the same thing."

"There would be one obstacle to my managing it, and
that is that I neither play the cornet nor can I do three
dangerous tumbles either forwards or backwards.

"No, but you've a good voice ; you could go along to
a cottage, strike a troubadour pose, and sing :

> ' My Fanchette is charming
>   In her simplicity ;
> Her piquancy disarming
>   Is better than beauty,'

and you'd get what you wanted. The first cottager would
give you butter, lard, and cream ; the second, a bit of bread ;
and the third would let you prepare your stew. The next
day you'd find another field of battle. That's what I
mean by the frog wheeze. And now, good-bye again !
I am leaving with an easier mind as I now feel myself
your benefactor ! "

The two youths said farewell all over again, and the morrow, before daybreak, M. Gustave was on his way to Paris.

CHAPTER XI

GUSTAVE AT THE BARRIER OF THE FAUBOURG ST.-MARTIN —DISAPPEARANCE OF MME. CARRÉ'S HOTEL—A GOOD NIGHT IN A CELLAR—A GENEROUS FRIEND—GUSTAVE ON THE ROAD TO CAEN—A VAN—HOPE AND DECEPTION —A RESTING-PLACE IN A LAUNDRY VAN—A WILD MARCH—ARRIVAL AT CAEN—HIS FATHER GONE—ONE LAST EFFORT—GUSTAVE IN HIS FATHER'S ARMS

THE fifth day after his departure, about two o'clock in the afternoon, M. Gustave was at the barrier St.-Martin, sniffing the odour of stews and kedgerees but without a sou to purchase a morsel of hare or plaice for his own eating. His last two halfpennies had been spent, that very morning, at Ile Adam, on a loaf of bread. Yet M. Gustave was resolved on one thing ; that he would not enter Paris till ten o'clock at night.

What was the reason of this ?

You shall hear.

M. Gustave counted on getting a lodging in the little rue St. Nicolas, at Mme. Carré's private hotel. He knew the house ; had studied it as a draftsman ; knew how the lights and shades fell. Now if he stood in the shade the state of his attire would be less visible ; then if, as was probable, there was no room for him at the hotel, instead of sending him off as they would be sure to do at one o'clock in the day when there was time for him to find another lodging, they would keep him, even if they had to let him sleep in a corner on a box of straw ; and that was the height of M. Gustave's ambition.

Here, I hope, are two good reasons, satisfactory even in the eyes of our readers, why M. Gustave acted as he did ; but if they are not enough, we can only be sorry, for we have no others to give.

M. Gustave, then, remained at the gate warming himself at the portable stoves of the hot-chestnut vendors ; and, when ten o'clock struck, he entered the town.

When you have done fifty-five leagues in five days it is not much of a walk to go down the faubourg St.-Martin, especially when you are anxious to reach Mme. Carré's hotel, standing at the corner of the rue St.-Nicolas all ready to receive you. Good Mme. Carré always used to call M. Gustave her little Étienne.

Should he present himself under the name of Étienne or Gustave ? Under the name of Étienne.

But where the devil was Mme. Carré's hotel ?

Oh, where ?

It was demolished—razed to the ground—surrounded by a palisade of planks.

Ah ! . . .

Gustave sat down on a post at the corner of the street. He might have been taken for Ulysses returning to Ithaca if he had found a dog who would agree to die of joy at seeing him again. As there was no dog he was simply M. Gustave ; but M. Gustave in a state of despair, this time.

However, he wasn't the man to let himself be utterly cast down ; and having made this resolve, our traveller rose.

There was a door in the palisade. That door was fastened within by means of a bent nail and a looped string. He slid his hand between two planks, found the string, undid it, opened the door and shut it behind him. Then he felt the ground with his feet, found a ladder leading into the cellar, went down a dozen steps and found himself in the damp atmosphere of a subterranean abode.

It never rains but it pours : M. Gustave had found a lodging ; he was also to find a bed.

The old mattresses of Mme. Carré's hotel had been emptied of their stuffing in one corner of this cellar. This made a bed as soft as eiderdown !

M. Gustave took off his overcoat for fear of spoiling it, and covered himself right to the neck in the straw. But for the pangs of hunger, that night would have been comfortable ; compared with the night in the sentry-box it was excellent.

The next day, at dawn, M. Gustave rose, shook his

handsome black locks, and went off to find a friend. The friend gave him breakfast and lent him thirty sous !

He now had to travel fifty-three leagues on thirty sous. Bah ! He had already done so many difficult things that surely he could once in a while accomplish the impossible. Gustave attempted it, not, like Nero, because he longed for the unattainable, but because he was constrained by necessity.

At two o'clock in the afternoon he left Paris.

At ten o'clock that evening he arrived at Mantes. At any rate, he had traversed fourteen leagues out of the fifty-three.

Our traveller now spent ten sous on a lodging and ten more on food ; this left him with ten sous for the remaining thirty-nine leagues. The next day he set forth as soon as it was light ; it was unpromising weather, grey, sombre, and threatening.

When one league from Mantes he overtook a tradesman travelling with his cart, which took up all the middle of the road. The tradesman, confiding in the intelligence of his horse, was himself walking along one of those footpaths that pedestrians wear at the side of the ditch.

Our Prodigal Son peered at the vehicle. It was a pretty little van covered with oilcloth, merely suspended on the axle, it is true, but the jolting was diminished by means of a stuffed seat hung on straps.

His examination of the vehicle determined him to get into talk with the tradesman. This good fellow met him halfway.

" Are you going far ? " asked he, after the first compliments had been exchanged.

" To Caen," replied the young man.

" To Caen ? You're not there yet ! "

Then, stretching out his hand, to catch the drops of rain that were now beginning to fall, " It looks like rain," he said.

" I'm afraid so ! "

" It's coming down now."

" Oh, the devil ! We shall get wet through."

" Not me."

" How's that ? "

" I shall get into my cart."

Adding example to precept, he mounted the driver's seat, cracked his whip, and departed at a trot.

Gustave had lost the trick.

Nor had the young traveller ever been out in such rain ; when he was fifteen leagues from Mantes he came to a stop.

The last ten sous would have to be spent on lunch and dinner. It was no use thinking of a bed.

A laundry van, unharnessed and standing in front of a house, supplied that.

Our traveller crept into the van and made himself as comfortable as he could.

There were still twenty-four leagues to do next day, and not a halfpenny left to buy a bit of bread or purchase a drop of brandy.

At four o'clock in the morning the cold was so intense, the water that filtered through the cover of the van so icy, that our traveller decided to take to the road again.

He still had twenty-four leagues to go, and it foolishly entered his head to do these twenty-four leagues in the one day.

By midday he had done fifteen ; but he was drooping with hunger and fatigue. He thought for a moment that he would sit down by the side of the road, but, though he was only speaking to himself, he said aloud :

"If you sit down, Étienne, you will die." And he continued to walk on.

By two o'clock he had done eighteen leagues. There were only six more to walk—it is true that, by now, he was almost delirious.

He walked like a man in a high fever, as if out of his mind, frenzied and feverish, his head raised, his eye fixed, his mouth open, and his teeth clenched. He breathed with a roaring sound.

Those who saw him pass—pale, his glance feverish, his fists clenched, and his arms rigid—got out of his way and whispered to one another :

" Is he a lunatic—walking like that ? "

Yet he walked on. His muscles obeyed his will mechanically ; he might have been called a machine started by Satan. It seemed to him now that the distance was unimportant ; that he must arrive, no matter what the distance.

Only, when he had got there, what was to happen ? The Greek from Marathon also had reached Athens, but when he did, he died !

By five o'clock in the afternoon his pace had not slackened ; he was taking not a minute more over each league. But the trees along the road, and the houses in the villages all whirled before his eyes. His temples were beating so that he almost thought an artery would burst. He had a roaring in his ears as if he stood near the Falls of Niagara. He saw red, as if he had a cloud of blood before his eyes.

All of a sudden he heard the beating of drums.

It was the tattoo.

He was nearing Caen !

He gave a hoarse laugh almost like ɬ cry of a hyæna.

Soon he saw the town in front of him—a black mass, pierced by lights.

Since four o'clock on the previous day he had eaten nothing, not even a crumb of bread, nor had he even drunk a drop of water.

He came down the faubourg Vaucelles like a ghost, went the whole length of the rue St. Jean, came into the rue des Carmes and rushed to his birthplace ; but not having the strength to go up to the third floor, he beat against a door and cried : " Is my father there ? "

A man opened the door.

" Why, it's Étienne ! " said he.

" My father ! Where is my father ? " the youth panted, leaning against the wall to keep himself from falling.

" He has moved."

" Oh, my God ! Where has he gone to ? "

" Rue des Postes, number twelve."

The unhappy boy made no reply ; he started off again.

There were about five hundred paces to go from the old home to the new.

These five hundred paces seemed to him at the moment more difficult to accomplish than the twenty-four leagues that he had just traversed.

The house in the rue des Postes had a court similar to that of the rue des Carmes.

Only he did not know where his father lived, whether on the ground floor, first, second, or third story.

He rushed into the court, crying :
" Father !   Father !   Father ! "
His father heard his cry from the second story, recog-
nized his son's voice, ran downstairs and reached him just
as he fell fainting.
" Oh, my poor boy ! " he cried.
Without another word, without a reproach, he took
him in his arms, carried him up to the second floor, and took
off his rags, washing him and putting him to bed like a child.
Étienne let him do as he pleased ; he felt as if his arms
and legs were broken.
He had not even strength enough to moan.

CHAPTER XII

The Packet of Hair—His Father tells Gustave about an Episode of his Youth

Étienne himself could not tell what happened that first
night of his arrival ; he had fainted, or nearly so. He felt
his lips parting from time to time and a strong spirit
moistening his dry throat ; then his father—who did not
show a demonstrative affection for his son as a rule—his
father pressed a trembling kiss upon his forehead. His
memory would not go beyond these few details.
The next day, when he came to himself, he found a pile
of books on a chair at his bedside.
His father had remembered that to read—to read again
and to go on reading—was one of the favourite amusements
of his son's childhood.
For eight days the youth kept his bed. Whenever he
wished to get up, no matter for what purpose, he had to
get out of bed hands first, dragging himself along like a
seal, as his lower limbs were as powerless as if a wheel had
passed over them.
One day, when his father was absent, he had opened, in
search of amusement, the old walnut cupboard, pulling out,
one after the other, all the drawers, looking for he knew

G

not what. At the back of one of these drawers he found a
packet of hair tied with a black ribbon and wrapped round
in a triple paper wrapping.

It could only be some family souvenir ; it awakened
his curiosity.

He put the packet on his bolster, and when his father
returned, coming to sit, as usual, by his son's bedside, he
drew the packet from its hiding-place, and asked, " What
is this, father ? "

His father had no need to take off the triple wrappings.
Directly he saw it he knew what it contained.

" Oh, that ! " said he. " That's nothing."

And he threw the packet into the fire.

" Oh, father ! " cried the young man, rising to rescue
the hair which he believed to be a souvenir more precious
than his father allowed.

But his father held him back till the paper with its
contents was completely reduced to ashes.

Then he lay back in his chair, sighed, and, closing his
eyes, let his head drop on to his breast. Then from his
closed lids two silent tears ran down over his cheeks. They
were followed by two more. It was clear that this man of
steel was looking into his memories, making a journey
through the country of his youth and treading again the
path of old illusions.

Astonished, the youth for a moment watched him weep,
then he, in his turn, lifted his head and did what he had
never dared to do before—he kissed the old man's cheek
just where the tears made a glistening path upon it.

His father opened his eyes, threw his arms round his
son, and kissing him in his turn upon the forehead, he said :

" Étienne, one day when you were playing with other
children, they asked you ' Why your father always looks
so grim,' and I heard you reply, ' Not because he's bad
tempered ; but I don't think, when he was young, that
any one taught him to laugh.' "

" Father ! "

" You were wrong, Étienne. When I was young I
laughed like any other youngster. When I was eighteen
I was a lively young fellow, and the first three years I was
with my regiment, when they had no other expression to
measure gaiety with, they used to say, ' As jolly as Jean.'

" Now I'll tell you how and why I ceased to laugh.

" I was older than my brothers and sisters, much older, and so when our father and mother went out, either to work or on business, they left me in charge of the others. So the smallest called me Mother John, the next in age Father John, and the elder ones Brother John.

" The one I loved best was a dear child called Catherine —fair, rosy cheeked, fresh, full of fun ; and she loved me as I did her, which is saying a great deal.

" When I joined up she was twelve—it was in 1791. I greatly regretted leaving my father and mother, my little brothers and sisters ; but the one I regretted most of all was Catherine.

" I set out and joined the army. I was fighting for four years—always light heartedly—for from time to time I had letters from Catherine in which she told me that she was well, and letters from the others who told me that Catherine was growing more and more beautiful.

" At the siege of Mayence I received a bullet in my leg. The surgeon wanted to amputate it. I took my sabre from under my pillow and told him that if he came near me with any such intention I would run him through.

" He took it for granted and left me to be attended by his students. I recovered, to his great regret.

" Every time I had to pass him I struck my thigh with my cane and said, ' You see this ? '

" ' Yes,' said he ; ' but you limp.'

" ' I should limp much more if I had only one leg.'

" Our conversation always stopped at that.

" Then we heard that there had been great victories in Italy ; that a young general called Bonaparte had beaten the Austrians and that peace had been declared.

" One day I received notice of leave with no time limit —a gallant attention that I owed to General Hoche, with whom at one time I had shared a bed.

" They gave me my arrears of pay, which had mounted up to a sum of four hundred and thirty livres ; that was another favour of the general's, for in those days they paid as seldom as possible.

" I took the coach to Strasbourg and, six days after, arrived in Caen. I got down about a quarter of a league from the town. I wanted to look about me a bit, and see the old places one by one. I was afraid that I should choke with emotion. So I entered Caen on foot.

"A friend of mine, a joiner, who was standing at his door, seeing a soldier come limping along, looking eagerly at all he passed, gazed at me attentively, recognized me, and called me. I went into his house.

"I was glad to have this chance, too, to get news of my people.

"'How is my father?' was my first question.

"'Very well.'

"'Mother?'

"'She is well too.'

"'And the little ones?'

"'All well.'

"'And—Catherine?'

"As I asked for news of her my voice trembled.

"'She has just gone by on her way to the cowsheds; you'll see her when she comes back if you wait five minutes. You know they call her all round here the Beauty.'

"'I will wait.'

"Five minutes later I saw her. She was, indeed, a beauty. All my heart went out to her. I was going to rush out of the house when my friend stopped me.

"'Catherine, come here!' said he. 'Here's some one who wants to speak to you.'

"Catherine came up smiling, singing the last couplet of a little song that I had taught her in olden days.

"She set down her milk-jug at the door.

"'Who wants to see me, neighbour?' asked she.

"Merely to hear her voice set me trembling in every limb. Though she was now a young woman it had retained the fresh pure tones of infancy.

"'Who is it? Why, a soldier! Look at him, my dear. Doesn't he remind you of some one?'

"Catherine turned to me, looked at me—hesitated—flushed and paled; then with shaking lips she said:

"'Why, it's John! My brother John!' And she stretched out her arms to me. But at that moment her eyes closed, her head fell back, she gave a little cry as if something had snapped in her heart, and fell to the ground.

"I cried out and rose hastily; but I was too late. I

couldn't stop her fall. I raised her in my arms, and
pressed her to my breast. She had fainted. I felt like
fainting myself.

"'Oh, Catherine, Catherine dear! Quick! Fetch a
doctor!'

"The cleverest doctor in the town passed at that
moment, in his cabriolet. They ran after him and stopped
him. He got down and came to the house, asked us what
had happened, felt the patient's pulse, and shaking his
head said :

"'Can't be helped, I must bleed her.'

"'My God! Bleed Catherine?'

"'Would you rather she died?'

"'If you let blood, will you answer for her life?'

"'Only God can answer for life or death.'

"'Do what you think best,' I said.

"They bandaged the poor child's white arm. I saw
the veins swell up, I saw the lancet gleam, I saw the point
approach her flesh, I saw the blood jet forth.

"Oh, I felt as if I should go mad. I wanted to kill
the man.

"I threw myself on a chair, ran my fingers through
my hair, and burst into sobs.

"I heard a sigh.

"I lifted my head.

"On the ground stood a salad bowl full of blood.

"Oh, my God! my God! I would willingly have given
all my blood for that which was in the bowl.

"Catherine looked round her, with haggard eyes.

"'It's I, dear,' said I. 'Catherine, it's I—John—
your brother.'

"She tried to speak ; her tongue at first could only
articulate unintelligible sounds.

"Then with a great effort, she stammered out these
words :

"'John, you are going away again?'

"'No, no.' I cried. 'I have returned for good, dear ;
I am going to stay with you, never to leave you again.
Don't worry, Catherine. There's not only brother John
here, but Father John, you know, and Mother John.'

"She tried to smile, but her mouth was contracted and
her smile terrifying.

" 'Mother John ? Father John ? ' repeated she—as an imbecile might search among his memories or, rather, might seek to understand what was said to him. ' No, always Brother John.'

" I looked at the doctor.

" 'Well,' said he to me, ' you see she is better. Just now she was practically dead ; she's alive now ; she was dumb, and she speaks.'

" 'Oh yes ; but in what state is she and how does she speak ? '

" 'She speaks as a girl would speak and is in the state a girl would be in who has just suffered from cerebral congestion.'

" 'And what is to be done now ? '

" 'Everything depends on her youth and Nature.'

" 'May we take her home ? '

" 'Oh yes ; if it isn't far and if the mode of transport is gentle.'

" 'The house is only a few hundred steps from here and I'll carry her in my arms.'

" 'Take care. You don't seem overstrong yourself, and you are lame.'

" I lifted Catherine in my arms as I would have lifted a child of five.

" 'Pardon,' said the doctor ; ' but where do you live ? '

" I told him.

" 'I'll come and see her every day.'

" 'And you will cure her ? '

" 'I'll do my best.'

" I gave a deep sigh ; the promise sounded vague. Then I carried Catherine away in my arms.

" The whole suburb already knew of Catherine's accident ; I arrived home followed by more than a hundred people.

" My return to the paternal home was a sad one. I came back alive, but I brought my sister back dying.

" How different from the return I had dreamed of !

" They put her to bed.

" From her pillow her eyes followed me, not leaving me for a moment.

" Every time I went to the door she stammered anxiously :

" ' You are not going away again ? '

" ' No, dear ! No ! Don't worry,' answered I.

" Whenever I left her room she kept crying, grieved and troubled, like a child :

" ' Brother John ! Brother John ! Brother John ! '

" And I came back again, saying :

" ' It's all right, Catherine. Don't worry. I am on leave.'

" It seemed as if she could not understand.

" The doctor came every day ; but instead of getting better, poor Catherine got worse and worse.

" One day the doctor said to me :

" ' It's your moustache, your pigtail and uniform that worry her. While she sees you looking like that you'll never be able to get her to understand that you are no longer a soldier.'

" I ran upstairs at once to my room, shaved off my moustache, cut off my pigtail, and threw my uniform to the back of the wardrobe.

" Then I slipped on a blouse and went back to her.

" When she saw me so transformed a gleam of pleasure passed over her face.

" ' Ah ! ' she cried, ' this really is my brother John ! '

" I went to her and took her in my arms. She leaned her head on my breast and murmured :

" ' When I am dead you'll return to the army, but not till then, will you, Brother John ? '

" Oh, when she said things like that I sobbed my heart out.

" From that moment she lay awake smiling, and smiled even as she slept.

" One day—one day—still smiling, she died !

" When I was quite sure that she was dead I went up to my room, took out my coat, hat, and sabre, and without saying good-bye to any one, neither father, mother, nor brothers, I rejoined my regiment.

" I did not come back for ten years.

" From the day of Catherine's death I have not smiled.

" You see that you were wrong, child, when you said that they didn't teach me to smile ; I knew, but the lesson was lost ! "

Étienne would never have heard this story if, one day,

as we have said, he had not found that packet of hair tied with a black ribbon at the back of a drawer in the old walnut cupboard.

CHAPTER XIII

GUSTAVE IS BORED—HIS FATHER'S ADVICE—DEPARTURE FOR PARIS—VISIT TO MLLE. DUCHESNOIS—GUSTAVE DECLAIMS A TRAGIC SPEECH—A LETTER OF INTRODUCTION TO SOUMET—KIND RECEPTION FROM THE POET—HE RECOMMENDS GUSTAVE TO THE BROTHERS SEVESTE—GUSTAVE APPEARS AT MONT-PARNASSE—HIS ENGAGEMENT

ONE morning the father looked fixedly at his son and said :
" You are bored, Étienne ? "
It was true ; Étienne did not answer.
" Come with me," his father added.
They went out together.
His father took him to the tailor's.
" Make me two complete suits for this young man," he said ; " one for every day and one for Sunday."
" When do you want them by, M. Jean ? "
" As soon as possible ; he is going back to Paris."
" By Sunday, then ? "
" You can't deliver them before ? "
" Impossible."
" Then by Sunday."
Étienne was not bored ; he was preoccupied.
What was he preoccupied about ? Why, things theatrical, of course.
But why should he be more than usually preoccupied with the stage just now ?
That's what we are going to learn.
In his absence on that unhappy tour in Flanders, Mlle. Duchesnois had been appearing in Caen and had had a great success. But in Caen they were talking even more of her kindness than of her great talent. Indeed, it would

be difficult to be more good-hearted than was Mlle. Duchesnois. Every one who had to do with her sang the praises of this great tragic actress.

Actors when on tour ought to be more careful about their private life and personal qualities. A touring actor becomes an object of universal curiosity ; his most trifling actions are spied upon and his lightest words repeated ; the walls of the hotel he stays at are as the eyes of Argus, and its doors have the ears of Midas. As long as he stays in the town they talk about his talent. But the day he leaves the town they talk about his disposition and his vices ; and for a week or a fortnight or even a month those form the principal subject of conversation. Why, even to-day, they say to strangers, passing through Caen : " Do you know Mlle. Duchesnois, sir ? "

The stranger will say " Yes " or " No " as the case may be.

" A charming woman, sir. A charming woman ! " declares the inhabitant of Caen, taking his pinch of snuff or removing his cigar from his mouth. " Not to look at. Oh no. One couldn't call Mlle. Duchesnois beautiful. On the contrary, one might even call her ugly without much fear of being contradicted ; but as for heart, why, she has a heart of gold ! A charming woman, sir. A charming woman ! "

What they say to-day in Caen, even though thirty years have passed, whenever the conversation happens to light on Mlle. Duchesnois, seems like an echo reawakened that has been slumbering since the first quarter of the century. One can understand that, at the time of her departure from the town, this was the general talk, the unanimous opinion.

It was this talk, this murmur that had been tickling both the heart and the ears of our Étienne. It was the thought that, if he stayed on at Caen, he could not go and call on Mlle. Duchesnois, which was making him sad ; so sad, indeed, that his father noticed it, took him to the tailor, bought him a new outfit, and said : " I see you are longing to return to Paris."

The youth made no reply, for fear of saying too much.

The day of his departure his father slipped a hundred francs into his pocket, and going with him to the coach, said : " So you are off again to Paris ! "

" Yes, father."

" You'll go back to M. Bochar ? "

" Yes, father."

" And work at the Madeleine ? "

" Yes, father."

" You've had enough of the stage ? "

" Yes, father."

" And you won't make a fool of yourself like that again ? "

" No, father."

" Then good-bye, you rascal."

" Good-bye, father."

Thus our young man took his departure, quite determined to doff the name of Étienne at the barrier and to present himself, the very next day, to Mlle. Duchesnois, under that of Gustave.

This time, as Mme. Carré's hotel had disappeared, he took up his quarters at the Hotel Recouvrance, rue Nôtre Dame de Recouvrance.

That very evening he went to the Théâtre-français to ask for Mlle. Duchesnois' address. She lived rue de la Tour des Dames, in la Nouvelle-Athenes.

At eleven the next morning he knocked at her door.

" What name shall I say ? " asked the servant.

" Say M. Gustave, please."

As you see, Gustave kept his promise to himself.

He was shown into a room where he awaited the coming of Mlle. Duchesnois.

She would come by and by.

Oh, how his heart beat ! How he would have repeated, if he had only happened to know it, Hamlet's impatient utterance when waiting for his mother : " By and by is easily said ! "

At last he heard a step, the soft swish of a frock ; the door opened and a servant announced Mlle. Duchesnois as an usher at Versailles might announce " The Queen ! " And Clytemnestra appeared.

Ugly, but gracious, with magnificent arms, a leg moulded on that of the Venus de Milo—she liked showing this leg in *Alzire*—Mlle. Duchesnois had the charm of good-nature. She smiled at this handsome young man, who advanced towards her, and questioning him both with glance and voice said : " You wanted to see me, sir ? "

" Oh, mademoiselle," replied he, blushing, " please forgive me. I come from Caen."

" A fine town."

" Every one there speaks in terms of adulation of your talent and your kindness, and as I am an artist—— "

" An actor ? "

" Well, something of that sort. I said to myself, ' Mlle. Duchesnois is so kind that I am sure if she can do me a service——' In short, as you see, I ventured to come, and here I am. Do you think you can do anything for me ? "

" Well, your appearance is good. Are you a pupil of the Conservatoire ? "

" Oh no."

" Have you ever played in public ? "

" Here and there—at fairs."

" At fairs ? "

" I mean in the provinces."

" Let me hear something—tragedy."

" What shall I say ? "

" Something you've never heard any one else do."

" Oh, I know. Something from M. Soumet's *Orestes*."

" Haven't you ever seen Talma in the part ? "

" M. Talma died before my first visit to Paris."

The young man threw down his hat, took the pose of an antique statue, and began :

" I stood within the tomb a vengeful God
Seemed to inhabit ; there I stayed and viewed
With pious recollection those soft veils
That lay so gently folded in its depths
Electra's tresses and the recent offering
Replacing the fond gifts of absent son.
Now fifteen years of exile had dragged through,
I there renewed my vows—there, on the altar
Where blood should flow ! A woman then appeared
In that sad place and sombre ; to observe
Her purpose, I did hide within the gloom.
To that abode of death it seemed she came
To bring not grief alone but something more—
Was it remorse that caused her steps to fail,
Her breath, uncertain, agitated, laboured ?
There at the foot of the altar did she pause.

The lamp that lit this place of grief and pain
Showed her all pale, her features all convulsed.
She gripped the altar with her crisped hand,
A prayer expiring on her trembling lips ;
And from her breast, as moment followed moment,
Came plaintive cries and long heart-broken shudders !
O Pylades, at this my reason tottered,
I seemed to see—O God, I seemed to see
The earth torn by the clang of Tartarus,
Vomit with lurid flames daughters of Hell
Who crouched twixt her and me ! ' Strike ! ' cried they.
  ' Strike !
Dost thou not see thy mother ? ' Yes, my mother !
And then the spectre of my father came
Rushing towards her, bearing her to share
With him the gulf of sin ; while I, oh, I,
The worthy son of Atreus and Tantalus,
Impatient witness of that fatal strife,
I felt within my heart, weary of virtue,
I know not what fierce craving to shed blood !
I knew myself the prey of unknown fury ;
I sprang—the altar lamp had flickered out ;
The goddesses of Styx concealed their torches ;
My very steps were lost in that vast tomb ;
A voice cried : ' Oh, remember thy poor father !
He waits thee now, to-night, at the funeral altar ;
Clytemnestra will be there ! ' This ghastly voice
Round that abode of death thus thrice re-echoed.
I left it dumb and frozen, filled with horror,
This terrible grim portent, that trembling woman,
Those ghastly sisters and that furious spectre
Pursue me still—— They are before my eyes——
I sink—— ''

" Good ! " said Mlle. Duchesnois when he had finished.
" You didn't lie to me, for I can see you haven't seen the
piece played."

" That doesn't sound exactly like a compliment."

" It is not a compliment ; no. But you would be wrong
if you took it for a criticism. You have a fine voice. Your
delivery is original ; it may not be good, but at least it is
neither vulgar nor mediocre."

" Then, mademoiselle—if that is so—— " hesitated
the young man.

" I'll give you a letter to Soumet ; he'll get you an
engagement to play minor rôles at the Odéon."

She sat down then and there at her bureau and wrote
the following note :

"MY DEAR SOUMET,

"Why haven't you been to see me? I am on the Committee next week, and I'll have you put into the repertoire.

"I want to recommend the young man who brings this letter to you; give him a line for the Odéon.

"If he proves a worker he should do well.

"DUCHESNOIS."

She gave the letter open to the young man, who read it aloud.

"Oh, I promise you I'll work," he cried. "Where is my hat?"

"Here it is."

"Mlle. Duchesnois, I don't know how to thank you. You do understand, don't you? But never mind. If I succeed I shall be proud to say that I owe it to you."

Saying good-bye to the good-hearted actress he ran out of the house.

If he had found Mlle. Duchesnois a gracious benefactor, he discovered in Soumet an equally good-natured patron.

Dear Soumet! I knew him, too late, but yet well enough to aid him in the production of his last two works, well enough for him to think that he owed me some gratitude.

He was a fine type of the poetic genius. Proud, as he might justly be, of his talent, full of faith in the Muse and of religious zeal for the art of poetry; kind, gentle, obliging, like the true genius he was. In 1828 he was still young, his large eyes still flashing with inspiration, his black locks floating in the wind, his heart open and pliable to every influence. Therefore he gave our young man a gracious reception in his elegant study, decorated with busts of the Great Masters.

He read the letter, and said, as the writer had said, "Let me hear something."

M. Gustave thought that the speech which had made so good an effect on Mlle. Duchesnois would succeed as well with Soumet.

Soumet listened with attention.

"It isn't minor rôles that you want; it is principal rôles. You ought not to be playing at the Odéon two or three times a month, but in the suburbs every day. I'll give you a letter to Seveste."

" Mlle. Duchesnois sent me to you ; do as you think best."

Yet, after having dreamed of the Théâtre-français, after having seen the Odéon almost within his grasp, he felt it a bad " come-down " to descend on Seveste.

Soumet understood what was passing through the youth's thoughts, however submissive he might seem.

" If you once start playing third-rate parts you will never get away from them again. Believe me, you should not appear at any Parisian theatre till you can make a hit there."

" Give me the letter for Seveste, sir, and I'll present it within the hour."

Soumet wrote the letter in his fine clear handwriting which resembled that of Lamartine. Great men write a characteristic hand.

The two Sevestes, Jules and Edmond—Edmond is dead, but Jules is now manager of the Théâtre National—lived then at rue Beauregard and ran all the suburban theatres. It was from this house in the rue Beauregard that the carriage loads of actors started every day, sent in this way from the centre of the circle to the circumference. They were called the Seveste salad.

Thanks to Soumet's name M. Gustave was taken at once into the presence of one of the brothers. It was Edmond.

Edmond read the letter, and for the third time in this one day, M. Gustave heard the portentous words : " Let me hear something."

This time, for the sake of variety, he gave Hamlet's speech from the First Act :

> " Angels and ministers of grace, defend us !
> Be thou a spirit of health or goblin damned,
> Bring with thee airs from heaven or blasts from hell,
> Be thy intents wicked or charitable,
> Thou com'st in such a questionable shape
> That I will speak to thee ! "

At the fourth line, as he was about to continue, a man appeared suddenly from an adjoining room. " Stop ! " he exclaimed. Gustave stopped at once.

" Sing something," said the newcomer.

" With pleasure," said M. Gustave.

He sang three vaudeville couplets to three different airs.

" What a fine bass voice ! " cried Jules Seveste. (The newcomer was Jules Seveste.)

" What rôles do you know ? "

" *Michel and Christine ; No Drum, No Trumpet ; Adolphe and Clara.*"

" That will do. You can rehearse to-morrow and play the next day."

" Where ? "

" At Mont Parnasse."

Two days after, in the evening, M. Gustave played *Michel and Christine* at Mont Parnasse.

The call boy was waiting for him when he left the stage.

" Please go to M. Seveste."

" What, made up like this ? "

" Yes. As you are ; he is waiting for you."

" Oh, I won't keep him waiting."

He went straight off to M. Seveste.

Two contracts lay on a table, duly signed by M. Seveste.

" Please sign these," said Edmond.

M. Gustave did so without even reading them.

" Good. Now you'd better read them," said the manager.

M. Gustave did read them. He was engaged for principal parts, leading juveniles, heavy fathers, light comedy parts ; to sing in musical pieces and appear in spectacular ones.

For all this he was to receive just the same salary as Zozo of the North had promised him ; that is, fifty francs a month.

But he had to find his own wardrobe.

M. Gustave went home as happy as a prince, pressing his contract with his left arm against his heart.

CHAPTER XIV

ORESTES AND PYLADES MEET ONCE AGAIN AT BELLEVILLE
—THE TEMPTER—GUSTAVE IS ENTICED AWAY—INDIS-
POSITION—ARRIVAL AT HAVRE—THE THREE-MASTER
INDUSTRY—GETTING UNDER WAY—WAITING AT HAVRE
A MONTH FOR A FAVOURABLE WIND—SAILING FROM
THE PORT

GUSTAVE became a member of the stock company at Belleville.

The very next day, as he was going on the stage at rehearsal, he was greeted by a cry.

" Why, it's Gustave ! "

" Why, it's Hippolyte ! "

Orestes had met Pylades again. Orestes approached his Pylades with requisite solemnity, saying :

> " Yes, since I have found again my faithful friend,
> Fortune must bear for me a happier face;
> Already seems her wrath 'gainst me abated,
> For 'tis her care that we encounter here."

Hippolyte had also been obliged to leave old Dumanoir ; the wretched life had become unbearable, and as the winter weather continued to be so bitter that the touring actor found, as the grammars say, " ponds and rivers alike frozen," he could not procure a single alleviation of his life by making use of the wheeze his friend Gustave had bequeathed to him either by fishing for frogs or singing :

> "My Fanchette is charming."

After this first outbreak of verse, and Racine at that, they took to plain prose.

" What are you doing ? " asked Gustave.

" I play the lovers," said Hippolyte.   " And you ? "

" I'm the bass ; do re mi fa so la si re."

As a matter of fact, Hippolyte played all the lovers, whatever they might be, humorous, dramatic, or sentimental.

Gustave played uncles and fathers, generals, governors, in short, " old men."

This lasted for six months. At the end of that time one of the two suits given by an affectionate father disappeared for good. The other was in a bad enough condition. A Greek cap (mortar-board) had taken the place of the hat, but that did not matter. Enthusiasm for the brave Greeks was at its height just then. But his boots let in the water and socks were being replaced by old day-bills. You will understand that Gustave, having only fifty francs a month, and out of that fifty francs being obliged to provide everything needed at the theatre, could not afford much in the way of clothes to be worn in the streets.

One evening, after he had been playing in three pieces, some circumstance, I know not what, had kept him there after his comrades, and he came out of the stage door at half-past twelve at night. As he took the first steps along the street a man who seemed to be waiting for him moved away from the wall and followed him. Although it was summer-time the night was dark and the street deserted. M. Gustave had nothing, absolutely nothing on him, for a thief to steal, yet he felt anxious at being followed in this way. He stopped short at a turning so that when the unknown turned the same corner that he had just rounded he and M. Gustave must find themselves face to face.

" Ah, pardon, M. Gustave," said the unknown.

" Pardon ? What for ? " asked our young man.

" For having followed you."

" Then you were following me ? "

" Certainly I was."

" And why were you following me ? "

The unknown began to smile.

" I wanted to ask you a question, sir."

" What question ? "

" Are you fond of travelling ? "

" That's an odd question to ask a man, especially at one o'clock at night."

" I'm sorry, sir, but I hadn't patience to wait longer."

" To know if I like travelling ? "

" Yes, sir. I attach great importance to your opinion on that matter."

" Well, sir, I am passionately fond of travelling. And you ? "

" Oh, it's my business to like travelling."

H

" You are a traveller ? "

" Indefatigable, sir. Have you any curiosity to see America ? "

" Which ? There are two : North and South."

" Neither the one nor the other ; Central America."

" The Antilles, then ? "

" That's it."

" That's odd. I'm dying to drink the milk of the coconut like Robinson and to eat guavas like Captain Cook."

" Well, sir, it's for you to say whether you do or not."

" What's that ? You say it is for me to say ? "

" All expenses paid."

" Oh, that suits me all right."

" And three hundred francs a month as salary ; two hundred and fifty more than you get from M. Seveste."

" I must say it's tempting."

" Then let yourself be tempted."

" Do you know, this dark night, standing here at the corner of a deserted street, I in my coat and you in your cloak, we suggest Faust and Mephistopheles ? I am Faust, of course."

" Hold on to my cloak and let us set off."

" What about Seveste ? "

" Has he paid you any salary in advance ? "

" None."

" Then your honour isn't engaged. And take note of this."

" You are an observer ? "

" Yes."

" Well, what am I to take note of ? "

" That each man has his own particular proclivity. You have a proclivity for deserting."

" What ? "

" It's true. First of all you ran away from M. Bochard's studio to become one of Dumanoir's Company ; then you left Dumanoir's Company to join that of Bertrand, known as Zozo of the North ; then you ran away from that company to go back to Dumanoir's ; then you left that to go back to your father ; then you left your father to become one of Seveste's Company ; now you are going to desert from M. Seveste's Company to join that of Victor Marest ;

indeed, you are deserting France for America, Guadeloupe, and Trinidad, where the lovely climate, the pure air, the charming women, the milk from the coconuts, and the guavas will cure you of the desire to desert, or so I hope."

"You seem to know all about me."

"I usually find out all I can."

"But Seveste?"

"Does he want to keep you very badly?"

"Less than you seem to want to get me, since he only gives me fifty francs a month and you offer me three hundred."

"Think it over."

"I have thought."

"Well?"

"I'll desert."

"Bravo!"

"But—wait a bit! We must desert as honourably as possible."

"Honourably—but effectively."

"Oh, the one thing doesn't preclude the other."

"So much the better."

"I shall have to be ill."

"What for?"

"They will have to get some one else for my rôles and so, when I go I shan't leave Seveste in a hole."

"Do you know that reassures me against the day when my turn comes round."

"I may be a deserter, but I am honest!"

"All right, that's understood. Then you are going to be ill."

"You'll leave me fifty francs."

"I'll leave you fifty francs."

"You'll set off for la Havre."

"I'll set off for la Havre."

"And two days before the ship sails—I presume you go by sea to the Antilles?"

"You have guessed correctly. Would you rather walk?"

"I might prefer it with a salary a hundred and fifty francs below that you offer me."

"Unfortunately——"

"Yes. It isn't possible. Well, two days before you sail, you'll write to me."

"I'll write to you."

"I shall be with you in time to embark and the thing is done."

"Here are your fifty francs. I can count on you?"

"Here's my hand on it."

"I have your word and that's enough for me."

"You are right; it's safer than a contract."

Mephistopheles departed to his destination and Faust to his.

The next day, M. Gustave was indisposed; the day after he was ill, the day after that, very ill.

They were obliged to get a substitute for all his parts.

Only the management pointed out, as considerately as possible, that when one is only drawing fifty francs a month salary one is not entitled to be ill more than eight days.

On the seventh day he received a letter from M. Victor Marest telling him that the ship was due to sail in two days' time. About six o'clock in the evening there was a ring at the bell.

M. Gustave was dressed and ready to start.

"Who's there?" he asked, through the door.

"It's me. Hippolyte."

"Oh, if it's you, you can come in."

Hippolyte came in. They were so intimate that each deprived the other of a syllable. Hippolyte was Polyte and Gustave Gugus.

"Are you better?" asked Polyte.

"I have never been ill."

"What? But your—indisposition?"

"Just a ruse."

"But why? I say——"

"Well, say away."

"You are dressed for travelling."

"I am just starting on my travels."

"You are? But M. Seveste——"

"It's on his account that I've been ill."

"I see. You want to get away without his knowing?"

"That's it."

"But he'll send after you."

"I shall run him out of breath; you needn't worry."

" Then you're going a long distance ? "

" To the devil ! To Martinique, Guadeloupe, and Trinidad."

" Oh, poor Seveste. And when are you going ? "

" Come and see me off. But mind ! Keep this to yourself."

" For greater safety perhaps I'd better tell them to-morrow that you are dead and then bury you the next day ? "

" Oh, you needn't trouble. The day after to-morrow I shall have started."

A quarter of an hour after they were at the Messageries royales ; ten minutes after that and the two friends had said good-bye, each wiping a tear from the corner of his eye ; then Gugus rolled off along the road to Havre.

The next day, at two o'clock in the afternoon, he greeted M. Victor Marest, singing the air from *The Deserter* :

"I gasp for air ; I must get my breath again."

This fine air was listened to by M. Marest with attention, for he was not sorry to get an idea of his new acquisition's powers in opera comique.

" When are we starting ? " asked M. Gustave.

" To-morrow, at high tide."

" What ship ? "

" The*Industry*; a fine three-master. Captain Chamblon. He has undertaken to do the voyage in a month."

" Can I sleep aboard the *Industry* ? "

" Are you afraid of being recognized ? "

" Perhaps—— "

" By all means, especially as high tide is due at six in the morning."

M. Gustave accordingly went off to make his arrangements on the three-master. It was rather a formidable undertaking for a man to be a whole month on the sea, when even the short distance from Delivrande to Trouville on a customs boat had caused him to vomit blood.

The next day, as soon as dawn appeared, the captain gave the order to set the sails. This is always an interesting sight even for those who assist at it every day, watching from the jetty ; it is far more so for Parisians who have never seen it and who are personally interested in the manœuvre in which indeed they are actors, the ship being their theatre. It goes without saying that the whole company, manager and stage manager at their head, were on deck.

Two ships sailing for Guadeloupe were due to start at the same time. When the moment for raising the anchor came round the second ship which, owing to its position should be the first to sail, began to float and passed without misadventure from the harbour, over the bar and so out to sea. But it was not the same with the *Industry*, who drew a hundred and fifty tons more than the first ship ; either the tide was not high enough or the boat was badly handled by the pilot, but she struck and could not get away. The start had therefore to be put off for the next high tide. But by the next high tide the wind had changed and was contrary. The other boat was lost to view the same evening.

For a whole month the wind remained obstinately fixed N.N.W., therefore for a whole month the *Industry* remained in the harbour. During this time Gustave wandered about the neighbouring country. He was flying from the emissaries of M. Seveste. The month passed without accident. At the end of that month he heard the drummer announce the departure of the *Industry*. He went on board again.

The next day, thanks to able handling and to a favourable wind, the three-master sailed happily from the port and triumphantly gained the high seas.

CHAPTER XV

Captain Chamblon—M. Gustave in his Berth—St. Cecilia—Dialogue between Two Ships—Ducks and Cocades—A Penance—Usefulness of the Academy's Dictionary—The Second Mate makes a Pennant or Penance—Gustave carves an Image—Dead Calm—Gustave's Image in the Sea—Guadeloupe—Bescherelle's Dictionary.

This delay of a whole month had put every one in a bad temper, particularly Captain Chamblon. He was a man of

from forty to forty-five years old, tall, cold, dry, grave and
even sad of countenance. He was a chevalier of the Legion
of Honour, and had gained his cross on a ship of war.

As for the rest, the wind was favourable ; this wind, so
contrary while they were in the Channel, became most
favourable directly they doubled Cape Finisterre. In
spite of the good weather, M. Gustave scarcely left his
berth, where, as they say on the sea, he was counting his
shirts. After seven or eight days at sea the manager, who
as an old traveller had his sea legs, came to see this member
of his company.

" Well, Master Gustave," said he, making the most of
an admirable bass voice.

" M. Marest," replied Gustave in lamentable accents.

" You're still here, then ? "

" I am quite aware of that."

He tried to raise his head.

" Well, I can see you ; that's enough for the moment.
I came to tell you that it is St. Cecilia's Day the day after
to-morrow."

" Well ? "

" Well, I hope you'll try to sing the poor saint a little
song."

" Oh, M. Marest, if the boat continues to roll like this
I give you my word I shan't leave my berth."

" Oh, don't worry. We shall have splendid weather.
I've arranged that with the stage manager."

In fact, the next day but one, when they arrived at
Madeira, the wind dropped all of a sudden. In two or three
hours the sea looked like a great smooth mirror. Towards
five o'clock in the afternoon, under a clear blue sky, in
sight of Madeira, they laid the table. The captain offered
his passengers an extraordinary repast, ornamented with
bordeaux and enamelled with champagne. The stage
manager had kept his word, the weather was magnificent,
and the ship scarcely moved.

Dinner over, every one went on deck. It was one of
those wonderful evenings such as fall from Heaven upon
Lake Majeur, or the sea off Sicily, or upon those gigantic
baskets of flowers which we call the Islands of Oceania.
At the sight of those perfumed isles, that sparkling sea, the
deep blue of the Spanish sky, no one remembered the bad

weather they had lately had, and every musician on board, tuning their instruments, played with the same *ensemble* as if they had been parts of an orchestra.   The entire company sang the chorus from the *White Lady* :

" Sound, sound, horns and bagpipes."

They sang and accompanied with the more spirit because they had an audience.

An English brig had come within three or four cables' lengths of them and the spectators who covered her bridge applauded this improvised concert.   Then when the chorus from the *White Lady* was done, two horns began a duet on the English brig, playing with rare execution.

It was now the turn of the *Industry* to applaud.

Then a conversation commenced between the two ships ; they were so close that one could talk from the one deck to the other.

" Have you an orchestra on board ? " asked the brig.

" I should rather think we have.   We are going to Guadeloupe with a comic opera company.   Have you ? "

" Oh, we've two artists on their way to New York for concert engagements."

" Oh !   Bravo ! "

Compliments began to fly from deck to deck.

Then the musicians on board the *Industry* gave the signal for another song ; and the chorus from *Joseph* rang out :

" God of Israel, Father of all created things."

In her turn the English vessel replied with a second concerto.

And this sort of thing went on for a good portion of the night ; that lovely night, perfumed, harmonious, which will linger long in the memory of all who shared it.

At last the French musicians played the air, " Vive Henri IV.," and the English ones replied with " God Save the King."   They said good night and wished each other pleasant dreams, then went slowly and regretfully down to their berths till no one remained on deck except the helmsman, who did not take his eye from the compass, and Captain Chamblon, who was leaning over the end bulwark, watching the course cut by the ship through what looked like waves of fire.

The next day, when the passengers came on deck again, the English vessel was no longer in sight, for its speed was greater than that of the *Industry*. It was merely visible as a tiny white-winged creature, like a seagull shaving the water on the horizon line.

In three or four days' time they had had more than enough of this calm which they had so longed for ; they were not making ten leagues in twenty-four hours; Captain Chamblon particularly was in a bad temper, almost all the time.

Captain Chamblon suffered, as did M. Jean, from the fact that his lesson to laugh when he was young was forgotten. But M. Jean, though grave, was calm.

Captain Chamblon never broke silence except to fall into a violent state of agitation.

The only time when he seemed to feel at all comfortable was when, bent, as we have seen just now, over the bulwark, he watched the course of the ship through the immeasurable abyss between high-crested waves.

It seemed as if at the bottom of this man's heart was either some deep grief or some terrible remembrance. Perhaps both. This calm weather irritated him in the extreme. On the other hand, the calm rejoiced our friend Gustave, since it allowed him to walk the decks and study with his artist's eye the wonderful equatorial sunsets.

One day when he was pacing along the deck with the other passengers, they all amused themselves by putting cockades on the ducks.

Ah, your pardon, reader ! If you have never made a long voyage you probably know nothing of this diversion.

We will tell you about it.

You make a cockade of white paper, or blue or yellow or red or green, the colour doesn't matter, but it must be about three inches across ; the size, like the colour, depends principally on the taste of the player. To the centre of this cockade you attach firmly a piece of string. At the end of this piece of string you tie a morsel of bread. You throw the whole contraption to a duck. The duck, naturally, prefers the bread to the cockade ; with characteristic gluttony, it devours the bread ; the string follows the bread and the cockade follows the string. When it reaches the bird's beak it hesitates a moment ; then it decides to travel to the right or to the left and ends up against one of its eyes. This gives the duck such a ridiculous appearance that every one has to laugh.

"It wouldn't make us laugh," you reply, disdainfully. Just try being out at sea for fifteen days; fifteen days without seeing anything except sea and sky, and in the sky only albatrosses and frigate birds, in the sea only bonitos and dolphins, and between sea and sky only flying fish; and I will wager that you won't need Ravel, Arnal, or Grassot to make you laugh, nor stipulate for your favourite actors in a play by my witty colleagues Duvert and Bauzanne.

Every one was laughing, then, at the sight of a dozen ducks promenading gravely on the deck each with a cockade on its forehead, each cockade being of different colour and size; when the captain was heard saying to the second mate: "What we want is a penance to see from which side the wind is coming."

The passengers looked at one another and whispered the question: "What does he mean by that?" No one knew. One of the passengers had an Academy Dictionary with him. He went down to his cabin and looked up the word "penance." "Penance, *n.s.*, act of penitence from one who is ashamed or remorseful."

The passenger went up to the deck again with his dictionary open at page 262, and pointed out the word in the third column to his companions. All agreed that it couldn't be the right meaning; so they went up to the second mate, who was obeying the captain's instructions.

This is how he was doing it.

He had found a cork from a bottle of bordeaux, the longest he could get; he had sharpened one end to a point, leaving the other end as it was. Then he proceeded to cut the cork into twenty round pieces. These circular pieces got smaller and smaller as they got nearer and nearer the pointed end of the cork. The biggest was the size of a coin of twenty sous value, the smallest no larger than a lentil.

Now this did not seem to have any noticeable connection with the definition given in the Academy.

Their curiosity was, accordingly, excited to the highest degree.

The proprietor of the Academy's Dictionary ventured
to address the second mate. "Please, is that thing you
are making what the captain calls a ' penance ' ? "

" Penance or pennant, I don't quite know which : I
think it ought to be pennant, though we sailors usually
say penance."

" Oh, pennant," said the proud owner of the dictionary.
Turning its leaves, he found on the first column of page 265 :
" Pennant, *n.s.* This was the old name for a standard or
banner with a long tail, which a knight with twenty men-
at-arms under his command had the right to carry."

The dictionary man turned to the second mate to see
if the object he was making bore any resemblance to a
standard or banner with a long tail, and he saw that the
second mate held a fowl between his knees, brought to him
by a cabin boy, and that he was plucking from the breast
of this fowl the softest, most golden feathers. Then when
he thought he had enough feathers the second mate gave
the fowl back to the cabin boy, who took it back to its cage.
It had uttered piercing cries during the operation.

" That can't be it either," said one passenger to the
other, and they formed a circle round the second mate,
passing the dictionary from hand to hand.

" But, my dear fellows," expostulated the owner of the
book. " The Academy Dictionary—why, it's the Law and
the Prophets ! "

The more serious the thing became the more fixed was
their attention. When he had cut the rounds of cork and
pulled out the fowl's feathers the second mate made a knot
at the end of a bit of string and passed it through the
smallest of the rounds of cork which he pushed right up along
the string to the knot at the end, then he slipped on the
second round which he pushed up the string to the distance
of about an inch from the first, then a third which was pushed
to about an inch and a quarter of the first, and so on, keeping
each round a greater distance from the preceding round as
they got bigger and bigger.

Then into the circumference of each round he thrust
the hard quills of some feathers, so that these feathers seemed
like the rays of a sun of which the round of cork was the
face, or solid orb. It goes without saying that the maker
of the penance or pennant suited the size of the feathers to

the size of the rounds of cork. The biggest feathers to the biggest rounds of cork and the smallest to the smallest.

Then he knotted the thread, or rather the string, to the end of a stick of about a foot and a half in length which he fastened on the bulwark of the ship. The slightest wind was sufficient to lift the rounds of cork and feathers and to show, consequently, from which quarter the wind was blowing.

" Bravo," said the captain ; " now at any rate we shall know with what we have to deal."

Gustave had noticed what importance the captain attached to his weathercock and he resolved to give him a surprise. He started by getting hold of a good piece of guaiacum wood about eighteen inches long. Then at the top end he carved with his knife a little man six or eight inches tall. He added to this man a movable arm of fir, the lightest of all woods, painting it the colour of guaiacum, the heaviest of woods. The rest of the wood formed a sort of Trajan column on which the little man stood. Then, when he had finished carving his little man on his column, he threw the stick of the " pennant " into the sea, stuck his column up in its place, and attached the string that held the rounds of feathered cork to the movable arm of the little man. At the slightest puff of wind the rounds floated in the air, not lifted by the arm of the little man but raising that limb.

When he saw this, Captain Chamblon's face was lit up by a smile ; the very first smile that they had seen upon his face. But this satisfaction did not last very long. That very day the wind fell so low that, though it had shown itself ready to be lifted by the slightest wind, the pennant remained absolutely motionless. The Sea of Aulis was not more dead under the galleys of the Greeks than was the Atlantic Ocean under the good ship *Industry*.

Captain Chamblon was very superstitious. When he saw this absolute dead calm he got it into his head that the little man carved by Gustave had brought bad luck to the ship.

Thenceforward he never passed the little man without addressing some threat or oath to him.

At last, one night, in his impatience, he took hold of the column, rounds of feathered cork and all, and threw the lot into the sea. An hour after this a terrible squall came on them and the ship, though running with furled sails, span along at eight knots an hour. M. Gustave, who had gone to sleep, believing in the continued calm, woke all of a sudden, tossed about in his cabin like a dried-up almond in its shell. His first cry was : " Tea ! "

Although the captain usually sent all the braying passengers to Jericho, he had recommended Gustave particularly to the care of the cabin boy, because of his talents. The boy came in with the Chinese infusion.

" Oho, so you've need of poor Gringalet's services now, have you ? "

M. Gustave had nicknamed the boy Gringalet in memory of the famous Gringalet of Caen.

" Why, what's the matter, Gringalet ? What's been happening ? " asked M. Gustave.

" Why, the captain's thrown your cursed penance into the sea, he said it was bewitching the *Industry ;* and now we're making three leagues an hour."

The squall lasted for fifteen days and the ship was nearly cast away on the coast of Senegal. The weather was so bad that they didn't even perform the ceremony usual when crossing the line. At last, on the sixteenth day, there was a moment of relaxation.

Mme. Dupuis, the baritone's wife, took advantage of it to have a baby. Her husband acted as midwife ; the captain performed the office of registrar, the manager of the company was godfather and the *prima donna* godmother.

From this date onwards they had fine weather again.

On the forty-fifth day after their departure from Havre the sailor in the crow's nest called out :

" Land ! "

They had sighted Guadeloupe.

" Damn that penance ! " cried the captain. " Just think, if I hadn't thrown it overboard we should still be hanging round Cape Bogador."

" Never mind, captain," said Gustave. " I won't carve you anything again. To think that I worked on my little man for three whole days and spoilt both blades of my knife as well ! "

" All right, M. Gustave," whispered Gringalet. " The captain's a liar ; he only threw the string and rounds of

cork into the sea ; I've seen your little man in the drawer
of his chest, and if you like I'll show him to you."

M. Gustave gave Gringalet a tip. Honour was saved!

As for the passenger who owned a dictionary, he didn't
return to France till 1838 or 1839 just when they were
publishing Bescherelle's Dictionary. Learning that a new
dictionary had just appeared, he went to see the publisher
and asked permission to turn over the leaves. It was
granted. He looked up the word that had been pre-
occupying him for ten years, and he found this :

"Pennant, *n.s.*, a sort of weathercock made of a stick
with rounds of cork attached to its higher end, round the
circumference of which small feathers are attached to show
the direction of the wind."

"Ah!" cried he. "Here is a man who knows more
than the forty Academicians put together ! "

CHAPTER XVI

ARRIVAL—M. GUSTAVE IN A CAFÉ—DIALOGUE WITH A
CREOLE—GUSTAVE, CHAMPION OF NEGROES, RECEIVES
A WARNING—THE GOOD-NATURED GENDARME—GUS-
TAVE IN THE COSTUME OF ADAM AFTER THE FALL—
CAPTAIN CHAMBLON FALLS INTO THE SEA—HIS FUNERAL
ORATION

As we have said, the land was Guadeloupe ; and you can
well imagine that the moment the cry of "Land!" was
heard, every one rushed on deck. But in the transparent
atmosphere of the tropics one can see land an incredibly
long distance away. This land, which was sighted at
seven in the morning, did not become really visible for three
hours after, and it was not till about five o'clock that afternoon that the *Industry* ran along the coast of the Arbousier.

At three or four leagues distance away they could make
out, with the aid of glasses, some hundreds of barques,
surrounding ·the French vessel which guarded the coast
and which was called the *Stationary*. These barque

seemed to be awaiting the *Industry*. As they gradually approached, demonstrations of joy were heard from these little boats, so expressive and so exultant that one wondered what could be the cause of this universal satisfaction which seemed to pass the limits of any ordinary manifestation of pleasure. But the first words that were exchanged between the barques and the ship gave the explanation of this enigma.

The ship which left Havre the day that the *Industry* should have sailed was also sailing for Guadeloupe.

She made the voyage in twenty-five days, and when she entered the port she announced the near arrival of the *Industry* which could not be long after her as she was starting on the same day. Having seen the three-master weigh her anchor, and not knowing that she had not been able to get away, it was natural to think that she was following. But, as you will remember, the *Industry* had had to wait a whole month at Havre. Now, the other ship had been anchored at the Pointe-à-Pitre for five days before the *Industry* set sail. Forty-five days taken up by the passage added to those five days made a delay of fifty days. The inhabitants of Guadeloupe, therefore, thought that the *Industry* had sunk. Now, among her passengers there were seven or eight Creoles from the island, almost all of them young people from the best families of the Pointe-à-Pitre ; so that this delay, which seemed as if it must be caused by some unknown disaster, had plunged the whole town into mourning. Therefore directly the look-out of the port signalled the three-master *Industry*, a great cry of joy went up from the whole town.

The *Industry* came in under full sail and nothing in her rigging or masts indicated the least damage. Moreover, far from her passenger list having suffered loss, the number of her passengers had, on the contrary, been augmented.

The Europeans thought it a marvellous sight to see this beautiful island with its luxurious vegetation outline itself against the golden background of the setting sun, while the transparent sea, thickly dotted with boats showering a spray of rosy diamonds from their oars, seemed a framed picture representing "A Fête to celebrate the Safe Return."

Boats and ships met near the *Stationary ;* there was an instant exchange of tender words, a running fire of kisses ; the people in the boats boarded the ship whilst some of the passengers leaped down into the boats even at the risk of falling into the sea. Arms were outstretched, while gentle breasts offered welcome and tender eyes suffused with tears.

Our travelling company was debarred from these demonstrations. Only curiosity welcomed them, and that curiosity was not exactly affectionate. They entered the town as night fell, looking with astonishment at the spectacle which to European eyes is so strange, of a black population, almost nude. The evening of their arrival was taken up with the search for lodgings. Yet there is nothing easier to find than furnished apartments at Pointe-à-Pitre. A crowd of beautiful negresses, from eighteen to twenty years of age, have no other livelihood except that which they get from letting out, furnished, the two or three rooms in which they live. They either take their own bed out of the room—or leave it in—whichever the lodger prefers ; there is a simple patriarchal touch about the matter.

M. Gustave went to the café directly he landed, thinking to find what he wanted there. Everything he saw astonished him ; he looked at all with avid eyes ; he listened with all his ears agog with curiosity.

Two Creoles were talking together ; he listened to their conversation. They were talking of a negro named Cicero.

" Sir," said one of the Creoles to our hero, " I see by your complexion that you are a European."

" By Jove, sir, you are not mistaken in that."

" And I should guess that this is the first time you have been to the Antilles."

" I landed at the Pointe-à-Pitre two hours ago."

" Well, sir, I'd wager one thing."

" What's that ? "

" I'll bet you are sorry for the negroes."

" Bet by all means, sir ; you would gain your bet."

" Yet it seems incredible that any one can pity such brutes."

" Why not, sir ? After all, they are men."

" Men ? A queer sort of men ! Why—look ; look there."

The Creole pointed to the man with whom he had been conversing.

" I'm looking, sir. What then ? "

" Well, he bought a nigger to-day—— "

" He bought a nigger, did he ? What then ? "

" He paid two thousand four hundred francs for him."

" Two thousand four hundred francs."

" The creature saw the money counted out before his face. You understand ? He saw it paid down."

" He saw it counted and paid. Well ? I'm following you."

" Then can you guess what he did ? "

" How can I guess ? "

" He has just hanged himself. This very night, sir."

" Hanged himself ? Really ? "

" As I have the honour to tell you. Now what do you think of a creature like that ? "

" I think him splendid, sir."

" You'd better not say things like that often, sir— especially when in the company of Creoles."

" Why not ? "

" Well, we are somewhat hot-headed in Guadeloupe, and we shoot pretty straight ! "

" And what has that got to do with me, pray ? "

The two Creoles looked at one another, as if to say : " Here's a revolutionary for you ! "

They left the café.

The next day, going out into the town for the first time, M. Gustave saw an old woman beating a negro on the head heavily with the stave of a barrel ; the blood was running down the sides of his head.

M. Gustave, alert to defend the helpless, sprang into the house and made the woman relax her grip. She thought it shocking that a white man should want to succour a black one, and ran to complain to the governor.

The governor sent for M. Marest, told him the scandal that M. Gustave's conduct had caused in thus posing openly as an abolitionist, and let him know in plain words that if a third complaint was brought against his employé,

I

that gentleman would be taken on board the first ship setting out for France and the captain would be asked to drop him as soon as possible either at Nantes, Brest, or Havre.

The manager, very much upset, sent for M. Gustave and told him to give up concerning himself with the affairs of negroes and negresses. Gustave, resigning himself to Fate, resolved to concentrate on his rehearsals, which were to commence next day.

Eight days later he made his debut in *Stanislas*, and had a big success.

M. Marest's Company had joined the remains of another company, who had come out before them and had for manager an excellent man called Verteuil, uncle or cousin of the Verteuil who is the present secretary of the Théâtre Français. He was also related to Mlle. Georges. Another thing that doubled their chance of success was that they exploited both Pointe-à-Pitre and the Basse-Terre, both at the same time. A little coasting ship which ran between the two places took the artists from one to the other in a few hours.

But my readers will remember M. Gustave's repugnance for the " liquid plain," as the poets of the Empire used to call it. Now, as our hero—as must have been apparent by now—was as good a walker as he was a bad sailor, and as the two towns were only about twelve or fourteen leagues distance from one another by road, he made the journey on foot on dry land that the rest of the company made by boat on the sea.

Between the two halves of the island, known to the natives as the High and the Low Land, and the bounds of which had been traced by Nature herself, swept some three torrential streams. The first was called the Three Rivers, the second the Guava, and the third the Mosquito. In ordinary weather—that is to say, in summer weather—M. Gustave, when he reached the banks of the Guava and Mosquito, contented himself with taking off his shoes and stockings, turning up his trousers, and jumping from stone to stone until he reached the other side of the stream. To cross the Three Rivers he not only took off his shoes and stockings, but also his trousers, and, walking with the utmost precaution, he got across, the water in places being up to his waist. But in exceptional weather—that is to say, in the rainy season—where he formerly took off his shoes and stockings he had to take off his trousers too ; and where he formerly took off shoes, stockings, and trousers he now had to take off everything, and making his clothes into a parcel, carry it over on his head as he swam across the stream.

The return journey was easy enough.

About a quarter of a league from the other bank of the stream—within the limits of the Low Ground—there was a village ; in this village was a shop where they sold dried fish, tafia, and tapioca ; in that shop was a gendarme ; in the gendarme's stable, a horse.

M. Gustave stopped at the shop to wash his feet in tafia and ended by becoming friendly with the gendarme. When he was on his way to the Low Land this friendship was useless to him, but it was quite another thing when he was going home from the Low Land. The gendarme mounted his horse, took M. Gustave up on the croup, carried him over the Three Rivers, the Guava, and the Mosquito, put him down again, and went back over the streams alone, returning to his own home to stable his horse, assist at the sale of dried fish, tafia, and tapioca, and serve the Government in his spare moments.

Now one day it happened that the rivers were so swollen that Gustave had to take off all his clothes to pass the Guava and the Mosquito, and as he swam across the Three Rivers he had to use both hands, with the result that the parcel of clothing fell off his head.

In this parcel, please remember, were his shoes, stockings, trousers, coat, waistcoat, and shirt. My readers will understand the value M. Gustave set on that parcel. He made unheard-of efforts to recapture it, but all in vain. The utmost he could accomplish was to avoid following his parcel which was carried away to the Gulf of Mexico, and to save his own skin.

He did save it and at first was inclined to congratulate himself on the fact.

But when he had done congratulating himself M. Gustave realized that he was as naked as a worm.

Still, there was always the gendarme and his shop.

But the gendarme's shop was situated in the very centre

of the village. It was therefore absolutely necessary to get to the centre of the village.

It is common enough to see negroes going about as naked as was M. Gustave and no one paid any attention, because of the colour of their skin ; but it was not the same thing for a white man.

M. Gustave found himself in the very situation of Robinson in his island or Adam in Paradise. But he had no animals' skins as Robinson had. However, he could lay his hands on leaves as Adam did. He therefore adopted the costume that Adam assumed after the Fall, and in this he made his entrance into the village and so to the shop of his friend the gendarme.

Once there he was saved. The gendarme lent him the insignia, tunic, and hat of the police ; and it was in this costume that he rejoined his company.

The public had heard of his adventure, and when he made his appearance they gave him a magnificent reception.

What had become of Captain Chamblon during this time ?

Captain Chamblon had taken his fresh cargo on board as quickly as possible and gone back to sea with his mate who was a master mariner and as experienced and skilful as himself.

One may ask, why this alliance of two certificated masters ? and the cleverest of us might be puzzled to answer. Yet three days after their departure from Guadeloupe the matter was explained.

The captain, according to his custom, was on the poop, leaning over the bulwarks and watching the ship's course through the waves as if in search of I know not what.

This time his preoccupation was so great that he forgot the laws of gravity, and, lifting his legs at the same moment that he chose for bending forward, he let himself slip gently into the water, falling without even a cry, which proves that it was a voluntary action and not an accident.

Five minutes after this event, which took place so quietly that the helmsman did not even turn his head, the mate came up the hatchway and looked round him as if in search of some one.

Then, not finding the man he sought, he asked the helmsman :

" Where is Captain Chamblon ? "

" At the stern, sir," replied he.

" At the stern ?   But I can't see any one."

The helmsman, astonished, turned round.

" Why, that's singular," he said.   " He was there a moment ago."

" Well, he is not there now," retorted the mate.

The two men looked at one another and shook their heads.

" The captain carried a load of trouble inside him," said the helmsman.

" Ah," said the mate.   " That's why for three days past he has been putting me up to everything till I know as much as he did himself."

" Better look in his cabin," said the helmsman.

" Think he's there ? " said the mate, shaking his head doubtfully.

" No ; but just to see if he's left anything behind him."

" Yes, you're right," said the mate.

He went down to the cabin.

Coming back after a few minutes, he said :

" It's all right.   He's made it straight for us."

" Then he did leave a note ? "

" Explaining everything."

" Then the poor captain—— ? "

" God rest his soul," said the mate, lifting his cap.

Such was Captain Chamblon's funeral oration.

CHAPTER XVII

THE COMPANY GIVES PERFORMANCES AT MARTINIQUE AND
TRINIDAD—A SNAKE HUNT—A CORAL SERPENT IN
A JAR — MLLE. MÉLANIE-FOR-THE-HOUSE — GUSTAVE
SHAVES OLD VERTEUIL

ON one occasion, however, M. Gustave was obliged to trust himself to the perfidious element. They were to

give performances at Martinique and Trinidad, and however ingenious one might be it was not possible to make the
journey by land.

They embarked about the end of July on the coasting
vessel, *Countess of Bouilly*, Captain Mandar. Two days
later, during the night, they anchored off Martinique;
and directly the dawn appeared, canoes swarmed round
the ship.

Martinique has no port. There is simply a roadstead, exposed to every wind. The lightest breeze floats
the ships stationed in those waters, even as it would waft
a flock of frightened birds.

A two months' stay at Guadeloupe had rendered our
actors familiar with all the strange things that had so
arrested their attention when they first arrived at the
Antilles. The one thing that struck them when they disembarked at Martinique was the quantity of snakes
hanging from the trees.

Not only has every one, as one will easily understand,
the right of life or death over these reptiles, but also for
every serpent's head a price was paid; naturally, therefore, the negroes hunted snakes with avidity and were
very adroit in the sport. Snakes usually flee from man;
the negro runs after them, catches them by the tail and
smashes the skull against the nearest wall or tree or stone
that he finds to hand; or sometimes against the earth
herself, our common Mother, who thus becomes a stepmother for the snake!

These reptiles are so common in Martinique that often
in the heavy rainy seasons you see snakes brought by the
streams which pour down the streets being rolled by the
torrent helplessly towards the sea.

Some time before the arrival of our company, a negro
in Martinique died from the bite of a coral snake, one of
the most dangerous of the whole Ophidian species. The
snake was hidden in a box of hay, and the negro, plunging
his fingers into the hay to give fodder to his master's
horses, was bitten by the snake.

These snakes, which terrify all Europeans, were much
sought after by old Verteuil. He was a handsome, goodhearted, and clever old man, with a serene expression and
beautiful white hair. He had to act with the disadvantage

of one leg that was almost paralysed, and he wrote really charming songs in his leisure moments.

But at Martinique he had no leisure moments. He collected snakes, iguanas, and alligators, which he kept, some in cases and some on boards, meaning to take them to the Marseilles Museum. M. Verteuil used to be manager of the theatre at Marseilles, and cherished a great affection for the Phocæa of antiquity.

He had with him an old servant who did not share his interest in natural history ; the first quarrel they ever had arose about a rattlesnake that M. Verteuil wished to keep as a live pet, and whose skull Mélanie-for-the-House had smashed with a broomstick.

"Why do you call her Mélanie-for-the-House? " the reader will ask.

Ah, that is true. You don't know, dear reader, what is familiar to our actors.

Old Verteuil's housekeeper was in the habit of signing the accounts : " Mélanie, for the House."

Half an ounce of butter : " Mélanie, for the House."

Half an ounce of lard : " Mélanie, for the House."

Half a pound of tapioca : " Mélanie, for the House."

From this all old Verteuil's friends had got into the habit of calling his housekeeper, Mélanie-for-the-House.

You see our explanations are clear and concise.

They remained fifteen days in Martinique ; then, the town squeezed dry, as they said in the days of old Dumanoir —whom we shall see again, so don't worry—they set off for Trinidad.

You know what Trinidad is, don't you? British Island, in spite of its Spanish name, situated facing the mouth of the Orinoco. Here old Verteuil was really happy ; but, on the contrary, Mélanie-for-the-House got into a state bordering on despair.

Trinidad is certainly the island that the Ark landed at ; in it are to be found a specimen of every sort of beast, and some of them, one must in honesty confess, have multiplied in a way that is out of all proportion. Among others, monkeys, parakeets, lizards, crocodiles, and snakes. Gustave, who was a good walker and loved walking for the exercise and movement it afforded, often stood gazing in ecstasy at the flight of parakeets of all colours and at the quantities of humming birds swarming round a cluster of flowers like bees round a hive, or at the passing of a great lizard, rapid as light and looking as if made from a single emerald.

One day when Gustave went to see old Verteuil he found him standing lost in admiration of a magnificent coral snake coiled round at the bottom of one of those jars that they call in the islands "pobans." He was standing on his good leg, resting both his hands on the table on which stood the jar, whilst Mélanie-for-the-House stood wringing her hands in a corner, gazing in horror at this new acquisition which had arrived to take its place with the stuffed parakeets, the crocodiles fastened to planks, and the lizards that were going yellow in bottles.

"Come here, Gustave! Come here!" said old Verteuil when he saw the young man who brought him a butterfly as large as a plate pinned on to his straw hat.

"I say, isn't this a pretty butterfly, M. Verteuil?"

"I dare say; what do butterflies matter?"

"You don't despise butterflies?"

"Oh, give it to Mélanie-for-the-House and come and look at my coral snake."

"Is it dead?"

"My dear fellow——"

"Well, I'm not like you; I loathe snakes."

"Oh, you're right, M. Gustave! I'm an unlucky woman to have to live with a man who likes nasty beasts like that!"

"Be quiet, you old fool. Go and get us two bottles of tafia."

"Don't you think one will be enough, sir?" said Gustave.

"It's not for you, M. Gustave. It's for his horrible reptile. He spends his whole profits on those things!"

"Mélanie-for-the-House!" said M. Verteuil in the tone of a man who might allow remarks on any other subject but who would not suffer the slightest reflection on this one.

Mélanie left the room; and M. Gustave, with a certain hesitation, approached the jar, and with his stick, which he thrust into the receptacle, began to tickle the reptile, which remained motionless, in spite of all his teasing.

"Good," said the young man. "He is dead!"

He then bent, in his turn, to take a close look at the magnificent jewel-studded creature that is known as the coral snake.

"One thing I don't like," said he to M. Verteuil.

"What's that?"

"Surely, as a rule, when these good people die, they lose the brightness of their colouring; and this joker persists in remaining magnificent."

"He only died this morning; so he hasn't had time yet to notice that he's dead. That's why I want to put him in spirit while he is still, as you may say, a trifle alive. Ah, Mélanie-for-the-House, give me that quickly and let's give this charming creature a drink."

The servant, who had just got back from the cellar, gave the two bottles to her master with a look of undisguised regret.

Gustave put his cane between his teeth and opened the bottles. Then, taking one in each hand, he began pouring a liberal dose of the spirit into the jar. But directly the alcohol touched the reptile it gave a sharp hiss, and standing on its tail like the heraldic serpent of the Viscontis, it slid out of the jar and fell on to the table. Luckily, with a movement as rapid as that of the snake, Gustave had dropped the bottle he held in his right hand, snatched his cane from his teeth, and held the reptile fixed to the table with a firm pressure.

That was a terrible moment. Old Verteuil took a hasty step backwards, but his paralysed leg played him tricks and he fell into the armchair in which he remained a prisoner only eighteen inches from the hissing jaws of the reptile.

Mélanie-for-the-House fled, calling loudly for help; and Gustave, still holding the serpent firmly down with his switch, called for a negro—any negro—with all the power of his lungs, accompanying his appeal with the most energetic curses he could remember from the vocabulary both of artistes and showmen.

"Neglo-man—come. Me want you!" he cried in pidgin English.

"Me here, massa," said the negro, running in.

"See there—coral snake!"

The negro did see there and understood at once the gravity of the situation.

" Sush ! Shut you' mouf, you actor-man, or you become dead mutton."

Then, seizing a whip, he addressed himself to the snake :

" What you doin' on dat table, massa snake ? Police-man teach you better manners. You sentence to a monf's hard labour, you is ! "

The negro now held the snake down with his whip, took the end of its tail in his fingers, and, in spite of its wriggling, put it back into the jar, where he left it to execute a " danse funebre " of the most frantic type, but without danger to others, thanks to the application of the lid, which was tied down securely with string.

Then at last old Verteuil ventured to breathe again.

" Thanks, thanks. We owe you our lives for that service."

" Please, massa, open bottle, give me little dlink of tafia. Hot work, dat. Me all sweat, shuh ! "

" No, you do not sweat, you rascal," said Gustave.

"Oh, massa," cried the negro, " but me sweat inside ! "

They gave the negro the flask and he went off, dancing with joy.

The reptile is probably still in the museum at Marseilles, and those who see and admire him there have little idea of the drama in which he was a principal actor shortly before rendering up his last breath.

This event chilled old Verteuil's enthusiasm for natural history and made Gustave more circumspect where ophidians were concerned ; but it gave Mélanie-for-the-House an attack of yellow jaundice !

They remained at Trinidad two or three weeks ; during the day stumbling up against millions of birds of the crow species who act as scavengers to the town, and it is therefore forbidden to touch them. They pass their mellifluous existence eating all they can devour and then perching on the roof-tops or on the arm of the gallows which is stuck up in the public square, to go through the process of digestion, pressed as closely against one another as if they were on the spit.

One night there was a great rat hunt. These animals gnawed the comedians' breeches and made lamentable rents in the tragedians' buskins.

But at last they had to leave this land of delight ; they embarked on the *Elisa*, Captain Lafargue, expecting the usual passage which takes from four or five days. They made their arrangements, therefore, to live on deck, in the air, swinging their hammocks there during those hot nights on the Gulf of Mexico where the heat is tempered by a sea breeze. Such nights are the most delicious of one's whole life. So our company thought when they came to Trinidad, and so they thought again during the first two days of the return voyage. But on the morning of the third day the captain showed some anxiety about a small black spot in the direction of New Orleans.

This black spot grew larger and larger till it blackened the whole sky. The captain at once gave two sailors the order to steer clear, to avoid the rocks, and ordered the passengers below so as to leave the sailors free to manipulate the vessel.

The first of these orders was easy to obey, the second almost impossible. Between decks the space was all encumbered by merchandise, for they had not expected twenty to twenty-five passengers. There was scarcely a space of two and a half feet between the packing cases and the forepart of the ship. Moreover this space was again constricted by the thickness of the mattresses.

They slid into this oven—no other word fits the case— they slid into this narrow oven as best they could. But they had to remain lying down, either on their faces or on their backs. They were allowed their choice of posture to that extent ; but no one was allowed to sit—not even the tenor, and you know tenors are the object of a manager's special care, more so even than leading ladies, even when the latter are in a delicate state of health.

They had scarcely settled themselves when an intolerable heat accompanied by an even more intolerable smell proved the forerunner of a host of black beetles, scorpions, and centipedes which ran over the boards over their heads like the Signs of the Zodiac. At first this worried them tremendously. Poor Mélanie-for-the-House gave vent to piercing shrieks.

Two or three of their company were bitten and stung ; old Verteuil handed them the little flask of lime-water that he carried with him for emergencies. They rubbed themselves till the places swelled up, then rubbed again, and again the places swelled up ; then they began to treat the beetles, scorpions, and centipedes with indifference, and then, as a climax of insult to the genus coleoptera, ended by paying no attention to them whatever.

But they were obliged to pay attention to the ever-increasing heat and the mephitic atmosphere to which a newcomer would have succumbed instantly, while our friends had been able to bear it for two or three days because they had got accustomed to it gradually.

But among these poor passengers, massed together like negroes on a slave ship, or like the souls of the damned in hell, there was one who suffered more than the others and consequently complained more. This was M. Verteuil, whose stiff leg rendered the cramped position absolutely unbearable.

But he was even more concerned about his beard— already eight days' old and growing up to his eyes ; it was as stiff as a brush and as white as snow. It was his habit to shave every day, but this operation, though easy enough on deck when weather was calm, became impossible in bad weather, and especially when one was forced to remain in a horizontal position. Therefore, though they all lamented their own fate, they all united in commiserating poor old Verteuil. But their pity, though unanimous, unfortunately brought no relaxation of his sufferings, which became so intense that the poor old man ended by begging them not, as before, to shave him, but to blow out his brains and throw his body into the sea.

As we have said, his moans touched every one, but particularly Gustave, who had for him the respectful affection of a son. So dragging himself to a place beside the old man, he said :

" Listen, M. Verteuil. I'll have a try."

" At blowing my brains out ? Do. But mind you don't miss ! "

" No, no. I mean I'll try and shave you."

" My friend, if you succeed, you will be my benefactor for life ! "

" I expect it'll be a bit uncomfortable in weather like this."

The ship was dancing on the waves to such an extreme that every time the framework creaked they thought it was going to fall to pieces.

" Oh, I don't care. Skin me if you like as they skin a side of bacon, but for Heaven's sake take away this furnace which is burning my face."

" Well, I can't answer for what will happen."

" All right."

" You absolve me in advance ? "

" Even if you cut my throat."

" You hear that, you fellows ? "

The others languidly replied that they did.

" Then we'll have a try."

Some one opened a trunk—the first that came to hand —and took out a razor.

" Here you are," said a voice.

" Here what ? "

" Here's a razor."

" Pass it to me."

They passed the razor from hand to hand, and at last it reached M. Gustave.

The ship was still dancing like a bouncing ball.

" Gringalet ! " called the barber. For Gustave every cabin boy was Gringalet in memory of the great Gringalet of Caen. (No one so soon gets used as a cabin boy to any name the passengers please to bestow on him.) The cabin boy ran as quickly as if he had received that illustrious name at the baptismal font.

" Water and soap ! "

" We only have yellow soap."

" Oh, that'll do ! " cried the patient.

" All right, sir, I'll bring water and soap."

" Oh, do, do bring my soap and water," moaned Verteuil.

The cabin boy came back with the desired objects.

" You've really made up your mind to be shaved ? " asked Gustave.

" I'm prepared for anything, my friend."

" All right. Keep still ! "

The young man bestrid old Verteuil, leaning on him and

resting on his left elbow, and in this position began to dab
his face with the soapy water.

"Oh," murmured the poor martyr. "That's good!
That's good!"

M. Gustave stopped.

"You wouldn't rather wait for a calmer sea?"

"Oh no! Oh no! Go on. Get it done at once."

The young man seized the razor and gave a sigh.

"All right," said he, "God help us!"

The razor ran along old Verteuil's cheeks.

"Oh," said he. "That's good! That's good!"

"My word, if it's as good as that let's get along with it."

And with an incredibly steady hand, with the sure hand
of the painter who only touches his canvas with the tip
of his brush, and of the sculptor who only touches his
stone with the point of his chisel, in the midst of the ship's
rolling and pitching, he continued his impossible task
which called forth more and more sighs of pleasure and
gratitude from his patient as it proceeded nearer and nearer
to accomplishment.

CHAPTER XVIII

Relative Happiness—Cayacou Roadstead—Gustave
takes a Header into the Sea, and with Three
Comrades swims to Shore—They bring back Fresh
Provisions—Return to Martinique—Tempest—The
Tricolour Flag—The Revolution of July—Dis-
persion of the Company

The operation took a whole hour, but was accomplished
without the slightest cut. The patient's skin was as red
as blood but perfectly unharmed.

"Ah, my dear Gustave," said he, "this is the second
time you have saved my life." (The first time, as my
readers will remember, was when the coral snake slid out of
the jar.) "Oh, by the by," cried he, "that reminds me.
What has become of all my lizards and snakes?"

" Oh, Heaven ! " cried Mélanie-for-the-House. " I feel something seize me by the leg ! "

" You're a fool," retorted Verteuil. " Why, the latest of them has had three days' immersion in spirits of wine."

" That's nothing," replied the housekeeper, very little reassured by this chronological reasoning, however convincing it might seem. " I've read in the Bible that the serpent is the most deceitful of creatures."

Old Verteuil was partly right, partly wrong. Most of the jars were broken in pieces, but the snakes and lizards lay about the ship motionless and lifeless. They did not find this out for some ten days, though directly his beard ceased to torment him he began to worry about his collection. It is so true that Man can never be perfectly happy !

When ten days had gone by, though, our passengers should have found themselves happy, if happiness, as philosophers say, is only the comparison of a better state of things with something that is worse. It is obvious that when, on the evening of the tenth day, the wind having dropped and the sea calm, the passengers returned to the deck instead of being couped below decks, and breathed the pure air of the ocean instead of the mephitic air of the hold, and had as horizon infinite space where the sun shone from clouds of purple and gold instead of those boards constellated with scorpions, centipedes, and black beetles ; it is obvious, I say, that the passengers should have found themselves happy or at least relatively so. But since Man must always be complaining—and by Man we understand also the Better Half that God gave him—these men and women, too, complained.

Of what did they complain ?

Of having had nothing but biscuit to eat for five whole days and of having had nothing to drink for the same space of time except lukewarm water which each day made not only warmer but more putrid.

On her part, the ship also complained.

She complained of having a mast smashed, and all her sails torn, and of feeling water coming through her splintered timbers.

They resolved, then, to gain the roadstead of Cayacou

and to stay there for twenty-four hours to repair damages. They therefore set their course for Cayacou.

As they advanced towards this place the passengers gazed with entranced eyes on the basket of flowers, for such the island seemed as it rose from the earth before them, surrounded by bosky hills and limpid, running water ; not one of them but dreamed of a bath in that water, a sleep beneath those trees.

Captain Lafargue cast anchor about a quarter of a league from the shore, but no matter how they begged him to send a boat to shore, he refused. Why? They never knew. Just a captain's caprice, that's all.

But the temptation was too great. At the risk of being cut in two by sharks or devoured by alligators, Gustave and three of his companions stealthily unrobed, and, actuated by the same impulse, each took a header into the water. One of them had knotted his handkerchief round his body and had slipped into it one or two dollars to excite the generosity of the inhabitants of Cayacou. The women cried out when they saw them go, not knowing why a sixth part of the company had thus thrown themselves into the water ; but when the four swimmers had told them that it was to get them fresh water and provisions and fruits of all sorts, that they had thrown themselves into the sea, the shouts of encouragement became universal.

The four swimmers reached the shore at varying distances from one another ; all had directed their course towards a sort of little fort, the whiteness of which had attracted their eye. It was, however, uninhabited. But, from this fort, they saw a village about a quarter of a league distant, and they walked off towards the village.

The four Europeans had been long enough in the Antilles not to bother any longer about their costume. It would have been silly to regard their nudity with more concern than the Cayacoutes, males and females, showed towards their own nakedness.

They acquired what they wanted quite easily ; no one could be more obliging than the Chevet and the Potel * of that island. For about half a dollar they purchased bananas, mangoes, cabbages from the cabbage tree, and tapioca bread.

Read "Harrods and Fortnum and Mason."—EDITOR'S NOTE.

The difficulty was how to transport all this.

A small bark canoe did the business. It was filled to the edge with fruits of all kinds ; then two Cayacoutes, who were to bring it back, swam out with the four Europeans, and all together they pushed it towards the ship. Never were conquerors received with louder acclamations of joy ; every mouth was dry, every throat on fire. They transported the canoe's cargo to the ship, sat round the pyramid of good things and attacked it with ardour, women and all, in spite of the pretence some of these latter made of never eating with an appetite.

Then they brought the mattresses up from the hold, shook and beat them, and spread them out on deck where they passed a voluptuous night, such as Cleopatra passed at Canope and Sextus Pompey in the Cyrenæa—the one in her royal barge and the other in his pirate's galley.

Then, the next day, they set off again with one of those delightful breezes blowing that do not make the sea rough and yet drive the ship before them.

Twenty-four hours after they were back in Martinique again. The aspect of the port was terrible to see. (When we say the " port " we mean the roadstead. Martinique, as we know, had no port.) The squall—every storm begins with a squall—had been so rapid and so violent that the ships had no time to gain the open sea.

Two three-masters and as many brigs, broken up and dismasted, had been driven on to the shore where they lay on their sides, and though no one appeared to be on board each rag that flapped on them gave vent to a piercing cry. The sea for about two leagues was covered with masts, yards, casks, hencoops, and other wreckage from ships, less happy than the ones referred to before, which had been broken up. The garrison under arms was drawn up along the coast. Sailors and negroes worked hard at salvage. Captain Lafargue did not want to be behindhand ; he cast anchor, and whilst the actors were taken on shore he sent his men to bear their part in the work of rescue.

Three days passed before they thought of opening the theatre. They hesitated to announce an entertainment in the midst of the sombre cares that had descended on the town. It was the town itself, as one may say, that demanded a performance from the actors. During the

K

company's six weeks of absence a taste for drama had had time to spring up in Martinique again.   M. Victor Marest announced, therefore, that in deference to the enthusiasm of the people of Martinique he would reopen on the 10th of September with the opera *Joseph* and the comedy *Brueys and Palaprat*.

The morning of the 10th of September, when the bill-stickers were busy sticking bills on all the street corners announcing the opera for that evening, the governor, followed by several officers and preceded by a drummer, came to the battery of the port and had the white flag lowered and the tricolour hoisted instead.

They watched this with profound astonishment.   No one knew what it meant.   However, as you will divine, they let him do as he pleased, while watching all his move-ments with extreme curiosity.   At last the rumour went round that there had been a revolution in Paris and that it was known as the Revolution of July; that Charles X. was dethroned and that the Duke of Orleans had accepted the office of Lieutenant-General, saying: " Henceforth the Charter shall become a fact ! "

The mulattoes shouted with joy.   What gain did they expect from a revolution at the capital, fifteen hundred leagues away ?   I will tell you.

They gained, or at least they meant to try and gain, the right to enter the pit and gallery of the theatre, aristocratic places reserved for Whites, and in which men of colour were not permitted to set foot.

At each revolution in Paris men of colour usually take a step forward.   The revolution of 1848, which freed the slaves, took them, not a step, but a bound forward, in con-sequence of which they have not only caught up with but in some cases passed the Whites.   In 1830 they had not got far enough for this.   They simply asked, as we have said, to be allowed to go into the pit and gallery.   As they asked this favour while threatening to take it, and as they were the strongest party and consequently could have taken it if they had been refused, the favour was granted to them.

But on the self-same day that the mulattoes acquired this right, which had been the summit of their ambition for two hundred years, the governor ordered M. Marest to bring his performances to a close. That evening, when they came to the doors of the theatre two hours earlier than usual so as not to lose a moment's enjoyment of their new privilege, the men of colour found the door of the theatre shut.

On their side, the company had been told by the manager that he had no further need of their services. Some of them wanted to bring an action and claim their rights ; but they were told that it was a matter of necessity.

Then, since they were separated from their mother country by some fifteen hundred leagues, each went his own way, calling to his help, as was the custom of artistes and showmen, his own particular " wheeze." The manager took a café. The *prima donna* became assistant to the manager. Elleviou, M. Bouzigue, the Dugazon, and Mme. Paul, having some savings, returned to France. The baritone, M. Dupuis, sang in the cathedral. Old Verteuil and his son started for Pointe-á-Pitre, where the old man died and his son became foreman in a printing office. M. Valdowski became a fencing master. The leading lady became dame de compagnie to the Governor. The heavy father, M. Salle, became porter to the masons, his brothers. Last, but not least, the second tenor, M. Gustave, after hesitating for a whole day as to which of his different " wheezes " he should adopt, decided to become a miniature painter.

CHAPTER XIX

M. Gustave, Miniature Painter — Happy Debut— Story of a Duel—Father Jean receives a Parcel from Martinique—His Astonishment—A Letter in a Snuffbox — The Portrait in Oils—The Canvas is replaced in an Ingenious Manner— Influence of Humidity on an Ass's Skin

The very day he took this resolution, M. Gustave went to a billiard-ball maker, bought three billiard balls, went to a cabinet maker and had each ball sawn into ten pieces,

and so found himself in possession of thirty ivory tablets
of different sizes.

At two doubloons the portrait, this made four thousand
eight hundred francs that M. Gustave thought himself
about to lock up in his drawer, without any further capital
expense than the fifteen francs for the purchase of the balls
and six francs for the sawing. As for the water-colour
paints and pastilles, he had paid for them long ago.

These preliminary preparations over, M. Gustave wrote
a circular which he sent round to the principal houses in
the town :

" M. Gustave, miniature painter, informs the inhabitants
of Guadeloupe and Martinique that he paints portraits
and guarantees a likeness."

It is well known that everything is just a matter of the
happy moment in this world, and that all depends, as a
rule, on the way an enterprise is set about.

M. Gustave's speculation began in a most propitious
manner. The first amateur who came to have his portrait
painted was a magistrate of Martinique who had become the
subject of general conversation on account of a terrible
duel. He was a man of from thirty-five to forty years
of age, small, slender, with charming features and that
soft Creole intonation which makes one think that those
whose speech is so musical must have a throat of velvet.
He had quarrelled with a professional swashbuckler ; or,
more correctly, the swashbuckler had sought a quarrel
with him. On this he had been to find his adversary and
had challenged him on the condition that they fought with
one loaded pistol and one unloaded, at the distance of a
pocket-handkerchief apart, the handkerchief to be held in
the left hand while the pistol was fired with the right.
The magistrate's adversary had accepted these conditions,
either because he could not or because he did not wish to
refuse.

Accompanied by their seconds the two champions met
on the ground. The two adversaries placed themselves
at three paces distance from one another, received a loaded
and an unloaded pistol from the hand of their seconds, and
stood armed. Fate gave the magistrate the right of the
first fire.

He pressed the trigger, but nothing happened. No detonation was heard. His bad luck had given him the unloaded pistol. On this his adversary fired into the air.

But he would not accept this generosity; he demanded that the pistol be reloaded under his own eyes; he himself, with his own hand, put the bullet into the barrel, and told his adversary to fire. Before this heroic conduct his adversary was obliged to yield; he did fire and the magistrate fell, his chest riddled through and through and his clothes singed by the powder.

By a miracle, however, he was not mortally wounded; and at the end of three months he was walking the streets of Martinique.

The Creoles are very brave, and, like all really brave men, they make a cult of bravery. The magistrate was the hero of the hour. If magistrates were not virtuous men, and if this one had not been strong, even among the strong, like the Sage of the Holy Book he might have been allowed licence to sin seven times a day and even more.

It was then incalculable luck to paint the portrait of this particular man. Good fortune never comes singly; the portrait was a success. It was on view at the art dealer's of the district in whose shop it obtained an immense success. From this moment M. Gustave's studio was never empty. Every shade of human skin, from a raven black to a tender rose, from the negro of Senegal to the fresh English girl of Plymouth or Southampton, came under his brush. M. Gustave had no preference, and showed no pride. Besides, as every one knew from the moment of his landing, if he had any prejudice it was rather in favour of negroes than against them.

Now while the son Étienne, under the name of Gustave, having charmed the Antilles with his voice and his acting was now ravishing them with the likeness and finish of his portraits—what was the father John doing?

He took the greatest interest in the completion of the Madeleine, and asked news of this from every one who came from Paris; from time to time, though, he felt a little surprised at getting no letters from his son. It is true that his son did not like writing, but surely Étienne might have found some occasion to say, "I am well," and to ask,

" How are you ? " It would have been such a pleasure to his poor father.

However, he never complained ; it was not a habit of Jean's to complain. He continued to murmur the Marseillaise, as he used to do under the Empire, and as he had done under the younger Bourbons, and from time to time, perhaps once a month or so, he was surprised to find himself saying : " It is none the less true that children are ungrateful."

One morning they told him a package had come from Martinique. From Martinique ! Who on earth could send to him from Martinique ? He knew no one in the Antilles.

This package contained a number of newspapers, a small cask of rum, a parcel of five hundred cigars, two pots of snuff, and a silver snuffbox. Father John opened the roll of newspapers and read :

" House for Sale.—Negro for Sale.—Negress for Sale.—Negro Child for Sale."

It was clear that this was no business of his. He pushed his investigations further and read :

" Theatre at Martinique.—M. Gustave gains daily in the favour of his audiences and he spares no pains to deserve the public's approbation. Yesterday he sang the famous air from the *Marriage of Figaro* with much talent and intelligence. His phrasing, above all, electrified the house."

" That isn't it," said Father John, who did not know his son under any name but Étienne.

He took up another paper and read :

" Spanish Trinity. French Theatre in Marine Square.

The lyric and dramatic artists under the management of M. Victor Marest will play :

Mahomet, or Fanaticism.

M. Gustave will take the part of Mahomet."

This name, Gustave, underlined for the second time, attracted M. Jean's attention.

" Why the devil do they bother me with this man
Gustave ?   I don't know any Gustave."

He continued to read :

" *The Dinner at Madelon's, or the Citizen of Marais.*"

Benoist, *old bachelor* . . .	Mm. Verteuil.
Vincent, *his friend* . . .	Salle.
A Corporal	Victor.
A Commissionaire. . . .	Gustave.
Madelon	Mlle. Moinet."

" M. Gustave ?   M. Gustave ? " repeated Father Jean.
" I believe that's where they have squats."

But as none of the other twenty newspapers told him
anything beyond what he had read in the first two he
passed from the papers to the packet of cigars.   He took
one, smoked it, and found it excellent.   " Oh, oh," said he ;
" It makes me want a pinch."

And taking a pinch of maccoboy from the large-throated
bottle he snuffed with a confidence which was justified by
his experience of the cigars.

" Excellent, by Jove !   Excellent !   Let us fill the snuffbox quickly."   He opened the snuffbox.   In the snuffbox there was a letter.

" Why," cried he, " it's Étienne's writing ! "

He opened the letter and read :

" It is I, papa.   As you wished, I have given up the
stage, where I was appearing under the name of Gustave,
and I am now a miniature painter, in Martinique.

" Your respectful son, who is making heaps of money,
                                                    " Étienne."

Father Jean was overwhelmed.   Nevertheless he told
two people about the letter, or rather the note, that he had
received ; first, the customs lieutenant, the design on
whose snuffbox was the first picture his son had copied,
and secondly, M. Odelli, who had secured for him his first
prize.

However, one thing consoled him a little—that his son
had ceased to be an actor and had become a painter.

During this time, M. Gustave—rare event—kept the
promises of his prospectus.   He guaranteed a likeness, and
his likenesses were such that one day a rich colonial desired

to have his portrait, not in miniature, but life-size, not in water-colour or pastille, but in oils. He came to see M. Gustave and asked him if he painted portraits in oil.

"I do everything connected with my art," replied M. Gustave.

"Then you guarantee a likeness full-size as well as in miniature?"

"I guarantee it all the more."

"And what difference will it make in the price?"

"Instead of two doubloons it will be four doubloons."

"All right. Four doubloons. We will begin to-morrow."

"To-morrow isn't possible. My whole day is booked up."

"Then the day after."

"I can't manage it till Monday."

"Then on Monday," replied the amateur, giving a deep sigh expressive of his regret at this delay of four whole days. He left, making Gustave promise that he should have his sitting on the following Monday.

M. Gustave had his reasons for putting off this first sitting till Monday. He was busy, it is true, but not so busy that he could not have stolen a couple of hours from his other sitters. His reason for asking for four days' grace was his fear of not being able to find a canvas suited to oil painting, and the necessity of setting his imagination to work to solve the problem if the requisite canvas was not forthcoming.

His forebodings were justified. No matter how he searched about the island he could not find a canvas on which to paint his portrait. Then he set about trying to find an old portrait which he could paint out. This research was as unprofitable as the other.

These two misfortunes which, as he had foreseen them, were only relative, did not abate his courage. Directly he had realized that he might not find the canvas, which was at the moment he took the engagement to paint the picture, he had an idea at the back of his mind, like Renard the fox in the fable.

M. Gustave went to the bandmaster of the National Guard and began hunting among the instruments which had been thrown aside. He found a huge drum, one side of which had burst.

That was exactly what he was looking for.

He bought the side that had not burst and nailed it to a frame of the same dimensions as the drum, stretching it as best he could.

Then he waited for his amateur, who came at the appointed time. (Gustave had got the best colours he could from the sign-painters.)   The amateur was astonished at first to find that his countenance was to shine forth on ass's skin, for that is the material that is stretched to form the sides of a drum ;   but M. Gustave told him, with imperturbable aplomb, that his chemical research work had taught him that ass's skin was preferable to canvas in the Antilles because of the saltness of the air ;   and his sitter was convinced by this reasoning.

M. Gustave began bravely using his oil paints, taking care not to tell his model that this was the first time he had ever worked in that medium.   The work made more noise than painting on canvas.   Each stroke of the brush resounded like a beat of the drumsticks and produced its characteristic symphony.

The painter took eight days to finish this portrait ;   but it was a *chef d'œuvre !* The sitter, as happy as could be, returned home to introduce the portrait to his family ; but he did not breathe a word of the material on which the portrait was painted ! He was afraid that if it came out that his portrait was painted on ass's skin he would lose status in the minds of his wife and children.

Unfortunately, unsuspected by any one, least of all the artist, a catastrophe menaced the portrait.   The winter—that is to say, the rainy season—came round.   To the hot weather which dried everything succeeded the damp that sops and softens things.   The portrait, so perfect that it seemed a living thing, seemed to watch this season come in with repugnance.   Its face, always serious, seemed to grow sad and old ;   not only did it wrinkle horizontally—which would have had the effect time produces on human beings—but it also wrinkled vertically, which had an effect unknown before.

The family took fright at a portrait with so ephemeral a life, while its original lived the life of other men.   They sent for the painter.

The painter approached the picture full of confidence,

and as his face remained calm the faces of the family regained their serenity.

"Why," said he, " I must have forgotten to varnish it." Then in the tone of a physician raising the spirits of afflicted parents, he said : " It's nothing. Come and see it at my house in three days' time and you will see it has all disappeared."

M. Gustave guessed at once that the damp had made the ass's skin go flabby and that the portrait was only suffering from " softening." This malady, usually fatal to man when it attacks the brain or the marrow, is not fatal to portraits.

M. Gustave shut up the portrait for three days in a room heated to thirty degrees, and at the end of the three days, as he had prophesied, nothing of the trouble was to be seen.

The family was enchanted ; all their superstitious fears vanished ; but they were warned that the portrait had a tendency to hydrophobia, and had this advantage over other portraits that it served at the same time as a picture and as a thermometer.

CHAPTER XX

THE DEMON OF " THE BOARDS "—M. GUSTAVE EMBARKS ON THE *URSIN*—ONE WAY OF EFFECTING A CHANGE OF WEATHER—A FAMOUS COOK—SATISFACTION OF THE CAPTAIN—DISAPPOINTMENT—THE CAPTAIN HANGS UP ALL THE COOKING UTENSILS—WHAT THE BASINS AND PIEDISHES SAID AS THEY CLANGED AGAINST THE RIGGING

M. GUSTAVE had again discovered the source of Pactolus.

But, what would you ? These miserable artists !— and this is the whole cause of their inferiority to other men in the present and their superiority when the present is forgotten in the future—instead of subordinating their

thoughts to their interests, it is their interests, on the contrary, that are constantly subordinated to their mental
qualities.

Now, as we know, M. Gustave was possessed by a
demon that gold could not exorcise ; the demon of " the
boards."

Oh, this is a terrible demon who seizes hold of you,
awake or sleeping, and with his wand transforms drawing-
rooms into theatres, candelabras into footlights, fireplaces
into a prompter's box ; who whispers the *Cid* into one ear
and *Figaro* into the other ; who is eternally pursuing you
with a distant thunder of applause and makes you say, as
Ninon did, in the midst of luxury : " What fine times I
had when I was so utterly miserable ! "

Well, M. Gustave, even as he daubed away at his
miniatures which were bringing him in thirty thousand
francs a year, was thinking of and sighing for the time when
he had the promise of fifty francs a month from Zozo of
the North and when he had to dine with Duke Humphrey.

When you are in this state of mind your future, for good
or ill, depends on the least circumstance.

Gustave made the acquaintance of a young man from
Rouen who had seen him play on a previous voyage.

" Hullo," said he, " so you're painting miniatures
now ? "

" As you see."

" But why aren't you on the stage ? "

" There is no longer a theatre."

" What a pity !   You had so much talent."

M. Gustave should have seen in this the trail of the
serpent, but he did not or would not notice it.

" What's to be done ? " said he.   " Man proposes but
God disposes."

" Oh, well !   If you liked I would—— "

(The serpent was gently trailing along !)

" If you like—I know Valter."

" Who is Valter ? "

" Manager of the theatre at Rouen."

" No ! "

" How do you mean—no ? "

" I don't want to play in the provinces."

" Oh, well, Rouen is on the road from Havre to Paris ;

on your way to Paris you can stop at Rouen ; it isn't an engagement, it's just a halt."

Oh, tempter ! Any but a son of Adam would have recognized your voice ; but alas, we are all sons of Adam !

" Well, yes. Certainly," replied Gustave, already half convinced. " It's tempting. But do you mean that I'm to present myself to this man without recommendation beyond a simple letter ? "

" Oh, I've something better than that to propose. I'm starting to-morrow."

" You are off to-morrow ? You are lucky ! "

" You think so ? It's a form of luck that you can make yourself a present of."

" Oh—me ! "

" Listen. I'm off to-morrow. Start yourself in a fortnight's time. When you reach Rouen you'll find your contract waiting for you."

" Really ? "

" Word of honour ! "

" May I have till this evening to think it over ? "

" Of course. I don't want to force you to come."

The demon was letting out a reel or two of line to the fish he had caught.

The man from Rouen took his hat and went out, saying : " To-night, then."

But he had not gone four paces from the door when Gustave opened it again and said : " You needn't wait till to-night."

" You refuse ? " asked the tempter with a Satanic grin, which would have betrayed Mephistopheles himself if Mephistopheles had not been sure of his prey.

" No ; I accept."

" All right," said the man from Rouen.

He disappeared round the corner of the street. The pact was signed.

The man from Rouen did not appear again. He had possession of M. Gustave's soul and was afraid of losing his grip upon it.

A fortnight after, to the day, M. Gustave embarked on the *Ursin.*

The passage cost four hundred francs, which included food. But, no doubt whatever, the captain had made

an arrangement with the sea to keep the expense of food for
the passengers as low as possible. No sooner had they
left the roadstead than the weather became execrable.
Moreover, the captain had a " wheeze."   When the weather
was altogether too bad he used to say : " I shall have to cut
up a cabin boy." According to him that was the best
recipe for procuring a change of weather.

" Boy ! " he would call.

The cabin boy, who knew the captain's pet superstition, in great trepidation, would just show the end of
his nose.

" Boy ! " he would repeat in a key of three sharps.

The cabin boy would appear.

" Boy, a glass of rum ! "

The boy would race off to get the desired object and
return again as slowly as possible.

" Here, captain," he would say with visible terror.

" Give it here, you fool."

The boy would give it there and flee, but never quick
enough to escape the captain's kick.

If the captain aimed the kick well he would say : " Now,
you see, the wind will turn."

The experiment was so often repeated that it was rare
if the wind did not turn once or twice out of every ten ;
and this was sufficient to keep firm the captain's faith in
his superstition.

Then to this " wheeze " he joined a mania that was its
complement.   There was a cook on board.   This cook had
cruelly deceived the captain.

At the very moment of their departure from the Antilles
he had charged his mate to find a cook.   The mate had
hunted for one and made inquiries, and in the end he found
a man who said he was a chef of the first order. " We are
all cooks, father and son. It's in the family," said he.
He had worked with Brillat-Savarin ; his father had
served under Cambacéres ; his grandfather with Grimod
de la Reynière ; and his great-grandfather with the Marshal
de Richelieu. This list frightened the captain at first
and it was with some hesitation that he asked what wages
the man wanted.

The man replied that his desire to travel and study the
ways of cooking in other countries was so great that he

would be content with a modest sum. They fixed it at £500 a year.

The cook had warned the captain that he would prob-ably be ill the first few days after their departure ; but once this tribute to human frailty was paid all would be rose-colour. The captain had passed the £500, but he stuck at these two or three days. However, the money paid and the days conceded he demanded from his cook the most delicate dishes, and, above all, exquisite sweets. The cook was delighted ; but he said that if the captain required all those recherché dishes he would need a con-siderable addition to the cooking utensils, especially in the way of piedishes, casseroles, and pannikins. The captain thought this just, and authorized the cook to buy these pannikins, casseroles, and piedishes up to the price of fifty crowns. The next day the cook was seen from the ship simply covered with a cuirass of cooking-dishes. The captain viewed these objects with admiration, not even knowing their names ; and as it was even more for himself than for his passengers that he wanted a comfortable ordinary, he passed his tongue eagerly over his lips at the thought of the unknown dishes he was about to enjoy.

They set sail.

One of the seductive promises held out to his passengers by the captain was that of a table such as they would not find even on dry land. He had, however, warned them that they must be patient for the first two or three days after setting sail, this voyage being the first the famous cook had ever taken in a sailing vessel, and every one, even the kings of the kitchen, are equal before the terrors of seasickness. The passengers understood this all the more because they could say with Dido :

"Unhappy in myself, I learnt to pity
The wretched state of others."

The three first days passed without a complaint even from the captain, and no one else thought of complaining. But towards the end of the third day, the captain sent to warn the cook that the next day would be his birthday and he wanted to have a good dinner ; therefore it would be necessary for the cook to leave his cabin and give some sign of his existence.

The sign of existence that he gave was like to prove the
death of captain and passengers. Each dish that he
served up, from the soup to the tarts and soufflés, seemed as
if it must have been cooked to win a wager. He spoiled
everything, except the apples, yet even apples that he had
cooked and served with some sort of sauce proved to be
uneatable.

So, between the coffee and liqueurs, the captain sent for
the poor wretch to make an example of him before the
passengers.

The poor cook did not forget that on his ship a captain
has the right of life or death. He threw himself at his
master's feet and confessed humbly that finding himself
at the age of thirty-five without resource and without
employment he resolved to adopt the calling of cook ; but
knowing that an apprenticeship of some sort is needed for
any calling he resolved to pass his on board a ship, the
captain of which was renowned for his good heart.

He also said that the expense he had put the captain
to for utensils was a proof of his desire to learn. He
swore that with God's help he would be able to use these
utensils one day in a fashion worthy of the honourable
captain whose service he had entered.

All these arguments were more touching than convincing,
so the cook received fifty lashes and was put in irons ;
after which, the principal steersman, who could do a little
cooking, was told off to teach him how to roast a leg of
mutton and boil an egg.

You will easily understand that the nervous irritability
of the captain increased, when there was stormy weather,
under the influence of the electricity in the air. The
thought of the bad dinners he had been giving to his
passengers and of the cooking utensils on which he had
sacrificed a hundred crowns of his good money kept coming
into his mind and urging him to deeds of vengeance. At
first these evil thoughts, which found expression on the
cabin boys, had a useful end since they served to change
the direction of the wind. But in the end they developed,
with an egoism, alas, only too natural to mortal man, into
mere personal revenge.

When the bad weather merely consisted of a passing
breeze, a cloud which the very wind which had brought it

would quickly carry away, the captain, satisfied at seeing the heavens clear and the wind change, limited himself to a few kicks. But when the breeze persisted and turned into a storm it was another matter. All the cause for complaint, legitimate in itself we admit, that the captain had against his cook crowded into his mind. Then, like the lion who beats with his tail against his flanks to excite his own ferocity, he excited himself.

"Boy!" he cried.

The cabin boy, recognizing by the intonation of the captain's voice that it was not he alone who was threatened and that the lightning would pass over his head to strike a loftier summit, ran up without fear indeed, almost with joy.

"Here, captain. What can I do for you?"

"My oilskins, donkey."

The boy disappeared, to come back almost immediately with the desired article in his hand. "Here you are, sir."

The captain muttered "Good!" Then he sent the boy away again.

The cabin boy, always afraid that the captain might bethink himself, retired backwards as one does before a king, holding both his hands crossed behind his back as low as possible.

Five minutes after the captain would cry, "Boy!"

"Yes, captain?"

"My sou'-wester."

The boy brought the curiously shaped hat, like that worn in our market-places, falling in a rounded form right down the back so that water should slide off as off the shell of a tortoise.

The captain put on his sou'-wester which gave him a formidable air. The boy retreated.

Scarcely had he disappeared when the captain cried, "Boy!"

The boy came back.

"Yes, captain?"

"My high boots."

The boy would bring the boots which resembled the seven-leagued boots of the fairy-tale. The captain put them on, glaring fiercely at the smoking chimney of the cook's galley, and murmuring: "Just like that fool of a cook! I wish a wave would sweep him off one day, and his galley too, and that neither of them would come up again!" The boots on, he stood a good three inches taller.

"Boy!"

"Yes, captain?"

"Come here."

"Yes, sir."

"Go and tell the cook for me that he's a d——d rascal."

The boy departed to fulfil this commission, and did or did not carry it out.

"What did he say?"

"He said 'Very good,' sir."

"Very good! Very good indeed! Good for him perhaps, but certainly not for me. . . . Boy!"

"Yes, sir."

Same business as before.

"What did he say this time?"

"He said 'Very good,' captain."

"Good! Indeed! His dinner wasn't good, I can tell you. . . . Boy!"

"Yes, captain?"

"Tell him from me—from me, you understand?—that he's a dirty dog."

"Yes, captain," replied the boy as calmly as before.

"Well, what did he say?"

"He said, 'Very good,' sir."

"Very good indeed! The poisoner! Oh, so he said 'Very good,' did he? . . . Boy!"

"Yes, captain?"

"Bring me a hammer, nails, string, and the whole caboodle from that rascal's galley."

Five minutes after the boy came back with all these things as asked. "Here you are, captain. Can I help you?"

"Hand me the nails and hammer and slip a bit of string through each of these cooking utensils. A hundred crowns worth, damn it! When I think of it—a hundred crowns! More than I gain on six passengers!"

He took the nails in his mouth, the hammer in his right hand and the netting of the ship in his left hand, and at the risk of being carried off by a wave like the hencoops which had been long floating towards the Cape of Good

L

Hope, he gained the canteen, knocked his nails into the outer partition and made a sign to the boy to pass him the basins, panikins, and piedishes ; hanging them up by the bits of string to the nails he had hammered in, and thoroughly enjoying the bacchanalian music they made as they dashed together at each roll of the ship like grotesque Æolian harps, each horrible clang, according to the captain, shouting to the cook this message :

" You can't cook! You can't cook! You can't cook ! "

CHAPTER XXI

M. Gustave at the Theatre at Rouen—The Statue of Corneille—Gustave's Success—Visit from his Father—His Farewell—Good Advice from Mme. Dorval—The Statue put up to Lottery—Departure for Paris

Rolling and pitching, after a two months' voyage, they reached Havre.

M. Gustave had managed to make a friend of the captain. M. Gustave was always very ingratiating when he was seasick. In his moments of relief he painted the captain's portrait. This wolf of the seas adored his mother, and the idea that, thanks to M. Gustave, he could now send her his portrait caused him to break through all his usual shipboard habits. Every passenger keeping his berth was supposed to have no food. M. Gustave alone had the right to eat while in bed. Yet in spite of the many little privileges that he enjoyed on board, the two months' voyage seemed to him very long. Therefore, though still seedy, he rejoiced when they arrived.

He began by giving all his bows and arrows, his boomerangs and whole Caribbean arsenal to the actors at the Havre theatre. Then directly he set foot on land a huge banquet celebrated his return to his mother country.

This was paid for by the doubloons that he had brought
from Martinique and Guadeloupe.

The next day he set out for Rouen. The man from
Rouen had kept his word. He was engaged in advance
at two thousand francs a year. He was to play all the rôles
that the management might please to give him and to
furnish all his own costumes. M. Gustave was quite
indifferent to this last clause ; he had acquired a magnificent
wardrobe abroad, and at the bottom of his bag he had
brought back fifteen or eighteen hundred francs which
was a fortune for an artist whose last wheeze had been to
fish for frogs and his last resource to beg a morsel of bread
from a poor cottager.

The elephant Kiuni was due to arrive in Rouen.

The debut of M. Gustave and of Mlle. Kiuni was
announced in a play called *The King of Siam and his
Elephant.* Both had a huge success. Then M. Gustave
created all the big rôles of modern drama ; the Duke of
Guise in *Henri III.*, Charles the Fifth in *Hernani*, Raphael
Bazas in *Clotilde*, and Buridan in *The Tour de Nesle.*

In the middle of all this, M. Gustave—whom work makes
work, and who is as lazy as a Neapolitan when he isn't in
a fever of rehearsals—in the middle of all this M. Gustave,
for the sake of having, as they say in good society, another
string to his bow, but as artistes and showmen would say,
to have another trick in his wallet, M. Gustave learned
engraving with Brevière the great artist who illustrated
"Paul and Virginia," and who has just engraved David's
Sabines in the "History of Painting." After this he, in
his leisure moments, set about illustrating the *Revue de
Caen.*

One day Valter came to find him.

Valter was the manager, a good fellow whom I knew
well and who recited the very first tragic lines I ever wrote.

Valter, then, entered his actor's room just when he was
putting a coat of varnish on a copper plate.

" Oh, that's not the thing to do," he said.

M. Gustave raised his head.

" What ought I to do, then, my dear Chief ? " he asked.

" Why, a month to-day will be the anniversary of
Corneille's birth."

" And you want me to recite something of his ? "

" Oh, that too."

" What else, then ? "

" Well, they usually crown a bust of him."

" Well ? "

" Well, this year the Rouen theatre must distinguish itself."

" How ? "

" By crowning a statue—— "

" Oh, and you want me to do the statue ? "

" I want you to do the statue."

" All right, I ask nothing better."

" A colossal statue ? "

" I can't make it more than six and a half feet high."

" Why not ? "

" Because my room is only seven feet high."

" Oh, I see. Yes, there is that. Well, then, make it six and a half feet."

" All right, it shall be six and a half feet."

As there was no time to lose since he only had a month before him, that very day they brought him the first cartload of clay.

M. Gustave was lodging on the sixth floor ; and at the twentieth cartload the house began to crack.

" The devil," cried Valter. " We shall have to look to this."

" I dare say I can manage with twenty cartloads," said Gustave.

He set to work. Twenty cartloads did suffice ; and the statue was moulded and cast for the day of the anniversary.

The work was not easy. To work at the feet, M. Gustave had had to lie down on his stomach as when he shaved old Verteuil.

On the day of the anniversary the statue was inaugurated at the theatre with loud applause from the whole of the crowded house. That evening Gustave's name was in every mouth.

The next day the statue was moved to the Town Hall, and all Rouen came to do it homage. Every newspaper had an account of the ceremony and exalted the name of Gustave. The young man collected all the papers that spoke of him and sent them to Father John.

Three days after Gustave was still asleep when, at six o'clock in the morning, he was awakened by a knock at the door. As soon as he really woke he leaped out of bed and ran to the door, crying : " That's Father ! "

He opened the door. It was, indeed, his father.

His father was not laughing—you remember that he never laughed ; he was crying. There are some scenes that one cannot even try to describe. Every man, even the worst, carries in his heart the memory of some such scene. Let him turn his thoughts to that ; his memory will tell him more than could my pen.

His father remained at Rouen for three days and saw his son play three different parts. It needed the applause of the whole house, repeated on each of these three occasions, to induce him to forgive his son for playing Corneille at the Rouen theatre instead of carving capitals for the pillars of the Madeleine.

The night before his departure, his son was the first to go to bed. His father had lit his pipe and was sitting by the fire thinking, his eyes lost from sight in the clouds of smoke with which he contentedly enveloped himself.

All of a sudden he rose, to take a seat at the bedside of his son, and holding out his hand he said :

" Listen, Étienne." (You understand that for Father John, Étienne was always Étienne and could not become Gustave.) " Listen, Étienne. I leave here to-morrow, and perhaps we may never see each other again."

" What ? Why do you say that ? " asked the young man, astonished.

" Well—who knows ? "

Étienne remained silent ; his father whistled two or three bars of the Marseillaise.

" Well," said he, " it doesn't matter."

" It doesn't matter ! " cried Étienne.

" What does it matter that the old go if the young remain ? "

" But, father, what has put this into your head ? "

" I have a feeling that, to-morrow, I shall say good-bye to you for good."

" But, father, then you mustn't go."

" And what about the customs ? "

" Oh, never mind about that. I made plenty of money over there, painting portraits."

" No more of that ! "

" I'm dumb ! "

" Suppose, one day, they told you—your old father was dead—— ? "

" Oh, what does all this mean ? "

" Silence ! I told you to be quiet."

" I obey."

" Suppose they told you one day that your old father was dead, you must start at once for Caen ; you must there go straight to the walnut wood cupboard, and in that drawer where I kept my pigtail you will find twelve hundred francs in my uniform cap."

" Why are you talking in this horrible way ? " cried Étienne, with a sob.

His father smiled a melancholy smile.

" Then," continued he, " you will send all the things that belonged to your mother to Paris. It is good to keep these family souvenirs."

Étienne was weeping.

" You'll promise me that ? " asked his father.

" I promise, father."

" Well, that's all I had to say to you. Good night, I'm going to bed."

He went to his bed without another word, took off his clothes and tucked himself in. Ten minutes after he was asleep. That was not the case with Gustave ; he had a sleepless night.

The next day, as was his habit, his father was on foot at five o'clock. The coach left at seven. Gustave, naturally, went to the coach with his father. He was not more sad than usual, but he seemed so to Gustave because he was more affectionate.

Before he got on the coach the father embraced his son several times. Then, just as the coach was starting, he put his white head out of the window and sent him a last kiss of the hand. At the corner of the street the coach disappeared from sight.

We said " a last kiss." It was, indeed, the last. Gustave returned to his rooms in deepest grief.

Frederick Lemaître had just arrived in Rouen to give

some performances. He was then at the height of his glory. He came to Rouen to play *Richard Darlington*, *The Tour de Nesle*, and *The Gamester*.

M. Gustave, naturally, gave up the leading parts to play the second or even third-rate rôles. In the prologue to *Richard* he played the doctor ; in *The Tour de Nesle* the idler who opens the scene by crying : " Here, Signor Orsini, you devil's taverner ! " and in *The Gamester* he played the Gamester's friend.

Then came Potier with whom he played *The Fierce Brothers ;* Arnal with whom he played the waiter in *The Private Room ;* and then Dorval with whom he played the archbishop in *The Incendiary*, the husband in *Antony*, and so on.

One night, when he went into the great actress's dressing-room to congratulate her, " Gustave," said she, after having watched him for some time with her beautiful clear eyes.

" Yes, madame ? " said Gustave.

" May I give you some advice ? "

" Please do."

" Will you follow it ? "

" I will try to."

" Then, believe me, you should go to Paris."

" I ask nothing better."

" If you remain in the provinces they will speak of you as a provincial actor, and once they do that you will never be anything else."

" I know that."

" You play heavy fathers ? "

" That's not my line, I know."

" Your line is lead."

" I think so too, but—— "

" Yes, but you want to have influence, you mean—— Eh ? "

" Yes."

" And you know no one ? "

" I know Mlle. Duchesnois."

" Well ? "

" She sent me to Soumet."

" And Soumet ? "

" He sent me to Seveste."

" And Seveste ? "

" Cast me for small parts and heavy fathers."

" You don't know Dumas ? "

" No."

" He is your man."

" But since I don't know him—— "

" I know him."

" Oh ! "

" I'll give you a line for him."

" But I am fixed here for six months more."

" Oh, you can arrange that with Valter."

" But if he won't hear of it ? "

" Have you never chucked a manager ? "

Gustave smiled. " That's one of my best rôles," he said.

The next day Gustave came to fetch his letter ; and the day after, he started for Paris, after putting his statue of Corneille up for lottery.

The statue was won by a tailor who stuck it up before his door and took for his sign : " The Great Corneille." It remained ten years at the door of this tailor's shop, and ended by losing its features under incessant drenchings with rain and snow and the buffeting of the wind.

The very day of his arrival in Paris M. Gustave came along to see me.

You have heard about his arrival and the story that he told me. This story made an impression on me as you see, such an impression that, after a lapse of twenty years, I am now telling it to my readers.

I looked at this handsome youth—only twenty-five— who had had such a rough life already.

" And then ? " said I.

" Well, you'll get me in somewhere, won't you ? "

" Where would you like to be playing ? "

" Why, at the Porte St.-Martin."

" All right, I'll do my best. Come and see me the day after to-morrow. I shall have had a chance to speak to Harel by then."

CHAPTER XXII

HAREL'S BAD TEMPER—GUSTAVE GOES TO SEE M. MERLE
— M. D'ÉPAGNY — *THE MALCONTENTS* — A LITHO-
GRAPH—MLLE. GEORGES

THE next day I went to see Harel as I had promised Dorval's
protégé I would do. I stopped a moment before going
in, halting before the Porte St.-Martin Theatre. The bills
bore this line at their head :
"Last performance of *The Tour de Nesle.*"
As a matter of fact, *The Tour de Nesle* has only been
played some six hundred times since then. Bocage gave
up the rôle and also the Porte St.-Martin.
I found Harel in a very bad temper. He refused point
blank the moment I began to speak of M. Gustave. I
could still have recourse to Georges, but when Harel was
in a bad temper it was usually because Georges herself was
also in a bad temper. I was intimate enough in that house
to know that. I therefore beat a retreat at the first repulse
I received.
The next day I saw M. Gustave again. "The wind
sets Hugo's way," I said. "There is nothing I can do
at the moment at the Porte St.-Martin. It seems that
Hugo has written a real play."
"Give me a line to Hugo."
"I can't ; we're not friends."
"Do you know M. d'Épagny ? They are playing a
piece of his to-morrow or next day."
"Yes. *The Malcontents.* I hear there's a magnificent
scene by Sechan to be used in that play."
"I asked if you knew M. d'Épagny."
"As we all know each other ; not enough to recommend
you to him. But wait a bit. Do you know Merle, Dorval's
husband ? "
"Yes. His wife gave me a letter to him."
"Then go and see Merle."
"I will."
M. Gustave went to see Merle. "Do you know M.
d'Épagny ? " he asked him.

" Why, of course.   He's a friend of mine."

" Then give me a letter to him."

" With pleasure."   Merle went to his bureau and in his charming handwriting, so fine and clear, he wrote a letter to his friend M. d'Épagny introducing Gustave.

It was then two o'clock in the afternoon.   " Don't go to-day," said Merle.   " He won't be at home.   He is sure to be at a rehearsal.   Go to-morrow."

" At what time ? "

" Ten o'clock in the morning."

The next day, punctually at ten, M. Gustave rang at d'Épagny's door.   A middle-aged woman opened it.   She was housekeeper to the author of *Dominique, or the Possessed*, a charming little piece played at the Théâtre Français admirably by Monrose Senior.

" M. d'Épagny ? "

" What is your business with him, please ? "

" I have a letter for him."

" From whom ? "

" From one of his friends."

The housekeeper would have liked to ask the name of the friend but apparently she did not dare.   She opened the door of her master's study.   " Here is a young man with a letter from one of your friends," said she.

" Where is he ? " asked d'Épagny, lifting his head.

" I am here, sir," said Gustave, advancing into the room with his most charming smile.

" You bring me a letter from a friend ? "

" Yes, sir."

" What's his name ? "

" M. Merle."

" M. Merle is no friend of mine, sir," said d'Épagny, rolling his eyes and raising his voice.

" M. Merle is not your friend ! " cried Gustave.

" No.   And the proof——   Here, read this article that he has written in his *Quotidienne* on the first performance of my *Malcontents*."

He began fumbling among his papers for the *Quotidienne* which at last—about a quarter of an hour later —he found.

" There, read that ! " said he.

" Oh ! " said Gustave.

" Well, what do you say ? "

" I say that he must have had some grudge against the Porte St.-Martin to write like this of such a good play."

" You saw it ? "

" I've been three times."

D'Épagny looked at M. Gustave.

" Hm," said he. " You've a good appearance."

" That's a good thing."

" Hand over your letter. Oh, you are a painter, are you ? Good."

" How do you mean—good ? "

" I know."

" I don't quite understand—— "

" Do you know Harel ? "

" I have not that honour."

" If I introduced you to him as an actor he wouldn't have anything to do with you."

" Oh ! "

" But if I introduce you as a painter he'll regret that you aren't an actor."

" Oh, that's what he is like, eh ? "

" Oh, I know him ! He is a clever devil, but we'll be cleverer."

" Speak for yourself."

" Wait a bit—wa—ait a bit ! "

D'Épagny sat thinking.

" I've got it."

" What ? "

" Do you understand lithography ? "

" I can manage a little of everything."

" In that case come and breakfast with me."

" I have breakfasted."

" What did you have ? "

" An egg and a cutlet."

" Well, you can manage two eggs and two cutlets. Boys of your age have an appetite."

" Too much, sometimes. There are occasions when it's a nuisance."

" Oh, so we've had to eat cat's meat sometimes, have we ? "

" We shouldn't have minded sometimes if there'd been even a cat to eat ! "

" D'Épagny rang the bell.

" Four eggs and four cutlets."

" But I've already had the honour to tell you—— "

" Hush ! "

" Oh, if you'll only get me a chance at the Porte St.-Martin I'll do anything you wish."

The four eggs and the four cutlets were brought in. M. Gustave prepared to eat his egg with some bread and butter.

" What are you doing ? " cried d'Épagny.

" Me ? Nothing. I'm eating my egg," said Gustave, alarmed.

" Is that how you eat eggs ? "

" I'm sorry—— "

" Hand it over." M. Gustave passed the egg to d'Epagny. " This is how you should prepare it." With this, d'Epagny put into the egg in equal parts a little butter, a pinch of salt, and a pinch of pepper, and turned the mixture round and round with his knife ; then handed the egg, all brimming over, to his guest. M. Gustave ate it as gravely as he could.

After breakfast d'Épagny rang the bell.

" Yes, sir ? " said the housekeeper, surprised.

" My coat, please."

" What for ? "

" I'm going out."

" You are going out, sir ? "

" Yes, yes."

" But you haven't a rehearsal, sir."

" I've business on hand."

" Business ? "

" Hold your tongue. I am going out."

" Oh, very good, sir." The poor housekeeper, astonished that M. d'Épagny could have any business that she did not know about, brought the coat which she handed sadly to her master.

D'Épagny is an excellent fellow with a heart of gold and fire in spite of his sixty-five or six years—he must be quite that—but twenty years ago he was only forty-five, and he was just as ready to take up a cause with zeal and render any one a service as he is to-day. And yet—who knows ? As they grow older, the good grow better.

He took M. Gustave by the arm and dragged him to
Cairo passage. It was there his play was being printed.
He took up a leaf and doubled it over.

" This is the size of my booklet," he said.

" Oh, good."

" You have seen my play ? "

" Three times, as I told you."

" Ah, yes. Well, I want you to do a lithograph of
Mlle. Georges in her big scene, and you needn't worry
about anything else."

As a matter of fact, M. Gustave had never seen either
Mlle. Georges or the play. But he went that night to the
theatre and from his stall he made a sketch of Mlle. Georges
in her big scene. For three days he kept his nose to that
stone ; but the third day, judging his *chef d''œuvre* to be
ready, he took off a print and carried it round to show
d'Épagny.

" Ah, that's the thing ! The very thing ! Thérèse !
. . . You lithograph very well, young man. . . . Thérèse!"

" Here, sir."

" Just stitch this in front of my play, will you ? "

" Yes, sir. Why, it's Mlle. Georges ! "

" You see, I didn't tell her. Yes, it is Mlle. Georges.
Do you think she'll like it, Thérèse ? "

" I should think she ought ! "

" Then everything will go on wheels, young man.
Come along this evening at eight o'clock to the stage door,
rue de Bondy."

" I'll be there."

" And now you'd better go."

" Till to-night, then, M. d'Épagny."

" Till to-night."

M. Gustave departed, his heart high with hope.

That evening, at the appointed hour, he was at his post.
Five minutes later he recognized d'Épagny in the darkness
and went to meet him.

" Well ? "

" Well, here I am. Now let's go up." They both
went up.

" Go on to the stage. I'll wait for Mlle. Georges at the
door of her dressing-room."

M. Gustave was not of a figure to pass unnoticed in the

wings. Five minutes after his entrance there was a murmur of voices :

"Who is that ?—Where does he come from ?—What's he here for ?—What does he want ? "

" Good-looking chap," said the women.

" Pooh ! " replied the men.

On this the curtain fell and Georges went to her dressing-room.

" Mlle. Georges ! "

" Why, it's M. d'Épagny ! " said the great actress with that slightly drawling intonation that gave such a great charm to a voice that issued from the most beautiful mouth and from between the whitest teeth in the world.

" Yes, it's I. I came to bring you this."

" What is ' this ' ? "

" It's our play."

" Oh, thanks."

Georges reached out a careless hand and let the little book fall on the sofa.

" Won't you look at the frontispiece ? "

" Is there a frontispiece ? "

" Look ! "

" What's it about ? "

" You, in your big scene."

" Oh, is it ? "

Georges opened the booklet. " Oh, that's good ! " she cried.

" You think so ? "

" I do. Who did it ? "

" A young painter I know."

" Where is he ? "

" In the wings."

" What's he doing in the wings ? "

" Well, you see, it's the first time he's ever been behind the scenes and he is taking advantage of the opportunity."

" Bring him up here."

CHAPTER XXIII

THE LINE IS BAITED—STRATEGY ON THE PART OF GUSTAVE'S
PROTECTOR—THE OCCASION SEIZED BY THE FORELOCK
—A RUN-THROUGH *THE TOUR DE NESLE*—M. GUSTAVE
PLAYS BURIDAN UNDER HIS OWN NAME AT THE
PORTE ST.-MARTIN

FIVE minutes after, d'Épagny came back leading M.
Gustave by the hand. Gustave was blushing like a young
bride.

" Oh, come here, sir," said Georges in her most charming
tones. " Do come here! It's admirable, sir. Couldn't
be more like. It's——" At this moment a key was
heard turning in the door of M. Harel's private office which
was only separated from Georges's dressing-room by a
partition.

" That's Harel coming in," said Georges. " Harel!
Harel! "

" What is it ? " asked Harel through the partition.

" Come here."

" Well, here I am." And Harel entered, rubbing his
hands as was his habit.

" Come and look at this! " And Georges showed him
the lithograph. " What do you say to that ? "

Harel usually waited till he knew Georges's opinion
before he dared to have one of his own ; so he took out his
snuffbox as he looked at the lithograph and rammed
snuff up his nose as he said : " Hum ! Why, that's a
lithograph! "

" Yes, of course, donkey. But what do you think of
the lithograph ? "

" Hm ! Hm ! Ha—Hm ! "

" Then you think it's charming too ? "

" Yes, yes, of course. Charming ! " repeated Harel.

" Adorable ? "

" Adorable ! " repeated Harel.

" Ravishing ? "

" Ravishing ! " repeated Harel.

M. Gustave drank in this flattery with eagerness, and
M. d'Épagny watched him. When the scene had lasted

long enough d'Épagny gave M. Gustave a poke with his elbow. M. Gustave, who knew his world, made his adieux and left. Georges followed him with her eyes. " Where's he going, that young man ? " she asked.

" I told you that he knows nothing about the inside of a theatre. The idea of passing an evening in the wings delights him and he doesn't want to lose a moment." Then, going to the door as if to make sure that M. Gustave had gone, he said to Georges and Harel : " What a pity it is he isn't an actor ! "

" Yes, it is a pity," said Georges.

" A great pity," said Harel.

" He has such a fine voice."

" Beautiful," said Georges.

" Magnificent," said Harel.

" Such a fine appearance for a leading man. Well, good-bye, Harel. Good-bye, Mlle. Georges ! I'll go down and join him in the wings. I told him to stop near the prompt side ; but he won't know which the prompt side is, and if he wanders about he may fall down a trap."

" Yes, you'd better go after him."

D'Épagny went.

" Well ? " asked M. Gustave.

" The line is baited ; be patient, the fish will soon bite."

" You really think so ? "

" I'm sure of it. But while you wait come along to the stage door every evening at eight or eight-thirty."

" All right."

" You understand ? "

" Oh, I ask nothing better ; I've nothing to do."

So, every evening all through the sixty performances of *The Malcontents*, they met at the stage door. Directly they met, author and painter went upstairs to the wings.

They always did this during an interval. D'Épagny went straight to the hole in the curtain. If there was a full house he would say : " Good. Let's go and find Mlle. Georges. Harel will be in a good temper."

If there were empty places in the auditorium he would say : " Nothing doing to-day. Remain if you like, but I shall go." And go he did. As to M. Gustave no one took any notice of him ; he was a painter.

However, day followed day ; till M. Gustave had used

up his doubloons and had begun on his costumes. The first he sold was a general's uniform. The epaulettes, shoulder knots, silver buckles, coat embroidered with gold lace, all went to a readymade clothes shop on the Place de la Bourse. Then, bit by bit, the rest of the wardrobe followed them.

The thinner became the wardrobe the more pressing was M. Gustave and the more M. d'Épagny said : " What a pity that instead of being a painter my painter isn't an actor."

And when d'Épagny had gone out, Georges would say to Harel : " Why does d'Épagny always say that ? "

" What ? " asked Harel.

" Why, that."

" I asked what that was ? "

" Weren't you listening ? "

" As if I listened to what d'Épagny says ! "

" He keeps saying : ' What a pity my painter isn't an actor ! ' "

" Oh, it's a nervous habit."

" Perhaps."

And Georges went on the stage again, saluting M. Gustave, whom she met on her way there and saying in her turn : " It is really a pity M. Gustave isn't an actor ; what a fine leading man he would make ! "

One day, or rather one evening, Harel decided to revive *The Tower of Nesle.* There was a full house. Delaistre was to play Buridan.

D'Epagny and M. Gustave came along as usual. (They were playing *Jeanne Vaubernier* as a curtain raiser.)

" Hullo, Harel ! " said d'Épagny.

" Good evening," replied Harel, brusquely.

D'Épagny turned, and saw behind him Mlle. Georges with a grave look on her beautiful face.

" My young man—— " he began, speaking to Georges.

" Oh, damn your young man," cried Harel. " Can he play Buridan to-night ? "

" What do you mean—play Buridan ? "

" Oh, here's M. Delaistre sent to say he's ill. He can't play to-night."

" If your young man could only act—— "

" He can ! " cried d'Épagny seizing the chance by the forelock.

M

" He can play Buridan ? " cried Harel, seizing d'Épagny by the collar.

" Yes, of course he can."

" But how's that ? "

" He's an actor."

" You say he's an actor."

" Yes."

" But you said he was a painter."

" He's both ! He's an actor-painter or a painter-actor, whichever you prefer."

" Where is he ? "

" On the stage."

" Go and bring him to me."

D'Épagny ran to find Gustave. He found him behind the first wing on the O.P. side. " Quick," cried he. " While it's burning ! While it's bubbling ! Come along ! Come ! "

" Come where ? "

" To Georges's dressing-room," cried d'Épagny.

They rushed to Georges's dressing-room. Harel didn't give Gustave time to enter. " Can you play Buridan ? " he cried as soon as he saw him.

" Of course I can."

" You know the part ? "

" I've played it twenty times."

" But I mean this evening—— "

" I'll be ready to play it in ten minutes."

" What, without rehearsal ? "

" Oh, I'll just have a run-through behind the blind with the others. And then—you—— "

" Yes—what ? "

" You'll be good enough to announce me."

" All right. Go up to the wardrobe and try on a costume."

" I've my own."

" Are they—all right ? "

" Oh, you needn't worry. I painted them myself ; it's cheaper and it's more effective. I'll be back in ten minutes."

" Off with you, young man."

M. Gustave rushed from the dressing-room. Harel turned to Mlle. Georges :

" Did you hear what he said, Georges ? "

" That he'd play Buridan."

" No, no. That's understood."

" What else did he say ? "

" He said that painted costumes are cheaper and more effective."

" Well ? "

" Well, suppose we put a clause in his contract that he is to paint our costumes."

" Oh, be quiet, you fool ! " cried Georges, throwing a cushion at Harel's head. " You understand nothing of management ! "

Five minutes later Gustave was back. His Buridan costume though ugly enough when seen close, was magnificently decorative at a distance. M. Gustave had painted it on calico after a Byzantine design ; then, on a hint from me, instead of wearing his sword suspended from his waist, he had sewn his belt to his doublet, which gave his dress a marked character of the thirteenth century. The rest of the costume had been copied in St. Evre's studio from a nobleman in his picture of " Inez of Portugal crowned after Death."

A quarter of an hour later Buridan was striding into the wings looking as if he had stepped out of some famous tapestry.

Georges gave a cry when she saw him. " Oh, he's magnificent ! Look, Harel, what a fine costume ! "

" You think so ? "

" Don't you ? "

" Why, of course. Magnificent ! Superb ! "

Then, in a whisper he added:

" I like mine best, though. . . . Now, boys, a runthrough ! "

They went behind the backcloth and had their runthrough. Whilst they were still at it the curtain fell on the last act of the comedy that preceded the drama.

" And about that announcement ? " suggested M. Gustave.

" Ah, yes," said Harel.

He called for " Moëssard ! Moëssard ! Moëssard ! "

" Here I am, M. Harel," said Moëssard, bowing as low as his alderman-like proportions would allow.

" Quick, Moëssard ; make the announcement."

" What am I to say, M. Harel ? "

" What you like, begad ! "

" Sorry, M. Harel. I make the announcements, but I don't write 'em. You word it, M. Harel, and I'll say it."

" Oh, it's simple enough. . . . Hm ! . . . Hm ! . . . Owing to sudden indisposition M. Delaistre unfortunately finds himself unable to appear, and as, by good chance, M.—What's his name—from Rouen happened to be in the theatre he has most kindly volunteered to play the part of Buridan. He asks the public to make all due allowance for the short notice, etc."

" But, sir," objected Moëssard, " I can't say M. What's his name ! "

" Oh, by the by, what is your name ? " asked M. Harel.

" Gustave."

" Oh, that's provincial, and won't do for Paris. Think of another name."

" I needn't think ; I have one. My own."

" Of course. And what is your name ? "

" Mélingue."

" That's a good name. A very good name ! Moëssard, you hear ? Owing to the sudden indisposition of Delaistre, M. Mélingue, just arrived from Rouen, being by good chance in the theatre, has most kindly volunteered to play the part of Buridan."

" All right, M. Harel. Ring up ! "

" Oh, Moëssard—add—— "

" Yes, sir. Add what ? "

" That he is wearing his own costumes."

" Yes, sir."

" M. Mélingue. Got it right ? Mélingue ! "

" Yes, sir."

.   .   .   .   .

This is the true story of the adventures and tribulations of M. Étienne Marin Mélingue, once companion in misery of M. Hippolyte Tisserand, from the day of his birth to the day that saw his first appearance in the part of Buridan at the Porte St.-Martin Theatre.

Dear readers, who have so often applauded him for these last twenty years, you know the rest of his story as well as I do, so there is no need for me to relate it to you.

MY ODYSSEY

CHAPTER I

My first introduction to the hallowed regions of the Théâtre Français took place when I was only two and twenty, on the night of the first performance of *Sylla ;* and my sponsor was Adolphe de Leuven, author of the *Postillon de Longameau.*

I was very greatly and justifiably excited. I—a wholly unknown youth—was to be presented to the great man whose flatterers called him sometimes Roscius, sometimes the French Garrick, but whose name has gone down to posterity as—simply Talma. It is enough—it is as well known as the other names.

De Leuven was an habitué of the place, and drew me after him through the densely crowded corridors. At length we reached Talma's room. Here the crowd was even larger. Possibly the dictator never had more clients thronging about him than the actor who represented him had admirers clustered near his door.

Fortunately de Leuven and I were both very thin in those far-off days, and we wriggled along like eels. The result was that we found ourselves in an ante-chamber, crammed with all the literary celebrities of Paris. I beheld for the first time : Soumet, Delavigne, Guiraud, Étienne, Lemercier, and four or five more.

While we struggled to gain an entrance to the inner room—the *sanctum*—a voice cried :

" Room for Mademoiselle Mars ! "

We at once squeezed as close to the wall as we could get. A vision glided by ! A gentle rustle of satin, a cloud of gauze, a perfume which filled the room, a pair of diamond eyes, two rows of pearl-like teeth, a voice low and sweet, uttering words of praise. The two—Talma and Mars—

embraced, and I believe I recall that the former used the
familiar " thou," while the latter kept to the more formal
and respectful " you."

Then the rustling sound was heard again. Mademoiselle
Mars reappeared, exchanged a few words with Étienne and
Soumet, made a sign to my sponsor—who did not seem to
be the least impressed !—and vanished.

" Come," said Adolphe, " we must get on."

" I dare not."

" Nonsense," said Adolphe. " He won't look at you ! "
Which was meant as an encouragement, but acted as a sad
damper.

We progressed little by little, and when at last we
reached the door I stood on tip-toe, and being above the
average height was able to survey the room.

Instead of Sylla wearing the dictator's toga and crowned
with laurels, I beheld a little old man bald-headed and
wrapped in a flannel dressing-gown.

I have related elsewhere how Talma baptized me
" dramatic poet," under the protection of Shakespeare
and Corneille.

CHAPTER II

Four or five years had sped, during which Talma had died ;
but his baptism of me had borne some fruit, for I, like
every one else, had composed a tragedy in five acts. It is
known, for I have related the fact, that I owed my inspiration to a *bas-relief* by Mademoiselle de Faveau, representing
the death of Monaldeschi.

I called my tragedy *Christine à Fontainebleau.*

It was not a classical piece in the manner of Æschylus
or Sophocles or Corneille, but was on the lines of the new
classical tragedy as expounded by Legouvé, Chenier, and
others. It is true that I had taken liberties in some of
the scenes, liberties at which Melpomene's hair would have
bristled, and that here and there I had introduced a touch
of humour.

But there it was! The question before me was how to obtain a reading. I hear that it is a very difficult thing nowadays to obtain one ; certainly it was very much more so then. If Talma had been alive, I would have gone to him without hesitation, although I had seen him only twice more, in his dressing-room, of course. On the stage, I saw him as often as I possibly could. I feel certain that in spite of its imperfections, *Christine* would have given Talma the opportunity of an entirely new part never acted before on any stage—I mean the part of Monaldeschi.

A coward!

No dramatist had dared to represent a coward.

I had dared—not that I had aimed at an innovation, inasmuch as I had found the character already drawn in Père Lebel's history.

I am convinced that Talma would have gladly accepted the rôle. He had, indeed, attempted something of the sort in the Leicester of *Mary Stuart;* but Leicester in *Mary Stuart* was not a coward, he was a man of ambition ; but to induce him to give the order—retracted in the following line—to arrest Mortimer, what innumerable preparations were necessary.

As I have said, Talma was no more.

I sought everywhere for help. Finally I obtained, after much difficulty, an introduction to the prompter of the Comédie Française. He was a good man, who perpetually took snuff, and whose name was Garnier.

It would take too long to relate how I made his highly important acquaintance ; and indeed the only point I wish to make is that one of the artists with whom Garnier, as prompter, had most frequent and intimate intercourse, was Firmin.

We all remember Firmin, a charming actor full of talent, warmth, and spirit. Unfortunately, Firmin could not rely on his memory. Well, it was precisely that failing which brought the actor to the prompter, which made a kind of alliance between them.

It was through Garnier, then, that I attained to Firmin.

A man of forty at that time, who enjoyed the prerogative of looking twenty-six or twenty-eight on the stage—such was Firmin. When almost a child, he made his debut on the stage of the *Jeunes Elèves;* from these he played with Picard's Company, and from Picard's went to the Comédie Française. There he played several parts—small parts—almost perfectly, but he nearly came to grief as Tasso in Alexandre Duval's rather poor drama of that name.

He bitterly complained of his chief, Armand, who would not allow him to play anything of the *répertoire*.

Firmin was short, his disposition fretful and quarrelsome, as becomes the man of five feet two ; but brave, and always ready for a fight.

In the course of his life he had occasion to give two or three thrusts with the sword, had received one himself—from a husband, I believe—right through his body.

One of his ambitions was to play the part of Bayard. A score of times he said so at the theatre, adding invariably :

" It must not be thought that Bayard was a colossus ; on the contrary, he was rather short than tall ; rather slim than fat ; Bayard, in fact, was a man of my own size."

The parallel, to Firmin's great regret, never attracted me sufficiently to influence me to write on the same subject as my contemporary du Belloy.

But, with his innumerable good qualities, Firmin—to my thinking—had one small defect : he was timid, where the Committee was concerned.

The theatre at that time was managed by a Committee, who assembled every Saturday. It was presided over by a royal commissary, Baron Taylor.

All the help Firmin gave me was this : " Get to know Baron Taylor." There was nothing compromising, as any one can see, in giving such advice.

Those who wish to know how I managed to get into touch with Baron Taylor, by what Jacob's ladder I climbed from the prompter to the royal commissary, can read my " Memoirs."

A reading of *Christine* was granted ; which of itself was a triumph. To obtain a reading at the Théâtre Français ! Good heavens ! there have been Academicians who never achieved more. I went in company with Firmin. It was the first time I was entering the *sanctum sanctorum*. I had been led through the obscure windings of the dramatic labyrinth, by Firmin. In those days, the stairs which led from the ground floor to the first story were absolutely dark. A lady was before us. As we followed her towards the illuminated regions, I was noticing, in what I could see of her, that charming motion of the hip called by the Spanish " menito." Floods of light presently reached us. Only then did she turn and recognize Firmin.

She burst out laughing. She had been at pains to attract, and the pains were lost. She reproached him with one word which, I thought, a rather free one for a " dame " of the Comédie Française. (Every one knows that in the traditions of the theatres one speaks of the " Girls " of the Opera, the " Young Ladies" of the Comic Opera, and the " Dames " of the Comédie Française.)

The Committee was in full force.

It was composed of Mm. Armand, Michelot, Monrose, Firmin, Granville, Menjaud, Saint-Aulaire, Sainton, and Mademoiselle Mars.

M. Lafon, also a member, was absent. His absence caused an incident which I will relate later on.

CHAPTER III

Christine was not refused and yet not accepted. Gustavus Adolphus' daughter showed similarities of temperament with Marie Tudor and Lucrezia Borgia, disclosing the author's tendencies towards the *monstrosities* of the modern drama. At least, that is what the critics said, the same who applauded when Jocasta married her son, when Orestes killed his mother, when Athea drank his brother's blood, and when Gabrielle ate her lover's heart. It is true that the heroes of all these dramas had been long since dead and had, therefore, achieved consecration.

The reading over, all the members, including Mademoiselle Mars, looked at one another. Two scenes— one between the queen and La Calprenède and the other one between Sentinelli and Monaldeschi—met with favour, and had to be repeated.

Not knowing better, I was waiting, when some one

remarked that I must do so in an adjoining room during the deliberations ; these never taking place in the author's presence.

I went out and waited.

After ten minutes, Firmin entered the room.

" Well," said he, " the Committee is most embarrassed."

" How so ? "

" They can't decide whether the play is classic or romantic."

" Why boggle about a question of words ? Is the play good, or is it bad ? That's all."

" They can't decide that either."

" Dear me ! That's a nuisance. Did they like it, or did they not ? "

" They have been very much interested."

" That's something."

" Of course ; but—— "

" But what ? "

" They dare not receive you."

" How so ? They dare not receive me ?

" No."

" Then, they refuse ? "

" They dare not decline."

" Well ! Will they accept it if I make alterations ? "

" Not quite."

" To what decision have they come ? "

" To seek Picard's advice."

" Advice from Picard, of all men ! He will find it execrable."

" Why so ? "

" Because Picard has no interest to find it good."

" Picard has a conscience."

" What ? An old dramatic author and an old comedian ; and what's more, an Academician ! Picard a man of conscience ? Come, come ! "

" You are mistaken there. Picard adores youth."

" Oh ! I know them so well, these good men of the Academy ; I usually meet some of them at M. Lethière's ; they also adore youth—but they abhor the young."

" You are quite wrong."

" To come back to my manuscript ; what has to be done ? "

" You will have to take it to Picard."

" I don't know him in the least."

" I will take you."

" You do know him, do you ? "

" I used to live with him."

" Is the Committee's decision irrevocable ? "

" No ; but my advice is, submit yourself to it."

" Then let us go immediately."

" You have decided at last, then ? "

" Certainly. We go to Picard. I am like the prisoner who on being told he was going to be tortured, answered : ' Very well ! that will help to pass the time for me.' "

" Let us go to Picard," said Firmin once again.

CHAPTER IV

WHERE did Picard live ? I don't remember. I only know that he lived on a second story, and that we were ushered into his *sanctum*—the name then generally given to the studies of dramatic authors.

This *sanctum* was an immense library whose walls were covered with beautifully bound books never intended to be touched.

Busts of Homer, of Sophocles, of Demosthenes, of Cicero, of Racine, of Corneille, and of Molière were placed on all the points of vantage of the great bookcases. It was, as it seemed to me, on M. Picard's part either a token of great humility or of self-confidence to live on terms of intimacy with those great men.

Picard, a small hunchback with a keen eye, a pointed nose and chin, was the very type of " Rigaudin " whom he had impersonated in a play written by himself, called *Maison en loterie*.

He was then supposed to be descended from Molière. I do not wish to dispute the legitimacy of his ancestry, but anyhow he had descended a long way.

Raising his spectacles so that they rested on his forehead, he looked at Firmin to bid him welcome. Firmin felt for Picard an almost filial respect. He explained to Molière's descendant the occasion of our visit.

Picard, turning to me, looked this time through his spectacles :

" Ah ! Here is the young man ? "

" Yes, sir ; here he is."

" And you have written a tragedy, young man ? "

" Almost so."

" On what subject ? "

" On Christine."

" Christine of Sweden ? The same who ordered the murder of her lover ? "

" Yes."

" There is one already written by our contemporary, Alexandre Duval."

" I know ; but not a good one."

Picard took off his spectacles.

" Oh ! Oh ! "

" I said not good," I repeated.

" And what assures you, young man, that it is not the subject itself which is not good ? "

" I think there are no good nor bad subjects."

" Ah ! Ah ! "

" It all depends on how the author offers them to the public."

" So you have got fixed ideas ? "

" Yes, sir."

Picard gave Firmin a look which seemed to say : " You hear ? This young man has fixed ideas," and if he had dared he would have laughed, rubbing his hands together— exactly like his Rigaudin. He resumed :

" Then you have written a *Christine* ? "

" I have."

" And the Comédie Française refers to me for an opinion of your work ? "

" I don't say they refer to you, sir ; I say they wish to hear your opinion."

" That's the same thing."

" Not quite."

" Give it to me."

I handed him the manuscript.

" Very well," said Picard.

" When will you have read it ? " asked Firmin timidly.

" In eight days."

" You hear ? " said Firmin. " In eight days. Come, we must not take up M. Picard's time."

I got up, repeating : " In eight days."

As for imposing myself on M. Picard, I promised myself he would never lose his time on my account.

" I am done for," said I to Firmin as soon as we had left the house.

" It was very wrong of you to talk as you did."

" Why so ? "

" Because he is a patriarch."

" I don't respect all patriarchs—Lot, for example."

" You are a misguided being."

" And your Picard is a malignant spirit."

With these words, we parted. I had trodden on forbidden ground. It was a miracle that I had not been struck dead on the spot.

Eight days later, at the appointed time, we presented ourselves to Picard. At a first glance, I saw my manuscript lying at his right hand ; a look at his face told me it was not as a mark of favour it had been placed there.

" I was expecting you," said he, smiling slyly, bareing as he did so the grey teeth that projected towards his nose and chin.

" Well ? " asked Firmin.

" Well ? " said I.

Picard was playing with my ill-fated manuscript as the tiger plays with a man ; or rather—for we can't compare small to great things (this is permitted to none but Virgil) —as a cat plays with a mouse.

" My dear sir," he began sweetly, "have you other means of support than a literary career ? "

" Sir, I have an employment in the establishment of the Duke of Orléans for which I am paid fifteen hundred francs."

" If that is the case," continued Picard, thrusting the roll into my hands, "go back to your desk, young man ; go back to your desk."

I bowed, and was leaving the room. Turning round, I saw him holding Firmin's hands in both his own and shrugging his shoulders, his head seemed to be rising from his chest.

Firmin joined me on the stairs.

" Didn't I tell you so ? "

He muttered something between his teeth.

We parted at the corner of the rue Richelieu, he to go back to his theatre, I to return to my work in the rue St.-Honoré.

CHAPTER V

As I was going in, the office-boy challenged me.

" You have been out ? "

" Yes, Féresse."

" During your absence an actor has called for you."

" What actor, Féresse ? "

" M. Lafon."

" M. Lafon of the Comédie Française ? "

" I don't know what theatre he belongs to, but he is an actor."

" What did you tell him ? "

" As he looked annoyed at not finding you here, I said to him : ' Oh ! he is sure to be back soon ; clerks at fifteen hundred francs have no business to stay away very long.' "

" How well you know the bureaucratic code, my dear Féresse ! And what did he answer to that ? "

" He promised to call again."

" That's good, Féresse. Now be off."

" What, go ? "

" Go about your business and let me alone with mine."

" You mean, with the office work ? "

" Yes, Féresse, you are right ; it's I who am wrong."

Féresse left the room grumbling.

What did M. Lafon want with me ? Why did he take the trouble to call to see me ? M. Lafon, a big wig of the Comédie Française ?

He held a curious post at the theatre. He acted the Chevaliers of France.

And what were the "Chevaliers of France"?

Why, chevaliers of France such as Bayard, Duguesclin, Raoul, Tancréde, and Marigny, who appeared dressed in a black toque and a white feather, a yellow tunic, tight pantaloons, high boots, and a cross-handled sword. Also Orosmanes, Zamore, the Cid, the Orphans of China, Hippolytus, Pylades, Britannicus, Achilles, etc., were classed among the "Chevaliers of France."

Now, once for all, it was allowed that Talma was at his best, or, to speak more correctly, had been at his best, as Hamlet, Nero, Macbeth, Charles IX., Richard III., and Othello—that is, in representing conscience-stricken villains, tyrants, and oppressors of the innocent; but Lafon, on the other hand, excelled in the part of a "Chevalier of France," and not only as Marigny, Tancréde, Raoul, Duguesclin, and Bayard, but also as Achilles, Britannicus, Pylades, Hippolytus, the Orphans of China, the Cid, Zamore, and Orosmanes, all of whom, though not actually "Chevaliers of France," were certainly worthy of being ranked among them.

Needless to say that this was not an article of faith of the best intellects. Casimir Delavigne had just written an appropriate verse which had met with a great success for its unquestionable truth:

"Fools, since Adam, are in the majority."

As has been said already, M. Lafon considered the part of a "Chevalier of France" his own; that is, any part of one who sides with the weak against the strong, and who expresses more or less generous sentiments in more or less hackneyed language.

He was a queer fellow, this M. Lafon, with whom no one could boast of having had the last word. He was a Gascon through and through, but it was impossible to say whether his "gasconnades" were those of a wit or of a fool.

One of the actors of the Théâtre Français, himself mediocre enough, who was, in theatrical expression, slightly gay more often than his due, was very clever at imitating Lafon's manner and accent.

Once when X. was performing in the comedians' green-room—and exciting the unrestrained laughter of the joyous assembly—Lafon appeared.

The actor stopped, but the laughter went on.

" Well," asked Lafon, in his Gascon accent, so exactly like his imitator's that it sounded as an echo of the first, " what are you doing here ? "

" Nothing, Monsieur Lafon. You see, we are laughing," answered X.

" Yes. It looks as if you were imitating me, X."

" Oh, Monsieur Lafon ! "

" I make no objection. Great models are useful to study."

" Monsieur Lafon ! "

" It is said that you imitate me wonderfully well."

" To be sure, Monsieur Lafon, as you have just said, great models are useful objects to study ; and by reproducing your manner—— "

" Let us see, my young friend, let us see."

" Oh, Monsieur Lafon, before your face ? "

" It will give me pleasure."

" Really ? "

" On the head of Orosmanes ! "

When Lafon had sworn by Orosmanes, he had taken the oath he held the most sacred in the world.

" Since you wish it," said X.

" I beg you—— "

And X. repeated the tirade.

Lafon listened with the greatest attention and many signs of approval. Then, after the mimic had finished :

" Well," he asked, " why don't you perform like that on your own account ? You would not be hissed so much then, my friend."

It must be owned that Lafon had the best of the encounter.

On another occasion. One evening—it was on the first night of *Pierre de Portugal*—I was behind the scenes in the theatre, with Adolphe de Leuven and Lucien Arnault. Between the first and the second acts, Lafon, who was playing Don Pierre, had to change. He had to doff the prince's costume, and go to visit Inés disguised as a soldier. Lucien Arnault, the author of the play, sees him coming in a costume embroidered all over, with a sun on his chest. Lucien, in despair, thinks that Lafon has made a mistake, which cannot be rectified or the second act will be delayed. He darts forward :

" Oh, my dear Lafon ! What have you done ? "

" What ! what have I done ? "

" Yes ; what costume have you got on ? "

" You don't like my costume ? You are difficult to please, my dear Lucien ; it is a brand new one."

" Too much so, by gad ! It's what I complain of."

" What do you object to ? "

" Why, I think a soldier—— "

" What ? "

" You have too much embroidery, too much satin and velvet ; that sun especially—— "

Lafon's hand on his shoulder interrupted him :

" My dear Lucien," said he with a smile that I can still see, " you must understand one thing, and that is that I much prefer to be envied rather than pitied."

He then turned his back ; and he had the satisfaction of playing the second act, not as a Portuguese soldier, not as a Chevalier of France, but according to the contemporary idea of a troubadour.

When Lafon talked of Talma, he used to call him " the other."

One day, M. de Lauraguais said to him irritably: "Monsieur Lafon, allow me to tell you that it seems to me you are ' the one ' rather too often."

Such was the man who had come when I was away and who was to call again.

What could Tancréde want of me ?

CHAPTER VI

As I was thus questioning myself, the door of my office was thrown open and Féresse announced :

" M. Lafon."

" Show him in," said I, getting up.

N

M. Lafon dismissed Féresse with a superb gesture, intimating at the same time his thanks and his sense of superiority. And he stopped on the threshold.

"Excuse me, sir," said he, "if I take the liberty of coming here without having the pleasure of your acquaintance."

"I unacquainted with you, Monsieur Lafon?" said I. "You are known all over the world."

"As an artist, sir, that's true. I ought to have said, when not personally known to you."

"Please be seated, sir."

M. Lafon bowed his thanks, but remained where he was.

"Sir, you have written a tragedy on Queen Christine."

The memory of my recent tribulations flashed across my mind. "Alas!" said I, "I can't deny it."

"It would not be right to deny it, sir. It is said that your manuscript contains beautiful things."

"You are very good."

"That is every one's opinion."

"M. Picard excepted," I added.

"Picard? What of him?"

"What of Picard? Don't you know Picard, Monsieur Lafon?"

"Oh yes; the author of *Petite Ville*. Well, but does M. Picard's opinion matter?"

"It does not matter to me, but it seems that it does matter to the Théâtre Français, since they have asked his advice before deciding about my play."

"Your play is accepted, sir."

"I think not!"

"It is accepted; and the proof of it is that I have come to ask you this question: Monsieur Dumas, is there not in your work a bold dashing gentleman who exclaims, as Christine, that wicked queen, is about to have the unfortunate Monaldeschi murdered, 'Majesty, you have no right to do that. No, no, no; you have no right'?"

"Upon my word, Monsieur Lafon, a happy suggestion; but it is too late. No, that part does not exist. I must admit that that part is missing, Monsieur Lafon."

"Oh dear."

"What can you expect? I am but an apprentice."

"And can't you put it in? I assure you it would improve it, sir, decidedly."

"I have no doubt ; but my tragedy was not written with that idea in mind."

"Why, sir ; was there not among the courtiers of Louis XIV. a Chevalier of France who pleaded in favour of that unfortunate foreigner, like Talbot in *Jeanne d'Arc ?* "

" I fear not."

" It is impossible, excuse me for saying so."

" In reality, it all happened as I relate it, Monsieur Lafon. The murder was sudden ; it took place fifteen leagues from Paris, nineteen from Versailles. Absence of premeditation is the queen's sole excuse."

"None can be made for her, sir," said the indignant Lafon.

"That's true, sir, and in the interests of morality I think as you do. No, she had no excuse ; but, if she had, the only one she could have would be her passion, her haste, her violence. It is clear that if she paused to think, Monaldeschi ought not to die. Now, you understand, since he is dead, one must make the best of it."

" But, Monsieur Dumas, it seems that M. Mazarin himself wrote a letter on that occasion."

" To which Christine answered with another, beginning thus : ' Most illustrious puppy . . .' You would not play Mazarin under such circumstances, would you ? "

" No, indeed, no. And what are the other parts ? "

" Well, there is Sentinelli."

" Sentinelli, Sentinelli. What does he do ? "

" He mercilessly murders his former friend."

" Oh ! The wretch ! "

" That does not suit you."

" No."

" There is Monaldeschi."

" The victim ? "

" The victim."

" Is the victim an interesting part ? "

" Not so much so as Iphigenia."

" Not so much so as Iphigenia ! And why ? "

" Because Iphigenia, like a true heroine of tragedy, advances towards the altar consoling her father and mother ; while Monaldeschi—— "

" While Monaldeschi ? "

" I must confess that he dies miserably."

" What ! He does not carry his head high while approaching the altar."

" There is no altar."

" Of course ; it is a figure of speech. How does he die ? "

" In the dust, Monsieur Lafon, imploring the queen's forgiveness, and dragging himself to her feet, shrieking for help."

" Then he is a coward ? "

" You say so. Well, yes, Monsieur Lafon, he is a coward."

" And you have dared to bring such a wretch on the stage ? "

" I have."

" And do you believe that your Monaldeschi will be tolerated ? "

" I hope so."

He shook his head.

" There it is, Monsieur Lafon ! We are reformers ; we want to bring back nature on the stage."

" Nature ? " said M. Lafon, shrugging his shoulders.

" Nature ! Well, yes."

" You know what M. de Voltaire said about nature ? "

" I know, Monsieur Lafon ; but I should like to hear that fine maxim from your lips."

" He said : ' My —— also is part of nature ; but I don't show it to the public.' "

" He showed them something very much worse than that, Monsieur Lafon."

" What did he show ? "

" He showed Othello disguised as Orosmanes, and Hamlet's mother disguised as Semiramis."

" Why, Monsieur Dumas, don't you admire Orosmanes ? "

" No, Monsieur Lafon."

" You don't admire Semiramis ? "

" Indeed I do not."

" But what is it you do admire ? "

" All of Æschylus, nearly all of Sophocles, a little of Euripides among the ancients ; all of Shakespeare, all of Molière, much of Corneille, much of Racine, *Le Mariage de Figaro* and the *Barbier de Séville*."

" And you do not admire Orosmanes when he says to
Nérestan : ' Wouldst thou flatter thyself to equal Orosmanes in generosity ' ? "

" No, Monsieur Lafon."

" You do not admire Tancréde when he tells Orbassan :
' Thee, proud Orbassan, it is thyself I do defy. Die
by my hand, snatch me out of life ' ? "

" No, Monsieur Lafon."

" You do not admire Fernand when he says to Zamore :
' Between the gods whom we serve, learn the difference.
Thine demand of thee murder, slaughter, and vengeance ;
and mine, when thine arm has slain me, command me to
pity and forgive ' ? "

" No, Monsieur Lafon."

" Now, sir, I begin to understand why you did not introduce into your *Christine* a bold dashing gentleman who
says to that Jezebel : ' Your Majesty has no right to
assassinate that man. No, no, no ; you have no right.' "

" And since I have not introduced that bold gentleman
in my *Christine*—— ? "

" Sir, my errand goes no further. Your most humble
servant, Monsieur Dumas ; I wish you success with your
Christine."

" I thank you for your good wishes, Monsieur Lafon,
and if ever I find a subject which allows it, and can put in
a bold spirited gentleman in a fine attitude—— "

" You will remember me ? "

" I will, I promise you, Monsieur Lafon."

The door closed behind him. Never since have I beheld
Lafon.

Eight days later, I read *Christine* a second time, when
it was accepted unanimously.

CHAPTER VII

SIX weeks or two months after *Christine* had been accepted,
there was the question of the rehearsals. I had been
given the preference over all those unhappy authors who

had been waiting their turn for the last five and twenty years. No one about me would believe it.

. One day, Mademoiselle Mars was announced, in the same manner as M. Lafon had been. This time, I must confess, I was fluttered. Mademoiselle Mars coming to see me in my poor little office !

" Mademoiselle Mars ? " I asked.

" Mademoiselle Mars," repeated Féresse.

" What Mademoiselle Mars ? "

" Are there two Mademoiselle Mars ? " came from the antechamber the sound of a charming voice I knew.

" Who is that ? You, yourself ? " cried I, leaping to the door.

" Of course. Since you don't come to see your actors, they have to come to meet their author."

" Ah, madame, I should not dare to call on you."

" When one is received at the Comédie Française, one is received by the actors."

" I did not know it, madame."

" Oh, there are so many things that you don't know. You don't know that I am here to have a talk with you ; that it will probably last some time, and, therefore, you ought to offer me a chair."

I rushed to get her a chair.

" Here it is, madame, here it is."

" And you, where are you going to sit ? Come, sit where you were."

I went back to my place.

" Sit down."

I sat dowm.

" Well, let us see ; how do you cast that play ? "

" To begin with, you are Christine."

" That's understood."

" Firmin, Monaldeschi."

" He is not quite up to it, but he will have good moments. All right."

" Périer, Sentinelli."

" Oh ! Oh ! Oh ! Oh ! Oh ! "

" Why not, madame ? "

" Does Périer play tragedy ? Come, come."

" But is my play really a tragedy ? And you your-self——— "

" I don't say I do ; but in my own part there is quite
a lot of comedy, whereas in Sentinelli's there is not the
slightest humour."

" That is true, I must admit."

" This arrangement is not your own choice, is it ? "

" No, I confess it again."

" Firmin made you do it."

" You have the gift of second sight, madame."

" No ; but I know the green-rooms, my dear sir. But
it was not Périer that you want in that part."

" Whom do I want, then ? "

" Ligier, it should be Ligier. He is a true Sentinelli ;
his faults are just made for that part. How is it that
you didn't think of him ? "

" But I did."

" Just so ; only they made you think of somebody else."

" Since I have started confessing, I won't tell lies. It is
true."

" Ah, my little Firmin, I recognize you there !
Believe me, my dear sir, you ought to give Périer a comedy
part, and when you want tragedy, give it to Ligier."

" Believe me when I say that you reduce me to despair."

" Oh, it doesn't matter to me ; it is only for your
sake I am speaking. What has it to do with me ? I
have no scenes with Périer."

" Rest assured, madame, that I am absolutely convinced that you speak for my benefit only."

" Then, if it's at all possible, you will agree to give the
part to Ligier. And now that the cast is practically
arranged, or nearly so, will you allow me to say a few words
on some of your verses ? "

" Of course, madame ! I'll receive them on my knees."

" Oh ! On your knees. I know that expression."

" And what have you to say about my verses,
madame ? "

" Well, first of all, in the first act, there is the scene
between myself and La Calprenède. . . . By the way,
who plays La Calprenède ? "

" Samson."

" Not bad. Well, there are about twenty verses in
that scene which I don't like."

" Twenty verses ? Gracious ! "

"Oh, I, you know, I am Saint John with the Mouth of Gold."

"You are much better than that, you are Saint John with the Mouth of Pearl."

She looked at me.

"Ah, it's true," said she, "that you and Demoustier come from the same part of the country."

"And what are those verses?"

"Wait a moment."

She took a roll of paper out of her pocket.

"What is that?" said I.

"My part."

"Written already?"

"Not only copied, but committed to memory."

"My compliments to you!"

Mademoiselle Mars opened the roll at the page where the verses which she did not like were written—the page was turned back at the corner—and she read—it goes without saying that it was not in a way to do them justice —the following lines :

"Oh ! lorsqu'il est écrit sur le livre du sort
Qu'un homme vient de naître au front large, au cœur fort,
Et que Dieu sur ce front, qu'il a pris pour victime,
A mis du bout du doigt une flamme sublime,
Au-dessous de ces mots, la même main écrit :
' Tu seras malheureux, si tu n'es pas proscrit ; '
Car, à ses premiers pas sur la terre où nous sommes,
Son regard dédaigneux prend en mépris les hommes.
Comme il est plus grand qu'eux, il voit avec ennui
Qu'il faut descendre vers eux ou les hausser vers lin ;
Alors, dans son sentier profond et solitaire,
Passant sans se mêler aux enfants de la terre,
Il dit aux vents, aux flots, aux étoiles, aux bois,
Les chants de sa grande âme avec sa forte voix.
La foule entend ces chants, elle crie au délire,
Et, ne comprenant point, elle se prend à rire ;
Mais, à pas de géant, sur un pic élevé,
Après de longs efforts, lorsqu'il est arrivé,
Reconnaissant sa sphère en ces zones nouvelles
Et sentant assez d'air pour ses puissantes alles,
Il part majestueux ; et qui le voit d'en bas,
Qui tente de le suivre et qui ne le peut pas,
Le voyant à ses yeux échapper comme un rêve,
Pense qu'il diminue à cause qu'il s'élève,
Croit qu'il doit s'arrêter où le perd son adieu,
Le cherche dans la nuit :—il est aux pieds de Dieu."

After twenty-eight or twenty-nine years I read these verses again. No doubt better ones have been composed, but also many worse. In those days, I looked upon them as the best ever written. They were composed as a sort of tribute of admiration, half to Hugo and half to Corneille. Nevertheless, I never dreamt that one of those verses would prove as applicable to Hugo as it was to Homer and Dante :

"Thou wilt be unfortunate even if not prescribed."

I confess I was struck dumb when these precise verses fell under Mademoiselle Mars's censure. I must own I defended them vehemently.

After a few minutes' discussion, Mademoiselle Mars rose to go with an air as stiff and sour as she had at first been charming.

" Very well," said she, " since you like them so much, they will be recited; wait and you will see what they'll be like."

Alas ! I did not have the pleasure of hearing what effect they would have had, at least not from those lips. For they were not only never spoken before an audience by Mademoiselle Mars, but furthermore she always omitted them at rehearsal when I was present.

During the first rehearsal, as the prompter, thinking she had forgotten them, reminded her of those verses :

" Go on ! Go on ! " she said ; " the author is going to cut them out."

After the rehearsal, I went to Garnier.

" I don't mean to cut those verses out," said I. " On the contrary, I wish them to remain intact and mean them to be recited."

" The deuce ! " said Garnier.

" Why 'the deuce ' ? "

" I say : The deuce ! "

" I hear, and I ask you what you mean by 'the deuce ' ! "

" I mean that if Mademoiselle Mars does not wish to recite your verses she will not recite them."

" What ! she won't say them ? "

" No. Listen to me ; I know her—— "

" I have no doubt you do."

" For thirty years I have prompted her ; that counts for as much as if I had been dressing her."

" However, if the play is given, she will have to say them."

" No doubt, if she acts it, but she won't do it."

" Well and good ; somebody else will play it. I have not offered her the part, she has asked me for it ! "

" That comes to the same thing ; she will not play it, and no one else will play it. Oh, I know her through and through, the siren."

" Listen, Monsieur Garnier. There is another rehearsal to-morrow."

" Yes."

" I'll not come."

" That's a mistake."

" Why ? "

" I am an old hand, you know."

" And what about it ? "

" Who leaves the game, loses it."

" Not at all ; I must go so as to escape from her fascinating charm."

" And then ? "

" Tell her that I beg of her to say those lines, since I am not going to cut them."

" I will deliver your message ; she will not say them all the same."

" She won't say them ? "

" No, not even at the rehearsal."

" Oh, that's really too bad ! "

" You will see."

" It seems that every one is his own master here."

" My dear Monsieur Dumas, listen to me. Thirty years of observation, study, and reflection have taught me that here, every one has rights and no one has duties."

" What you say is profoundly true, Monsieur Garnier."

He let his hand fall on my shoulder.

" When you know better, you will be of the same opinion."

" I am already, Monsieur Garnier."

" And you will cut out those lines."

" I'll stick to them."

" You won't be played, then."

" I won't be played, or else I shall be played with those lines."

" Then, you won't come to to-morrow's rehearsal ? "

" No."

" And you persist in my giving your message ? "

" I do."

" Adieu, Monsieur Dumas."

" Au revoir, you mean ? "

" Adieu."

" How so, adieu ? "

" To-morrow's rehearsal will be the last."

" The last ? "

" I know what I say."

" Look here ! "

" You will see."

" We shall see."

" There is time yet."

" Monsieur Garnier, Mademoiselle Mars will say all the lines, or else she shan't play the part."

" She will not play the part ; and the play won't be given, at least at the Théâtre Français."

" *Habent sua fata libelli.*"

" My dear Monsieur Dumas, I can't say whether you make a mistake in your Latin, but your arithmetic is at fault, of that I am sure."

After which, we separated.

CHAPTER VIII

MADEMOISELLE MARS came to the rehearsal. As she had done the day before, she skipped the same verses ; and again, as he had done the day before, Garnier prompted her.

" No," repeated Mademoiselle Mars, as on the previous day ; " the author will take them out."

" I am afraid you are mistaken, Mademoiselle Mars ; he will not cut them."

" What, he will not cut them ? "

" No."

" Are you sure of that, Garnier ? "

" I answer for it."

" Good ; then, go on."

And she went on, without passing more remarks, but she left out the lines.

That same night I went to the theatre.

" Will there be a rehearsal to-morrow ? " I asked the secretary.

" Of course there is a rehearsal.   Why do you ask me ? "

" Nothing.   I only wanted to know."

" Yes, yes, yes," said he, " there is a rehearsal."   And he went on writing.

The following day, I was there at the appointed time. " You see," said I to Garnier, " there is a rehearsal."   He did not answer, but started humming an air from the vaudeville, *Le Mariage de Figaro :*

> " Jealous Jean Jeannot."

" Don't you hear ? "   I exclaimed.   " There is a rehearsal."

He went on :

> " Who loved a quiet life."

" And you said there would be no rehearsal."

> " Bought for his yard a savage dog."

" And there *is* a rehearsal."

> " To guard his pretty wife."

" Now then, gentlemen ; ready ! " called the usher.

" Now then, gentlemen ; ready," said I again.

A voice inquired: " And Mademoiselle Mars ? "

Garnier continued obstinately :

> " But what a frightful row !
> Thieves !   Towzer, down, I say ! "

" Mademoiselle Mars does not appear in the first scene," said I.   " She will come in time for the second."

> " The dog has Jeannot by the leg."

" Come, come, Garnier.   Get to your place."

> " The gallant gets away,"

finished Garnier, sliding into his recess.

The first scene began, went on, and was concluded. A silence followed.

" What now ? "

" Mademoiselle Mars has not arrived."

" Let us wait a moment."

" A letter from Mademoiselle Mars," called a second usher.

" For whom ? "

" For the director."

" He is not here."

" Where is he ? "

" In his study."

The usher disappeared.

Five minutes later, the director himself made his appearance.

" Monsieur Dumas," said he, " Mademoiselle Mars sends you her excuses. She does not feel well, and she asks you to go on rehearsing without her or to postpone the rehearsal till to-morrow."

" To rehearse without her ? " cried I. " Impossible ! Hers is the most important part."

" Then," said the director, " better postpone till to-morrow."

" Yes, to-morrow, that'll be better." And turning to Garnier :

" To-morrow, Garnier ; you hear ? " said I.

" Yes, I do."

And with an inimitable expression, he hummed :

> " To-morrow,
> To-morrow, to-morrow, to-morrow,
> Till to-morrow, quite early
> The match is postponed.
> To-morrow,
> To-morrow, to-morrow, to-morrow,
> Of your tragedy
> The end we shall see ! "

Next day, Mademoiselle Mars not having recovered from her indisposition, there was no rehearsal ; nor the day after, nor the days after, nor ever after !

So that *Christine* was performed at the Odéon by Mademoiselle Georges, instead of at the Théâtre Français by Mademoiselle Mars. It also happened that Ligier, who had left the Théâtre Français because he was not given the part of Sentinelli, played that character at the Odéon.

O great prophet Garnier ! Thou who hadst the

advantage over thy predecessors Ezekiel, Daniel, Jeremiah, Habakkuk, and Saint John being as clear as crystal ; how right thou wert to say that thou knewest Mademoiselle Mars as well as her dressmaker did !

CHAPTER IX

I HAD fully recognized that I must resign myself to my fate.

At the same time, M. Brault, a dramatic poet as well as a prefect, after he had lost his prefecture wrote a tragedy entitled *Christine*, which was read by him at the Théâtre Français.

This was a play modelled on the classical form, whose only fault was to have been written twenty years too late.

Yet what would have been a fault at another theatre was a recommendation at the Théâtre Français.

M. Brault's play was accepted in a spirit of antagonism to mine.

I was clearly predestined to be hated. I aroused hatred even though so far I had accomplished nothing.

I was within my legitimate rights ; with Roger I could have sung :

"In my good cause I have confidence."

But three reasons prevented my singing thus. The first was that the opera of the *Huguenots* had not yet been composed. The second, that I never did sing, not even the final vaudeville of *Figaro*. The third, that I never felt confidence in my good cause.

In the end—it is true that I took Garnier's experience as my guide through the maze—in the end I made up my mind to go into mourning for *Christine*. And this proved to be the only thing to do.

There was at the Théâtre Français an actress called Madame Valmonzey, whose talent has left no trace, but whose beauty is still remembered. Madame Valmonzey had been chosen for the part. She was the friend of

M. Evariste Demoulin, a man of letters, who 'did' the
Théâtre Français for the *Constitutionel*.

The *Constitutionel* has always been fatal to me.

It was through M. Evariste Demoulin's influence that
M. Brault's *Christine* was rehearsed.

I might have lodged a complaint, brought an action,
and possibly won it.

They sent me M. Brault's son, a charming young man,
who begged in the name of his dying father that I would
yield him my turn. Whether I have been earning fifteen
hundred francs a year or a hundred and fifty thousand I
have always liked to act *en grand seigneur*. But at that
moment my mother and I were awaiting the first performance of *Christine* to enjoy a satisfying meal.

I ceded my turn to the expiring M. Brault. If I
remember aright, I think he had the pleasure of living to
see his play performed. This was compensation to me.

But my play now succeeded one by M. Fulchiron, which
had been accepted in 1806. Its turn had come ; it was
just, since I had given up my own. It is true that Garnier
whispered to me : " Write another, and give the leading
part to Mademoiselle Mars. Don't make your lines thirty-
six feet long instead of twelve. Don't oppose her in anything, and your play will be performed."

" Well," said I to my mentor, " one writes the lines
one can, my dear Garnier. I have half a mind to write
in prose."

" That will be better."

" I must find a subject."

" Haven't you already got one at the back of your
head ? "

" Indeed, I have not."

" Go and look for one."

" I am going home for that purpose."

And I really did go home.

Before shutting myself up in my room, I went to see
a friend to whom I confided what had occurred. That
confidant was my good friend de la Ponce, who had taught
me a good deal of Italian and a little German. Under the
flimsiest of pretexts, I entered the accountant's offices,
situated on the third floor. Mine was on the second floor.
De la Ponce was not at his post, but I found instead, open

on his desk, a volume of Anquetil. Letting my eyes fall
unconsciously on the book, I read the following lines on
page 95 :

"Though attached to the king, and therefore a natural
enemy of the Duke of Guise, Saint-Mégrin nevertheless loved
the Duchess Catherine of Clèves, who is said to have returned
his affection. The author, from whom we have the anecdote,
relates that the husband was indifferent to the infidelity
—real or supposed—of his wife ; he resisted the entreaties
of his relatives to take vengeance, and was content to
punish the duchess's indiscretion or crime with a jest.

"He went early one morning into his wife's room,
holding a dagger in one hand and a cup in the other. After
awakening her roughly and reproaching her for her conduct :

"' Make your choice,' he exclaimed, ' between death by
the dagger or by poison.'

"In vain did she plead for mercy. He forced her to
make her choice. She swallowed the contents of the cup
and fell on her knees, commending herself to God, and
waiting for the death agony. An hour passed in fears and
tremors. Then the duke comes calmly back, and informs
her that what she took for poison was nothing more deadly
than an excellent consommé. No doubt, it taught her to
be more circumspect in future."

I don't know why that anecdote, as M. Anquetil calls
it, stuck to my mind. I borrowed the book and consulted
the Biographical Dictionary, article " Saint-Mégrin," which
directed me to the " Memoirs of l'Estoile." I was absolutely ignorant as to what the " Memoirs of l'Estoile "
might be. A friend of mine, an old student, gave me
not only all the information I wanted, but also the book
to read.

I went home, and in the first volume, page 35, I came
across the following paragraph :

" Saint-Mégrin, a young gentleman from the Bourde-
lais, handsome, wealthy, and of good lineage, and one of the
king's *mignons*, was leaving the Louvre, where the king
for the time was visiting, at eleven o'clock at night, when
he was attacked in the rue de Louvre, close to the rue
Saint-Honoré, by twenty or thirty unknown persons,
armed with pistols, swords, and cutlasses, who left him for
dead on the pavement. He died the following day ; and it

was a marvel he lived so long after having received thirty-four or thirty-five mortal blows. The king ordered that the body should be borne to the house of Boisy, near the Bastille, in which house also his companion Quélus had died ; and he was interred at Saint-Paul with pomp and solemnity equal to that of the funerals of Quélus and Maugiron, his companions, in the same church.

"And no action was taken upon this assassination, for it was well known to His Majesty that it had been decreed by the Duke of Guise, owing to the rumour that the *mignon* was his wife's lover ; and the man who struck the blow was said to resemble in his beard and general appearance the Duke of Mayenne, his brother.

"On the news reaching the King of Navarre, he said :

" ' I think well of my cousin, the Duke of Guise, for not having suffered himself to be made a cuckold by a *mignon* like Saint-Mégrin. That is the right way to deal with all little danglers of the court, who flutter round the princesses, ogling and making love.' "

"By Jove !" said I, after reading that paragraph. " If the duke played off a joke on the mistress, it was no joke he had with the lover."

Then, as the " Memoirs of l'Estoile," at once naïve and picturesque in style, had aroused my curiosity, I went on reading. A few pages further on, I came across the following :

" On the Wednesday, 19th of August, Bussy d'Amboise, first gentleman of M. le Duc, governor of Anjou and abbot of Bourgueil, who had assumed such haughty airs on account of his master's favour, and who had committed so many acts of pillage and wrong in Anjou and Mayne, was killed, together with the *lieutenant-criminal* of Saumur, by the seigneur of Monsoreau, in a house belonging to the said seigneur of Monsoreau, whither the said lieutenant, who acted as his go-between, had brought him to spend the night with the said Monsoreau's wife, for whom Bussy had, for a long time, entertained a passion, the said lady having intentionally given this false appointment so as to enable her husband, Monsoreau, to fall on him ; to which appointment he appeared towards the hour of twelve, when he was immediately surrounded and assailed by ten or twelve men

o

who accompanied Monseigneur de Monsoreau, and who fell on him with fury to take his life. That nobleman, on seeing himself so teacherously betrayed and being quite alone (as one does not as a rule wish for company on such occasions), nevertheless defended himself valiantly to the end, showing that fear, as he had frequently said, never entered his heart ; for, so long as he had a stump of sword in his hand he went on fighting up to the hilt, after which he defended himself with tables, seats, chairs, and stools with which he felled two or three of his enemies ; until, overpowered by numbers and entirely weaponless, he succumbed to their blows near a window through which he was endeavouring to escape. Such was the end of the captain Bussy."

By what correlation of my brain cells was Bussy's death connected with that of Saint-Mégrin, it is impossible to say. What I do know is, that with these two fragments of the " Memoirs of l'Estoile," and a scene from the " Abbot," by Walter Scott, where Murray tries to induce Mary Stuart to sign her abdication, I wrote my drama of *Henri III.* in two months. The little page is entirely my own creation, as well as the development of the characters of Saint-Mégrin and the Duchess of Guise ; to which may be added the entire plot.

I read *Henri III.* at the house of Nestor Roqueplan. It met with great applause. Firmin was there, and the plaudits impressed him greatly. He arranged a reading at his house to which were invited Taylor and Béranger, as well as Michelot, Samson, Mademoiselle Mars, and Mademoiselle Leverd.

The second reading only confirmed the success of the first. It was decided, on the spot, that on the morrow, the day of the Committee's sitting, the actors there present should demand a special reading, and on the strength of the precedence I had obtained for *Christine*, and which I had ceded to M. Brault, a second one should be granted.

That same evening Firmin buttonholed me :

" Listen," said he. " I have a favour to ask you."

" And what is it ? "

" That you will give me the part of the page."

" You ? "

" No, not me. I want it for this pretty little girl."

And he motioned towards Louise Despréaux, who later became Madame Allan.

"Very good!"

"She is a pupil of mine, and I can answer for her."

"Consider it done."

"Your word of honour?"

"Sacred word of honour."

He called the girl. "Louise!"

Louise, who no doubt well knew what we were talking about, came at once.

"It is yours," said Firmin.

"Oh, I am so glad!" cried she, jumping in her delight.

"Kiss him."

"Rather!" And, in her joy, she threw her arms round my neck.

"But, seriously," said she, "may I have it whatever Mademoiselle Mars does to take it away from me?"

"Mademoiselle Mars? Why should mademoiselle do anything to take away your part?"

"Whatever Mademoiselle Mars does to take it from me?" repeated Louise.

I looked at Firmin. "She knows what she is about," said he.

I made a gesture which meant: "Since she knows what she is about, there is no need for me to know."

"You shall have it, whatever Mademoiselle Mars may do to take it away from you," said I. And I was kissed a second time.

On the morrow I received my notification. *Henri III.* was read on the 1st of September, 1828, and received with acclamations.

After the reading I was called to the director's office. I found Mademoiselle Mars there. She came to her point with her habitual abruptness.

"Ah, it is you," said she. "The thing is now to avoid a repetition of the bungling you made over *Christine.*"

"What bungling, madame?" I asked.

"In the cast."

"Ah, that is true. I had the honour to allot you the part of Christine, and you did not play it."

"Maybe; there is much to be said on that subject; but I promise you I will play the Duchess of Guise."

" Then you cast it to yourself ? "

" Why, of course.   Was it not meant for me ? "

" Indeed it was, madame."

" Well, then ? "

" Then I most sincerely thank you."

" Now, the Duke of Guise. . . . To whom are you going to give the Duke of Guise ? "

" To Ligier."

" He is no longer here."

" Where is he ? "

" At the Odéon.   In his absence, there is only Michelot who can play that."

" Excuse me, madame, Michelot is like Périer, he only plays comedy."

" He will play the Duke of Guise very well."

" Madame, he will play it neither well nor badly."

" How so ? "

" For a very simple reason : that is, he will not play it at all."

" And what will he play ? "

" He will play Henri III."

" Henri III. ?   The fat Michelot ? "

" Henri III.   Yes, madame."

" Don't say so !   Armand is the man for Henri's part."

" It may be so, madame ; but Michelot will play it."

" But what have you got against Armand ? "

" I, madame ?   Nothing at all.   I have not the honour to know him—— "

" Well, then ? "

" You do not allow me to finish.   I have not the honour to know him, except by report."

" You believe those calumnies ? "

" What calumnies ? "

" You know very well what I mean."

" No, madame, I do not believe them.   I am only afraid that others do so."

" I must tell you.   I talked to Armand about it."

" You should not have done that, madame."

" And I have engaged him."

" You will have to disengage him."

" Oh !   You are a strange being, don't you know ? "

"Not at all, madame; only I am resolved that *Henri III.* shall be performed."

"Ah! . . . Well, now let us see. . . . Catherine; who is to play Catherine? Madame Paradol?"

"No; Mademoiselle Leverd."

"Leverd? She won't accept the part."

"She has."

"She'll never play it!"

"She shall have an understudy."

"Good. There remains the page."

"Quite so."

"I play three scenes with him. I tell you beforehand that I want some one for this part whom I like."

"I will try to please you, madame."

"We have Mme. Menjaud, who will play it splendidly."

"Madame Menjaud has much talent, but she has not the physique for such a part."

"Oh, that's too bad! And, no doubt, that part also has been cast."

"Yes, madame; it has."

"And to whom? Is it an indiscretion for me to ask?"

"To Mademoiselle Louise Despréaux."

"To Mademoiselle Louise Despréaux?"

"Yes, madame."

"You have chosen Mademoiselle Louise Despréaux for the page?"

"Why not?"

"Because . . ."

"Isn't she pretty?"

"Oh, very! But it is not enough to look pretty."

"Hasn't she talent?"

"They say she is promising."

"Ah, madame, a good part may help one's talent to develop."

"But to see that little girl playing the page!"

"I am still waiting for a good reason to convince me she is not fitted for that part."

"Well," said Mademoiselle Mars, "you shall see her dressed in her tights."

"Very good! What shall I see?"

"You'll see that she is shamefully knock-kneed."

"In that case we would not have her."

" While Mme. Menjaud, on the other hand—— "

" Is not knock-kneed. I know that ; but she has other defects from which Mademoiselle Despréaux is free."

" I see. You have made up your mind for Mademoiselle Despréaux ? "

" Yes, madame."

" Let it be so, then. What does it matter to me ? The play may go as it pleases. I am not going to play that part anyway. And don't suppose I can't see where this obstinacy comes from."

" Where does it come from ? "

" It doesn't originate with you ? "

" Possibly not."

" It comes from Firmin."

" You told me once, madame, that you were Saint John of the Golden Mouth. . . . I am his brother."

" He wants to push his own pupil."

" Like a good professor."

" It would serve you right if I threw up my part."

" Mme. Dorval would take it."

" Mme. Dor—— ! Mme. Dorval ! Who is she ? "

" She is a very talented woman, madame."

" Who plays in *Les Deux Forçats* at the Porte Saint-Martin. Oh, gracious goodness ! "

" The play is bad, but the actress is good."

" And why didn't you take your play to her before ? "

" Because I had agreed to a sort of engagement with the Théâtre Français."

" Then, you don't care whether you are played by us or not ? "

" On the contrary, I do care, madame, since I have come back to the Comédie Française after having been so badly used there."

" Wouldn't it be said that you had been shown the door ? "

" Perhaps."

" You are a spoilt child. Come, be sensible ! Your place is here ; you must stay. Only you will think again, won't you ? "

" About what, madame ? "

" About the cast."

" No need to think when the thing is done."

" And it is done ? "

" It is done."

" You won't change your mind ? "

" It is possible that my mind may change ; but the cast will not."

" Well, you are the most stubborn author I have ever met."

I bowed.

" But, my dear friend, do ask to see the legs of your page."

" Although that will be most indiscreet, madame, I promise you I will do it."

I bowed a second time, and left the office, leaving Mademoiselle Mars stupefied. It was the first time that an author had asserted himself against her. Nevertheless, I must admit that the page's legs kept running in my head. I hastened to Firmin :

" You know what is going on ? " said I.

" No, I don't."

" I have just had a scene with Mademoiselle Mars."

" Ah ! better take it lightly ; it won't be the last."

"The deuce ! You don't prophesy a bed of roses for me."

" What was it all about ? "

" The cast."

" Tell me about it."

" She wanted the part of Henri III."

" For her chatterbox, M. Armand, I wager."

" Precisely. She wanted Michelot to have the part of the Duke of Guise."

" She might rest assured that he would not be too dramatic."

" Then she wanted the part of the page for—— "

" For Mme. Menjaud ? "

" For Mme. Menjaud."

" She would have felt safe from any danger of that lady's being too young and pretty. They say that Mazarin, on his deathbed, said to Louis XIV. : ' I have set you up again on your throne, I have restored peace in your kingdom, I made you marry the Infanta of Spain, by my will I have bestowed upon you all my property ; well, sire, I am going to give you a piece of advice of more value than all the rest put together : never take a prime minister.' "

" Which means ? "

" Never ask the advice of an actor on the cast of your play."

" Not even you ? "

" Not even I. I am no better than any other ; every one of us has his own interests, you see. Thus, Mademoiselle Mars, who is in her sixties, does not want Louise's pretty fresh face at her side. She would prefer Mme. Menjaud."

" But, tell me ; she says that Louise—— "

" What does she say ? "

" She says that Louise is knock-kneed."

" Listen, my dear fellow. Louise's knees are mysteries to me ; but Louise will wear tights, and you'll be able to see them."

" I don't conceal from you that I shall be much pleased to do so."

" No doubt ! "

Three days later I was dining with Firmin, and, at the end of the meal, Louise Despréaux came in dressed as a page.

Louise Despréaux performed the part of Arthur, and gained tremendous applause from the audience. But, before that happened, my God ! what rages, what despairs, what gnashing of teeth !

Oh, the Théâtre Français ! It is a circle of the Inferno omitted by Dante, where God keeps those unfortunate authors who are haunted by the singular idea of earning there one half of the money they could get elsewhere, of being allowed twenty-five performances instead of a hundred, and in their declining years receiving the Cross of the Legion of Honour in recognition, not of their success, but of their sufferings.

CHAPTER X

You know, dear reader, the custom of the hare, which, however far it may run, returns always, in the end, to its form, so that the sportsman has only to wait, for he is sure to bag it in the end, or at least to get a chance of a shot. Well, the Théâtre Français was my form, and in spite of being fired at, I was always returning to it. Meanwhile, yielding to a sort of uncomfortable feeling which was floating in the air, and which is the usual precursor of a political crisis, I had written *Antony*. Under what personal circumstances had I composed that work ? That you may read in my " Memoirs." As soon as it was ready, I wrote to the Théâtre Français that I had committed myself to a new drama, and that I was desirous of a reading. *Henri III.* had met with an immense success. Mademoiselle Mars, personally, having received much applause. I had reason to believe that, having filled the coffers of MM. the Royal Comedians to the tune of three hundred thousand francs, my reception should be enthusiastic. Forgive me, dear reader ; I was only twenty-six years old.

On the appointed day I arrived with my manuscript, full of confidence in my genius and convinced that I had written a masterpiece.

Are you a swimmer ? Have you ever dived into a river and felt, as you were going deeper and deeper, the water getting gradually colder.

Well, the reading of *Antony* produced the same effect on me.

It was accepted, thanks, perhaps, to the success of *Henri III.*, but especially for this reason, that the play did not necessitate any outlay, and therefore the theatre would lose nothing.

The two leading parts were given to Mademoiselle Mars and to Firmin, who did not seem wholly flattered by the gift of them.

The second woman's part, that of the viscountess, was cast to a charming woman, then at the Théâtre Français, whose name was Rose Dupuis. (She is the mother of our excellent actor, Dupuis, of the Gymnase.) Menjaud played, or was to play, the poet.

I have said that the play had been accepted in consideration of two things. I ought to have said in consideration of three things, and I ought even to add, that the third was the most important. They had whispered among themselves: "We can accept it, what does it matter! The censor will never pass such an enormity." But MM. the French comedians had not reckoned on the revolution of July.

Came those three days which, in upsetting not a few other things, unwittingly upset censorship. We say unwittingly, because in reality, as soon as it was discovered that there was no more censorship, it was re-established. But, after all, for two or three years the benumbed hydra remained hidden in its lair at the Home Ministry, so that during that period, *Antony, Richard Darlington, La Tour de Nesle, Marion Delorme, Angèle, Lucrèze Borgia,* and *Marie Tudor* made their appearance. Were it not for that interregnum it is probable that those dramas, which played such havoc with society, would still be unpublished. In short, the revolution of July abolished the censorship, so that the Théâtre Français, who thought itself secure against me, beheld me appear one day at the Committee, and heard me utter these formidable words: "And *Antony?*"

I had been incautiously granted the precedence in favour of *Antony,* always in expectation of the censure, and now they had to comply with my right of precedence. It is true they had, as a last resource, the possibility of —to use theatre's phraseology—choking me off.

To do them justice, I must say that MM. the actors of the rue de Richelieu did all they could to that end.

While the great guns were rehearsing, the others listened, and although there is not the least attempt at a joke in *Antony,* every one present was taken with hilarity, except a good fellow who, from a porter, had been made property-man, and who was called Marquet.

I want to record his name here, so that posterity should go halves with me in the gratitude I owe him.

Also we must take care not to forget one detail which

has had a great influence on the interior of the green-rooms of the Comédie Française.

The revolution which had carried away the senior branch and the censure, had, at the same time, sent the Swiss * back to the ancient Helvetia—as the poets of the Academy still call it to this day. That was justice from the revolutionary point of view, the Swiss having fired on the people.

We said that Marquet was a doorkeeper † at the Théâtre Français; but let us make it quite clear—he was a doorkeeper like him of Racine's *Plaideurs*, except that instead of coming from Amiens, he came from Pontoise. Of course, Marquet had not fired at any one, and there was no reason for sending him back to the antique Pontoise. I know very well that after a revolution reasons are not necessary for sending people away. Nevertheless, Marquet remained, with the difference that, from a guard, he was made property-man.

This brought about a great change in the etiquette of the Théâtre Français.

During the period when the senior branch reigned, and Marquet was porter, it was forbidden to keep one's hat on one's head in the green-rooms of the Théâtre Français.

As soon as any one happened to forget that rule and failed to remove his hat, Marquet, dressed in his majestic uniform, would come up and say, in a tone of extreme politeness : " Sir, you are here in a royal theatre ; be so good as to carry your hat in your hand."

And one removed one's hat and talked to the actresses, holding it in one's hand, as is fitting, for these two reasons : First, because they are women ; secondly, because they are, sometimes, talented women.

To-day one talks to the women of the Théâtre Français hat cocked on one side, and one's hands in one's pockets. Were it not for fear of setting fire to the place, they would be talked to cigar in mouth.

Thus, in the time of *Christine* and *Henri III.*, Marquet held the post of doorkeeper ; in the time of *Antony* he was property-man.

---

* "Suisse" in original.—EDITOR'S NOTE.

† "Suisse" in French—a pun on "Suisse," the Swiss Guards, and "suisse," a doorkeeper.—EDITOR'S NOTE.

But although he had come down a step lower, and no longer carried a halberd, Marquet was none the less proud.

And so Marquet remained there, and to his credit I must add that in all the ups and downs I experienced with MM. the comedians, he remained the same towards me.

Well, in every passage of the drama, I was sure to see two things which I was not supposed to see : the head of Marquet through the crack of the door at the lower end, and the fireman's helmet appearing in the wings.

Young authors who wish to dedicate yourselves to the theatre, do not neglect the following lines, which have reference to the fireman's helmet. The fireman's helmet is, you see, the symbol of the success of a pathetic passage. The fireman's helmet is equivalent to the man-and-wife barometer. If the weather is to be fine, the wife comes out and shows her smart bonnet. If the weather is threatening, the husband appears with his umbrella. So the fireman who pokes his head out of the wings, you understand, represents the interest of the public.

If you get the fireman interested to the point of forgetting his duty and he emerges from the wings, mingling with the supernumeraries, your case is clear ; you have made a success. The further he comes out, the greater the success. That is why I say that the fireman's helmet is a symbol of the success of a pathetic passage.

Now, throughout the dramatic situations of *Antony*, I could see the head of Marquet, who was holding the door at the lower end half open, and the helmet of the fireman, who was showing himself at the wings.

CHAPTER XI

MEANWHILE the rehearsals of *Antony* continued amidst the indifference of the two leading actors, the ironical whisperings of secondary characters, and the unfailing interest of the property-man and the fireman on duty.

And thus they dragged on for three whole months ; the
street riots being a good pretext for such unprecedented
delays.

During those three months, with a persistency and skill
of which she alone was capable, Mademoiselle Mars had
succeeded in reducing the part of Adèle to the proportions
of a part by Alexandre Duval, or Scribe, of *La Fille
d'Honneur*, or *Valérie*.

For his part, Firmin was acting Antony as best he could,
as he had done that of Monaldeschi two years previously,
and was taking off all the rough edges.

The result was that, the three months over, Adèle
and Antony had become two charming lovers of the
Gymnase, answering to the names of M. Arthur and
Mademoiselle Céleste.

In spite of this the play seemed decidedly a daring one.

· But you will ask me, my dear reader, how is it that you,
who fought so determinedly at the time of settling the cast,
who opposed yourself like a block of granite against
Mademoiselle Mars, when she wanted to give Mademoiselle Louise Despréaux's part to Madame Menjaud, and
that of Michelot to M. Armand, how is it that you yielded
to the observations of Mademoiselle Mars and Firmin,
to the extent of distorting your work ?

Ah ! how indeed !

How is it that iron is corroded by rust, that rock is worn
smooth by the caresses of the waves, and that monuments
are defaced by the moonshine ?

You know the story of the drop of water, which, falling
regularly every second on the same spot, ends, after a
thousand years, by making a hollow in the marble.

So it was with *Antony ;* so much so that the leading
artists were looking much more contented, that the
secondary artists were laughing and were whispering less
also, but that, on the other hand, Marquet was not pushing
his head through the door, and I no longer saw the gold
of the fireman's helmet gleam from behind the scenes.

After the rehearsal, my friends were saying to me :

" It is a pretty play, a charming work. We would
never have thought you capable of writing in that style."

I, in consequence, was feeling deeply wounded. I
would simply sigh and answer :

"Nor I. I would never have thought I was capable of writing in that style."

The day of the performance was drawing near, do what they could to postpone it.

The poster announced :

"*The Day after to-morrow, Saturday, first performance of ' Antony,' drama in five acts, in prose.*"

I had stopped, as all authors stop, in front of a poster, and I had read, with that oppression of the heart mingled with a certain gladness, the announcement of the approaching performance of my drama, and then I entered the theatre for the last rehearsal.

Every one looked strange. It is true I was ten minutes late. I went to Mademoiselle Mars.

"You know," she said, "that you have been keeping us waiting ten minutes."

"It is true, mademoiselle," said I ; "but I found myself in a block of traffic, and my coachman was obliged to go a roundabout way."

"Oh ! Well, it does not matter."

"You are very good."

"I mean ——. You have been advised of what is——? "

"No."

"You have not been told ? "

"Has something happened ? "

"They are laying on the gas."

"So much the better."

"They are making a new chandelier for us."

"Pray accept my compliments."

"Yes ; but it is not that."

"What is it, then, mademoiselle ? "

"I have spent twelve hundred francs for your play."

"Bravo ! "

"I have four different dresses ——"

"You will look superb."

"And you understand—— "

"No, I don't understand."

"I want them to be seen."

"Quite right."

"And since we are to have a new chandelier—— "

"When ? "

" In three months' time."

" Well ? "

" Well, we shall play *Antony* to inaugurate the new chandelier."

" Ah ! Ah ! "

" Yes."

" That is to say, in three months' time ? "

" In three months' time."

" In the month of May ? "

" In the month of May ; that's a very good month."

" A very fine month, you mean."

" Very good also."

" Then you get no vacation during the month of May, this year ? "

" Of course I do."

" At the end of June, then ? "

" No ; the first of June."

" Therefore, if we start on, say, the 20th of May, I shall have three performances."

Mademoiselle Mars calculated :   " Four.   May has thirty-one days."

" That's good ; four performances ! "

" I'll recommence when I come back."

" Yes ? "

" Truly ! "

" Thank you ; that is very nice of you."

I turned my back to her, shrugging my shoulders, and found myself face to face with Firmin.

" You have heard ? " said I.

" Perfectly.   Did I not tell you that she would not play her part ? "

" But, why not ? "

" It's a rôle for Mme. Dorval."

" I have often thought of that."

" But, nevertheless, it is not so bad, you see, that the play is postponed."

" Why ? "

" Because you will have time to make a few corrections."

" Bless my soul !   I have made only too many of them."

" Don't complain ; the play has gained nicely by it."

" Yes, very nicely, as you say."

Firmin was spurred on :

" Listen," he went on. " Since we are on this subject, let me tell you my opinion of the play."

" Ah ! I know it. You have played it out of kindness to me."

" You understand perfectly. I could not very well say to the man who had written the part of Saint-Mégrin for me : ' I don't want to play Antony.' "

" It would have been better to tell me."

" No ; one mustn't say such things."

" Well, then, what does one say ? "

" You want my very frank opinion ? "

" Say on."

" Well, your Antony, if you must have it, is a mad man."

" I know it."

" A monomaniac."

" That's his only excuse. When he is tried at the Court of Assizes, that will be his lawyer's only chance to save him."

" Ah, yes ; but, for me, you know—— "

" No, I don't know."

" Well, that makes my part monotonous ; I repeat the same thing over and over again."

" Such was my intention."

" Intention, intention. . . . That is like the play—— "

" Good ! The play ? "

" Yes, the whole, the scheme of the play."

" Go on."

" That is not done as you usually do ; it is not done as *Henri III.*, as *Christine.*"

" Ah ! Poor *Christine !* Do not speak of her here."

" And if I were you—— "

" Well, if you were me ? "

" Since you are allowed the leisure—— "

" Since I am allowed the leisure ? "

" You are going to jump to the ceiling."

" Oh no ! Be easy. Since I came to the Théâtre Français I have heard so much—— "

" Well, I would take my play to Scribe."

I received the stroke full in the front without flinching. I was, as you may see, like those Scots at Waterloo, who had not only to be killed, but had to be pushed in order to make them fall.

However, I recovered my speech.

" Your advice to take the play to some one is good."

" Oh, you see it ? " said Firmin joyously.

" Yes ; only, I won't take it to Scribe."

" To whom will you take it ? "

" To Crosnier. In reality, I am beginning to be of the same opinion as yourself. I think that the part of Adèle is a Dorval, and I will add that the part of Antony is a—— "

" A—— ? "

" A Bocage."

Firmin burst into homeric laughter.

While he was laughing, I went to the prompter, who was still in his hole.

" My dear Garnier," said I, " do me the kindness of lending me my manuscript."

" Here it is," said Garnier, who was altogether unsuspicious of what was going on.

" Thank you, Garnier."

I rolled it and put it under my arm.

" Farewell, Firmin ! Farewell, Mademoiselle Mars ! "

Then, shaking hands with Marquet :

" Farewell, my dear Marquet ! If agreeable to you, I'll tell you one thing."

" What ? "

" That you are the only person I regret leaving."

" Are you really going, Monsieur Dumas ? "

" Yes, Marquet, I am going."

" Well, I will say that it is most unfortunate for the Comédie Française."

" Thank you, Marquet ! "

Five seconds later I was in the street ; ten minutes after, at Dorval's.

On the morrow the play was read to Dorval and Bocage.

Six weeks later it was produced at the Porte Saint-Martin Theatre.

P

CHAPTER XII

ONE day Anicet Bourgeois came to see me.

" My dear friend," said he, " I have come to propose something big for the Circus."

" What ? "

" I am leaving Franconi."

" You mean Adolphe ? "

" Yes, Adolphe.   He has a marvellous horse, with which he does whatever he likes with a lump of sugar."

" Well ? "

" Well, I have an idea of which I have told him, and of which he approves."

" Let us have the idea."

" It is to make a great play of *Caligula* in which the horse will play the leading part."

" The horse Incitatus ? "

" Yes, to be sure ; the horse that Caligula makes first consul."

" Well, my friend, that really is an idea ! "

" What about writing the play together ? "

" Willingly."

" When shall we start ? "

" By Jove, my dear fellow, you go at a fine rate !   I must study the period first."

" How many days do you require ? "

" Fifteen days ; is it too much ? "

" Fifteen days, good."

" Then, in fifteen days—— "

" You want me to go ? "

" I have no time to lose ; I am going to study.   You on your side must study also, and then what one does not know the other will."

After ten days Anicet reappeared.

" Well ! " said I, " it is not the fifteen days yet, my dear fellow."

" Ah," said he, " our play has ended in smoke ; and I have come in to tell you—— "

" What ? "

" Incitatus has had a kick from one of his stable companions—a fatal kick ; and has had to be shot."

" The deuce ! "

" Thus, my dear fellow, you have had your pains for nothing."

" Not at all. I have got most interested in my study of the period. I will write a drama without a horse in it."

" Would you like to write it with me ? "

" Thanks ; I should prefer to write it in verse."

" Then we will say no more."

" Ah, but, indeed, let us talk about it. The idea having been suggested by you, it is only right you should have a share in my work."

" You must arrange that as you please.'

" Then you leave it to me ? "

" Yes."

" So be it."

We shook hands, and that was all. I set at once to work.

Now, the Duke of Orléans had invited me to stay with him at the camp at Compiègne, so long as he was there himself. I thanked him and explained the work I had in mind, and that I should feel cramped besides being an encumbrance at the castle ; but as he insisted on my going, I accepted and begged of him to allow me complete freedom.

So to Compiègne I went and inquired there for a nook where I could work in peace.

Caligula obsessed me.

I was informed of a keeper's lodge at Saint-Corneille. This was a piece of luck.

I went to Saint-Corneille and negotiated with the keeper's wife. She gave me two rooms and arranged to prepare my food, for three hundred francs a month. One can't spend much money when one relies on tragedies for a living.

The day following my move in I set to work ; and at the end of thirty-six days the tragedy was finished.

The Théâtre Français had got wind of it. I must explain that, in the meantime, I had not entirely lost touch with it.

M. Thiers, being minister, had invited me to call on

him at the Ministry, and I had complied with his request. He had then asked me why I was writing for the theatres of the boulevard instead of for the Théâtre Français. To which I had answered that the kind of literature I wrote was better acted on the boulevards than at the Théâtre Français. He had insisted on the point of the pecuniary advantages resulting from writing for that theatre. In answer to which I proved to him that it was at that theatre that one got the least of all. And, as M. Thiers is a man of great intellect, he had at once understood what I am going to explain to you.

With plays which attain a great success the Théâtre Français makes an average of four thousand francs on each performance. The play will have a run of, say, forty performances, with an average return of one hundred and sixty thousand francs.

The Théâtre Français pays nine per cent. of the takings to the author; but it always manages to make a slight profit on that nine per cent. by giving a short play by a dead author. The living author then gets only seven per cent.

Seven per cent. on four thousand francs makes one hundred and eighty francs. Seven per cent. on one hundred and sixty thousand francs makes eleven thousand two hundred francs. A play at the Théâtre Français which has forty performances in three months and eighteen days brings, therefore, to its author eleven thousand francs.

"Why three months and eighteen days?" you will ask.

That is very simple. All the other theatres give a representation of a new play every day, Sundays included; whereas the Théâtre Français gives a performance only every second day and none on Sundays.

The result is that all the other theatres give the authors thirty performances per month against twelve at the Théâtre Français.

Now, a play ages, not on account of the number of its performances, but only by reason of the date on the poster of its first appearance. This is why, after three months and eighteen days, any play which has had forty performances during that time is just as old as that which, on another stage, has been performed every day, that is, for the whole one hundred and eight performances. Furthermore, on the theatres of the boulevards, the authors get ten per cent. Let us say that all the performances put together—that is, one hundred and ten—bring an average of two thousand francs per night, which makes exactly half of what the Théâtre Français makes. But, on the other hand, the ordinary theatre will have made altogether two hundred and sixteen thousand francs, which, at ten per cent., make twenty-one thousand six hundred francs or ten thousand four hundred francs more than at the Théâtre Français ; nearly double, you see.

I was telling you, then, that M. Thiers, who was quick at figures, understood all this at once. Besides, he understood also that we men of letters are won not by money merely, but by consideration shown to our feelings and by the flattering of our pride. So he asked me :

" What actors will you choose ? Which of your plays will you have rehearsed ? "

To which I answered :

" I want Madame Dorval engaged, and I want *Antony* performed."

I well knew that the engagement of Madame Dorval would be most disagreeable to Mademoiselle Mars. And really, she had caused me so much suffering that I was not sorry.

M. Thiers kept his word. I arranged to write two new plays, a tragedy and a comedy, on the condition that *Antony* should be performed, and that Madame Dorval should take Adèle's part. And *Antony* was once more put into rehearsal.

This time, the *élite* of the Comédie Française had accepted their parts in the play ; it was as if MM. the actors had guessed what was going to happen.

The announcement ran once more : " Shortly, *Antony*." Then : " Next Saturday, *Antony*." Finally : " To-day, First performance of the new production of *Antony*."

This time, in spite of a certain feeling of insecurity with regard to the Comédie Française, I was almost convinced that *Antony* was going to be played. But, at two o'clock in the afternoon, Jouslin de Lasalle came to see me ; he looked scared, and carried in his hand a letter, signed Thiers, and written on paper with the heading of the Chamber of Deputies. It contained these few words :

"The Comédie Française is forbidden to play *Antony*.
"THIERS."

"Well, and what now ? " I asked Jouslin de Lasalle.
"Well, you have just seen what——— "
"How did it happen ? "
"This morning, the *Constitutionel* published an article denouncing *Antony* to M. Thiers."
"Yes, because he kills Adèle. But M. Thiers knew that already."
"That is not all."
"I imagine not."
"It appears that twenty deputies have gone to M. Thiers, telling him that if *Antony* should be performed, they would refuse to vote the subsidy for the Comédie Française."
"I follow you. That is serious indeed. It is fortunate that I negotiated direct with M. Thiers and that I have kept his letters."
"Well, what are you going to do ? "
"Goodness, what a question ! I will sue him."
"The prime minister ? "
"Why not ? "
"In which court ? "
"In the *Tribunal de Commerce*."
"It will declare its incompetence in such a case."
"We shall see."

I brought an action and the court declared itself competent to try the case. In the result, judgment was given in my favour, and M. Thiers was ordered to pay ten thousand francs damages which the Théâtre Français paid for him. That is how I had kept in touch with the Théâtre Français.

Périer, whom I had known in the days of *Christine*, was sent to me by the Théâtre Français, which had heard that I was writing a tragedy, and which wanted to know on what conditions I would give it *Caligula*.

He went back to Paris carrying this ultimatum : "A premium of five thousand francs and the engagement of an actress in whom I was interested." Three days later he brought back the agreement signed by the Committee. I put my signature below that of these gentlemen, and I appointed a day for the reading.

I came back to Paris. I read and was warmly applauded, and the rehearsals were to begin at once. From the very first day I was in difficulties.

"What are you looking for, Monsieur Dumas?" remarked the machinist to me when he saw that I was looking round.

"I want to see where the horses will come in."

"What! horses?"

"Yes, horses."

"What horses?"

"Those attached to Caligula's chariot."

The machinist turned on his heel and left me to my search. Five minutes later, the director came.

"You were speaking about horses?" he asked.

"Yes; I was speaking of the horses which are to draw Caligula's chariot."

"The Comédie Française never understood that the chariot was drawn by horses."

"And what did it understand the chariot should be drawn by? By asses?"

"Oh, don't demand such a thing; the Comédie Française will never allow it."

"What! I shan't get it done?"

"No."

"But it is indispensable to my staging."

"The Comédie Française is not a theatre for staging."

"That is where it makes a mistake."

"The Théâtre Français was established to play the Masters, and the Masters had no need of horses in their tragedies."

"Yes; but the Masters' masters had need of them."

"What do you mean by the Masters' masters?"

"Why, Æschylus, Sophocles, Euripides."

"Never, I say, never! You will do what you please, you will say what you like, but never will horses tread the stage of the Comédie Française."

"We'll go to the courts, Monsieur Vedel, and you know that the Comédie Française is not very fortunate when I sue them."

" We'll go to the courts. But, think of it ; horses on the stage of this theatre ! If ever such a scandal took place, there is not one member who would not tender his resignation."

" Take care ; you are making me more obstinate."

" Well, I will transmit your request to the Committee."

" Do so."

On the Saturday my request was preferred to the Committee, who unanimously decided that it could not be granted, and as horses were out of the question they suggested women instead. I composed the Song of the Hours, and the chariot of Caligula was drawn by women ; a more moral proceeding, gentle reader.

CHAPTER XIII

IN every well-organized theatre there is a man with whom authors are advised to get into touch when the day of a first performance approaches. That man is the head of the paid applauders, and his name at the Théâtre Français is Vacher.

It was with Vacher, therefore, that I established relations. It was my first occasion for so doing at the Thèâtre Français, for in the days of *Henri III*. the applauders or clappers were not yet organized. That institution, inaugurated in the time of Nero and so popular in Rome, was not in favour in 1828.

In 1828 part of the pit had been disposed of among my comrades of the Duke of Orléans' establishment. In 1837—that is, nine years later—I had kept away nine years from the Théâtre Français, except for the short appearances which have been recorded. In 1837, I say, the pit was left entirely to the head-clapper, and, to use the green-room's colloquialism, he had to " answer " for it.

I don't know any greater abuse than that which I here describe. The three hundred seats of the pit are in the hands of the head-clapper, so as to prevent the entrance of ill-disposed persons. Of these three hundred seats, two

hundred and fifty are sold at a higher price than if bought
at the box-office, a proceeding much resented by the pur-
chasers, so that instead of those ill-disposed by nature,
those who take the seats are ill-disposed by nature and by
art alike. There could hardly be a worse system than this.
Special terms are made with the head-clappers, who get
usually a *gratification* of one hundred francs, which makes,
along with the tickets sold by them, a sum of from three
to four thousand francs for the first performance. In
addition, such or such an actress is especially recommended
to them, which means another fifty francs being given.

They are told : " You'll remember Madame So-and-so,
or Monsieur So-and-so after this or that act." They clap
and recall, and Monsieur or Madame So-and-so says : " See
how I have been applauded ! "

As I have said, I had not failed to see Vacher, and he
had promised his support without fail. He seemed most
delighted with *Caligula*. So I relied on him implicitly.

The first performance of *Caligula* took place ; and a
strange one it was. After a lively, animated prologue,
full of surprises—too lively, too animated, too full of surprises, as evidently it did harm to the rest of the work—
came the play itself, simple, calm, antique.

First, I should tell you, dear reader, who, perhaps, were
not present on that occasion, that the habitués of the
Théâtre Français had never before witnessed their heroes
at a meal or seen them drinking, unless, indeed, it were
poison. And I must let you know that those same habitués
had been already scandalized in the prologue by a drunken
Roman, stumbling about, and using rather free language.
Indeed, if that Roman had not been magnificently acted
by Menjaud he would have been hissed. He was not
hissed, but my troubles lost nothing by being deferred.

We were in 1837 at the time of the Jesuits' recrudes-
cence of power and of a daily fulmination against the
" black-robes " in the *Constitutionel.*

In the fourth act there was a scene between Stella, a
Christian, and Aquila, a pagan ; they think that they are
to meet their death together. It is probably the best
scene in the whole play. When the following line was
spoken : " I baptize thee in the name of the Holy Trinity,"
a voice called from a box : " Jesuit ! "

It was also the opinion of the pit, for two catcalls began at once as if in answer to the well-dressed gentleman's remark. I couldn't very well say anything to the well-dressed gentleman ; he was in a box and he, perhaps, had paid for it ; but I doubt it, for, generally, people who pay for their seats like to see the end of a play in order to get their money's worth. I had, then, nothing to say to that well-dressed gentleman, but I had to argue the matter with Maître Vacher, to whom had been allotted the pit, and whose duty it was to answer for it.

I went down and found quite a mob at the box-office.

Jadin, to whom I could only give standing room, having contrived to get into the pit, found himself seated beside one of the interrupters. As a protest, he had collared this individual and taken him to the box-office, from whence he wished to have him removed to the police-station as a disturber of the peace. The man was struggling vigorously, but Jadin had made up his mind that he should be securely locked up. Policemen came in, and were carrying the man off with them. Thus constrained he then confessed that he was one of Vacher's gang.

It was at this moment that I arrived.

" Oh, indeed ! " said I ; " and what does this mean ? "

The poor wretch explained to me what he had just explained to the policemen. I secured two amongst those present to bear witness to his declaration, if necessary.

In the meantime, *Caligula* was going badly ; Mme. Paradol got not only herself, but the play hissed. The curtain fell amidst great disorder. Was it a success ? Was it a failure ? No one knew ; myself, no more than any one else.

I wrote to the Committee asking for an explanation ; a hearing was granted. I presented myself at the appointed time ; I explained my grievances. The Committee declared that I was mistaken. I asked Vacher to be called in ; they complied with my wish, and in Vacher was ushered.

" Monsieur Vacher," said I, " on the night of the first performance of *Caligula*, one of your men hissed and was caught red-handed."

" You think so ? " asked Vacher.

" No, I do not think. I am quite sure of the fact."

Vacher shook his head in denial.

" You see," cried the members of the Committee,
"Vacher says that it is not true. . . . You may go, Vacher."
" Not at all. M. Vacher says no ; and I say yes.
And I am going to prove that what I say is so."
I opened the door and called my witnesses. They
gave evidence. Vacher hung his head. Among the
Committee ran a murmur of protest. Vacher raised his
head.
" But really, gentlemen," said he, in a tone of protest,
" it is necessary to come to an understanding."
" What do you mean ? "
" I mean, am I in the service of the administration of the
Théâtre Français ? "
" Yes, certainly."
" Is the Committee part of the administration ? "
" Of course."
" Must I obey the members of the Committee when they
give me orders ? "
" That is indisputable."
" Well, the half of you who acted ordered me to
applaud ; the other half, who did not, ordered me to
hiss. I obeyed everybody."
A fact ! The persons in question are still living ; it is
only *Caligula* that is dead !

CHAPTER XIV

IT was in the year 1833 or 1834 that Brunswick, on his way
from the theatre of the Porte Saint-Martin, where a play
of his, which he had just read, had been rejected, came to
see me. He was furious, as is usually the case with an
author whose work has been refused.
" Here," said he, throwing, as he spoke, his manuscript
on my table, " read this. Say what they like, there is, in
that, a subject for a play."
I read the vaudeville. It was about a girl who having
spent a night out in order to visit her father in prison,

when she refuses to say what she has been doing finds her reputation compromised. The subject had been treated from the comic point of view.

Brunswick called again a few days later.

" Well," said he, " have you read the thing ? "

" Yes, I have."

" What have you got to say ? "

" If the form were changed, there would certainly be something to work upon."

" Would you mind talking it over together ? "

" No. You know how I work : when an idea pleases me, I don't like to have it broadcasted ; on the contrary, I keep it to myself, let it germinate and grow in my brain till it knocks at my head ready to get out."

" Then—— ? "

" Then, my dear Brunswick, I promise you to work. When it is ready, it will appear. And when the play is read and received, I'll let you know, so that you can go to my agent and get one-third of the receipts."

" But I shall have done nothing at all ! "

" You have done a lot, you have brought me an idea."

" An idea, an idea—— "

" That is the acorn of the oak, the seed from which the tree springs."

" Very good."

And Brunswick went away. One year, two years, three years went by. From time to time, Brunswick appeared.

" Well, does the idea grow ? " he would ask.

" You have no idea how difficult your cursed play is to get right."

" Confess that you have given it up."

" Not at all. Look here."

And I would tell him how far I had gone ; I would show him parts of the work, which was developing gradually, and he would say as he left me :

" You see, if only you would buckle to it, it would be finished in a fortnight."

" I can't work in that way, my dear Brunswick. I don't make plays, plays make themselves in my brain. How so ? I don't know. Ask a plum-tree how its plums

are made, and a peach-tree how it makes its peaches ;
you'll see if either can solve that problem."

One more year, two more years went by, and Brunswick
still called at intervals.   One evening as he was leaving my
house no better satisfied than usual, he met the publisher
of my plays, a man called Charlieu, who was one of my
very good friends.

"Tell me, Charlieu," said Brunswick, as he was
going.   "I am entitled to one-third in a play that Dumas
is writing.   Will you buy that third for one hundred
écus ? "

"Will he write it, do you think ? "

"Well, I have his promise ; but it will soon be four
to five years since he gave it me."

"Well, come to see me to-morrow.   I dare say we can
do something."

"All right.   Then good-bye till to-morrow."

They parted ; Charlieu came in and we talked business.

"Now that I think of it," said he, when we had finished
our talk, "you have a play in partnership with Brunswick ? "

"Yes."

"Are you going to write it ? "

"Certainly."

"When ? "

"One of these days."

"In a month's time, six months, a year ? "

"It is quite impossible for me to fix a date ; but all I
can say is that I shall certainly write it."

"That is all I wanted to know."

The following day Charlieu was announced.

"Let him come in !   Let him come in ! " I cried.

I was happy, for I had just found the only thing that
had been wanting to finish *Mademoiselle de Belle-Isle.*
That is the scene of the sequin.

"Look here," said Charlieu, giving me a piece of paper,
" you owe me one hundred écus."

"One hundred écus !   I expect I owe you more than
that."

"Then you can add a hundred to the total."

"How so ? "

"Read."

I opened the paper and read :

" Received from M. Charlieu the sum of three hundred francs for all my rights in the third of a play which Dumas is going to write, and very likely never will.
" 5th of February, 1839.

" BRUNSWICK."

" Well ? " said I.
" Well, I have bought that third again in your behalf ; that makes a hundred francs that you owe me ; that's all."
" Keep it, my dear fellow, since you have bought it."
" I like that ! Do you think that's the way I do business ? "
" You are wrong if you don't."
" Well, give me two tickets for the first night, and we'll cry quits."
" Let me write just a word on that piece of paper ; you can open it the day after the first performance." And I wrote :

" M. Dulong, my dramatic agent.
" This is an order to pay M. Charlieu the sum of three thousand francs, from the authors' rights in *Mademoiselle de Belle-Isle*.
" Paris, this 5th of February, 1839.

" ALEX. DUMAS."

I folded and sealed the letter and gave it to Charlieu, who took it, not knowing its contents.

What had kept me so long at a standstill was that confounded scene of the sequin. I was not content with a commonplace beginning, and so I had waited five or six years for the scene which had just formed itself in my mind.

A fortnight later the play was all ready in my head, scene after scene, even to the leading phrases. When a play reaches that state, my custom is to write it in five or six days.

For the last year, the Théâtre Français had been making advances to me. De Mornay, a friend of twenty years' standing, had helped to make my peace with Mademoiselle Mars, who was getting old, and at whom the authors were beginning to look askance. Finally, I had decided to run the risk of another shipwreck on the rocks of the rue de Richelieu. I chose a Saturday, the day of the Committee meeting, to go to the theatre. They welcomed me warmly when they saw me ; it was two years since I had been there. And the shouts redoubled when I told Vedel—Vedel was then director—that I had come to ask for a reading. He pushed me into the committee-room where I had not been since my last explanation with Vacher.

" Gentlemen, here's good news ! " said he. " Here is Dumas who is bringing us a new play."

" A comedy or a tragedy ? " cried several voices.

" Thank you ! I have had enough of tragedies ! No, a comedy."

" Ah ! Hurrah ! You are a master of comedy ! "

" Is it because my works have always been dramas or tragedies that you say that ? "

" No ; but because there is always something of comedy in everything you do. The prologue to *Caligula*, for instance."

" Yes, I know. And the failure of that tragedy is due to its prologue."

" But what is *La Tour de Nesle* ? A comedy ? "

" Why not a vaudeville ? "

" Then you have got a comedy for us now ? "

" I have."

" And it is ready ? "

" Ready and waiting."

" Yes ; but what we mean is, *written* ? "

" Written ? No. There is not one word of it written."

" In that case, you have not come to ask for a reading ? "

" But I certainly have."

" For what date ? "

" For next Saturday."

" For next Saturday ! And not a word of your comedy written ! "

" Not one."

" You won't be ready by Saturday, then."

" Why not ? "

" You won't have time."

" That's my business."

" What a boaster you are ! "

" Why so ? "

" Well, you tell us that your comedy is ready when there is not a word of it written."

" To me a play is ready when it is all planned out in my head."

" And it is planned out ? "

" Entirely."

They burst out laughing again.

" Look here," said I, " I'll tell you one thing."

" What ? "

" Are the members of the management the same men as the members of the Committee for reading ? "

" Very nearly so."

" Shall I read my play to you, to-day ? "

" Without a manuscript ? "

" Yes."

" That would be curious."

" I will do it, upon one condition. The thing will count as a reading, and you shall vote on it at once."

" If only on account of the rarity of such a thing, gentlemen," said Vedel.

" By all means ! "

" Do you agree ? " said I.

" Agreed. Gentlemen, we'll begin ! "

" Will you have a glass of water ? "

" Thank you."

I took up a position leaning against the mantelpiece ; they gathered round in a circle and I began relating *Mademoiselle de Belle-Isle*. I was in my best vein and I did it full justice. At each act, I was greeted with a round of applause. After the fifth, I got two rounds.

" Well, gentlemen," said Vedel. " Shall we vote ? "

" Of course ! " all the members of the Committee answered.

They voted and *Mademoiselle de Belle-Isle* was accepted unanimously. Supposing I had fallen dead as I left the Committee, the Théâtre Français would never have got their play.

CHAPTER XV

REPORTS of what had happened soon spread abroad. I
received an invitation to dinner from Mademoiselle Mars.

" Ah ! So it's you ! " she said on seeing me.

" Of course it's me. Have I, by chance, mistaken the
day ? "

" No. Then you have written a comedy ? "

" Ah ! Don't scold me, my dear friend. One act
only is written and I should very much like to go no further
with it."

" Good ! Amiable as usual. Do I play in your
comedy ? "

" Well ! Who do you think is going to play in it ? "

" Who knows ! Authors are always so nice to me ! "

" If I may judge from what I have suffered myself, my
dear lady, I must say they have had some very hard times
at your hands."

" Oh, come ! And what part have you reserved for
me in your play ? "

" Whichever you choose."

" Answer my question."

" Good Lord ! And if I were to give you one which
would not suit you ? "

" Have you two leading parts ? "

" For my sins, unfortunately I have, mademoiselle."

" What sort of part is that of Madame de Prie ? "

" I see you have already heard that it ought to be
yours."

" Just so."

" So much the worse, since it is not the one you will
take."

" Then, do you want me to be Mademoiselle de Belle-
Isle ? "

" The deuce ! my dear friend, how well you are
informed ! "

" What do you expect ? Don't you know it's a miracle
to see you at the Théâtre Français ? and when you are
there it gets talked about. Now tell me which part will
suit me best ? "

Q

" You want to know which part you are to play, don't you ? "

" Yes."

" Well, you will play Mademoiselle de Belle-Isle."

" You have a way of answering that I find immensely irritating."

" Listen, my dear friend," said I. " Next Monday I am going to read to the actors ; I had to postpone my reading for two days. Will you come and dine with me next Sunday ?"

" Agreed."

" On Sunday evening I'll read to you *Mademoiselle de Belle-Isle*, and you shall choose ; but I must tell you beforehand, that you will play Mademoiselle de Belle-Isle."

" That is what you want me to do."

" Yes, I want it ; for the cast will be perfect with you as Mademoiselle de Belle-Isle ; Mademoiselle Mante as Madame de Prie ; Firmin as Richelieu, etc. Whereas if you played Madame de Prie I should have no one for the part of Mademoiselle de Belle-Isle."

" Why, you would have Mademoiselle Plessis."

" Is that your advice ? "

" I don't know the play as yet."

" Well, my dear friend, on Sunday you will make its acquaintance."

On the Sunday I brought the manuscript to Mademoiselle Mars. As soon as I entered the drawing-room I was taken aside and it was whispered in my ear :

" Tell her to play Madame de Prie ! . . . Tell her to play Madame de Prie ! . . . "

But Mademoiselle Mars's dame de compagnie, Julienne, herself an old actress of comedy, said to me :

" I warn you that if you give her the part of Madame de Prie, she won't take it."

" I know," said I. " Be easy."

" Very good," said Julienne."

I began reading. There was not a word uttered by Madame de Prie which did not enrapture every one ; on the other hand, Mademoiselle de Belle-Isle was coldly received. I was watching Mademoiselle Mars, and it was easy to see the truth of Julienne's remark, for Mademoiselle

Mars was listening intently to Gabrielle. At the end of
the play, every one gathered round her and praised the
character of Madame de Prie.

" Yes ! Yes ! " Mademoiselle Mars said, " very charming. It is a pity she does not appear in the fifth act ! . . .
Dumas."

" Mademoiselle ? "

" Do you think it would be possible to have Madame de
Prie reappear in the fifth act ? "

" No, mademoiselle."

" Why not ? "

" Because Mademoiselle de Belle-Isle's part would
suffer."

" Do you think so ? "

" Suppose you were to play Mademoiselle de Belle-
Isle, would you be pleased to see the interest in the fifth
act divided between you and Madame de Prie ? "

" Certainly not, if I were to act Mademoiselle de Belle-
Isle. It's true that from the point of view of the part—— "

" Well, you are going to play Mademoiselle de Belle-
Isle."

" Then," said Mademoiselle Mars, " you really wish it ? "

" Of course I do."

" You see, the author is master where the cast is concerned."

" And it has already been arranged."

" What ? Do they know down there ? "

" No ; but it is all fixed now ; for I was only waiting
for your approval."

Mademoiselle Mars looked askance at the list of the cast
and saw her name opposite that of Mademoiselle de Belle-
Isle.

" And you will not let yourself be persuaded ? " said
she.

" Now, am I, as a rule, persuaded with regard to my
cast ? " said I.

" Oh, certainly not by me ! "

" Mademoiselle de Belle-Isle is yours, madame, and you
will play Mademoiselle de Belle-Isle or *Mademoiselle de
Belle-Isle* shall not be acted.

Mademoiselle de Belle-Isle was played six weeks later,
and you all know with what success. But if I had accepted

the opinion of those who called themselves friends of Mademoiselle Mars, and had given the part of Mademoiselle de Belle-Isle to Mademoiselle Plessis, and that of Madame de Prie to Mademoiselle Mars, *Mademoiselle de Belle-Isle* would have been played at the Odéon, like *Christine*, or at the Porte Saint-Martin like *Antony*. But my insistance set me at variance, or nearly so, with the most influential members of the Committee of the Comédie Française, who wanted to get rid of Mademoiselle Mars, and who had even had funeral wreaths cast at her feet on the stage.

CHAPTER XVI

IN spite, or perhaps because of the success of *Mademoiselle de Belle-Isle*, I was not asked for another comedy. In consequence of the great injustice shown towards Mademoiselle Mars I had become deeply attached to her and resolved to stand by her to the very last. Naturally, as after the success of *Mademoiselle de Belle-Isle*, the Comédie did not ask me for another play, it was not for me to offer them one. Instead I had arranged to spend two or three years in Italy.

A few days before I left I met Mérimée at Cavé's house.

"Well met," said Mérimée. "I have not seen you for a long time, but I have seen *Mademoiselle de Belle-Isle*. I congratulate you very heartily, my dear fellow."

"Thank you! Congratulations from the author of *Colomba* and *Matteo Falcone* are something to be proud of."

"Why don't you write another comedy?"

"Because I have not been asked."

"What! you have not been asked?"

"No."

"Would you like to be asked?"

"What do you mean?"

"Would you like to be asked?"

"Very much."

"And if they ask you, will you write one?"

" My dear fellow, you know the saying : ' Whosoever has tasted drink, will drink ; whosoever has gambled, will gamble.' "

" Very well ! I take it upon myself to get them to ask you."

Three days later I received an invitation to dinner from M. de Rémusat, who was then Minister of the Home Department. I guessed that Mérimée was at the bottom of it, and I accepted the invitation. After dinner the minister drew me aside. " I am told you are going to Italy."

" Yes ; in a week or ten days."

" Would you have time between now and then to write a comedy for the Théâtre Français ? But I don't want to bother you at the last moment ; you have your passport and your packing to attend to. Send it on to us from Italy, will you ? "

" With pleasure ! But on one condition."

" If it is one of money, it is granted beforehand."

" Not at all ; it is one of *amour propre.*"

" Oho ! Well, let me hear it."

" That the reading before the Committee shall be a simple formality ; that the play is accepted from this moment, and that the rehearsals will begin eight days after the reading."

" Right."

" And you will send me a letter through Cavé setting out this agreement."

" I'll write it myself."

" All is well, then."

The following day I received a letter from M. de Rémusat in the sense arranged between us. I left, taking my letter with me.

After settling down in Florence, among my flowers in the Via-Rondinella, I bethought myself of my promise, not to the Théâtre Français, but to M. de Rémusat. At the back of my head I had an idea of a marriage in the time of Louis XV., not too original a subject for a play, but which, with the aid of some witty situations, could be made to serve. I set to work, and at the end of a month I wrote to Lockroy, asking him to read my comedy at the Théâtre Français.

Not only does Lockroy write charming plays such as *La Marraine, Un Duel sous Richelieu,* and *Le Chevalier du guet,* but he reads admirably. He is an " *empoigneur,*" to use the slang of the theatre. Lockroy rose to the occasion, read at his very best, and was refused unanimously.

In those days, telegraphy had not yet been discovered, and it took me eight days to hear the news. When I did hear, I immediately packed a portmanteau, put M. de Rémusat's letter in my pocket, and started. At the end of five days I was in Paris. Just time to take a bath and change my clothes, and I was off to the Théâtre Français. I had arrived at five in the afternoon, and at half-past eight I was at the theatre. In the corridor I met Mademoiselle Mars. " You ! You in Paris ? "

" Just arrived."

" Come, I must speak to you before you see any one else."

" Good ! You'll give me all the information I require."

" Oh ! I have a lot of nice things to tell you."

" I have no doubt."

And I followed Mademoiselle Mars who, having no change to make between the first and the second acts, was able to give me all her time.

" So you have been refused ? "

" Well, yes, so I have."

" Without being told why ? "

" I presume they found the play bad," said I, doing what I could to look as naïve as possible.

" But it's a good piece."

" What am I to think, then ? "

" My dear, you have been refused because you said that the part of the countess was to be mine. You indiscreet fellow."

" And—— "

" And as I am a great burden to them, they said : ' If she plays in a new part, it means another year of her.' "

" How ridiculous ! . . . Who will they have when you are gone ? "

" It will be as it was when Talma had gone. I told you not to mention my name ; but you could not hold your tongue. . . . What can we do now ? " . . .

" Don't be distressed."

" And the play is said to be charming."

" Oh, I never said so."

" No, that is what they say ; that is why I am so angry."

" Well ? "

" Well, isn't it too bad to lose a play in five acts ? "

" Perhaps we shan't lose it. Who knows ? "

" You really are astounding ! "

" You know, I am like Béranger : I have the greatest confidence in the deity who watches over simple souls."

" Since you are one of them. A plague on them."

" Mademoiselle Mars, you don't do me justice. If I were a plague on them, there wouldn't be one of them left."

I saluted her and I went into the lobby. No one seemed to know me, and I passed on into the secretary's office. Verteuil, the secretary of the Comédie Française, was there.

" Verteuil," said I, " does the Committee meet as usual on Saturday ? "

" Yes ; but, as luck has it, an extraordinary meeting is to be held to-morrow, Wednesday."

" Will you be so good as to let these gentlemen know that I will have the honour of paying them a visit ? "

" So you have come back to Paris ? "

" As you see, dear boy."

" You had a pleasant journey ? "

" Splendid ! "

" Then, to-morrow."

" To-morrow."

At two o'clock, the following day, I was announced to the gentlemen of the administration ; and on coming into the room, I saw long faces such as one sees in the house of mourning when the coffin is on the point of being borne away.

" Well, my boys ! " said I, beaming. " Here I am ! "

" So it seems."

" Haven't you any idea of why I have come ? "

" No ! . . . Indeed, no ! "

" I have come to ask when we are to begin the rehearsals of our play."

" Which one ? "

" *Un Mariage sous Louis XV.*"

" Don't you know what happened ? "

" No ! . . . Has something happened ? "

The members of the Committee looked at one another.

" Some misfortune ? " said I.

" You were refused."

" Indeed ! "

" Why, haven't you been told ? "

" Yes."

" Well, then ? "

" I would not believe it."

" You wouldn't believe it ? "

" No ! "

" And why wouldn't you believe it ? "

" For two reasons : first, I refuse to believe you refused the man who gave you *Henri III.* and *Mademoiselle de Belle-Isle,* two of the greatest successes you have ever had."

" And the second reason ? "

" Oh, you want a second one, because the first isn't sufficient for you ? Well, the other is that I have signed an agreement, not with you, gentlemen, but with the minister, and here it is, signed Rémusat. The eight days allowed after the reading are over. I am expecting my ticket for the rehearsals. Au revoir, gentlemen."

The next day I received the ticket. On the following Monday the rehearsals began.

CHAPTER XVII

Now, how did Mademoiselle Plessis come to take the part instead of Mademoiselle Mars ?

I am going to tell you in a few words.

A very good friend of mine who was looking after my interests in business matters, but who knew nothing whatever of the theatre world, thought Mademoiselle Plessis a very charming actress, in which he was quite right ; but he had also been told that Mademoiselle Mars was getting old, and he believed the report, in which he was wrong ; for who has genius like that of Mademoiselle Mars never

grows old. My friend, who was living in the country where
he kept a few goats, used to send, every morning, goats'
milk to Mademoiselle Plessis, who had a weak chest ; then,
in the evening, he would go to the lobby and people would
gather round him and say :

"Can you understand that old Mars, who, at the age of
sixty-five, plays the part of a girl of seventeen ? Really,
some one ought to tell her, to her face, that she is forty
years too old for the part."

These continual remarks made an impression on him,
and one day he answered :

"But if she ought to be told, why don't you tell her
yourselves ? "

"One of us ? She would say, as she always says, that
we want to get rid of her out of jealousy."

"Well, then," said my friend, "I will speak to her."

"You ? "

"Yes, I myself."

"You wouldn't dare."

"I will dare."

"When ? "

"Not later than to-morrow."

"Why not to-night ? "

"To-night ? "

"Yes. . . . Look, there she is going to her room."

"To-night ? "

"Ah ! now you draw back."

"I ? "

"You draw back ! "

"I ? "

"Yes, you."

"I am going ! "

And my friend, pushing his hat down over his eyes, went
straight to Mademoiselle Mars's room. She was changing
her dress.

"What is it ? " asked Mademoiselle Mars, holding her
chemise between her teeth.

"It is me, mademoiselle."

"Who are you ? "

My friend gave his name.

"Well, what do you want ? Why do you come here
without having been announced ? "

" I have come to say what none of your friends dare tell you, mademoiselle."

" What ? "

" That you are too old to play the part of the countess, and that you would do wisely in giving it to Mademoiselle Plessis."

" Mademoiselle Plessis shall have the part to-morrow, sir. No, leave me, if you please ; I must change."

The next day, Mademoiselle Mars sent back the part and announced that she would not renew her engagement with the Comédie Française.

And that is how it was that Mademoiselle Plessis, and not Mademoiselle Mars, acted the part of the countess in *Un Mariage sous Louis XV.*

CHAPTER XVIII

THE *Mariage sous Louis XV.* was first performed on the 1st of June, 1841. Its fair success, which in all probability would have been more considerable if Mademoiselle Mars, in taking the part of the countess, had made it the occasion of her last appearance, wounded no one's susceptibilities and consequently left me in good relations with the Comédie Française.

When I say " good relations," I mean nothing else.

I have just said that the success would have been more considerable with Mademoiselle Mars in the cast. Not that the part of the countess was not well played by Mademoiselle Plessis, on the contrary, she did it charmingly ; nevertheless, it would have been interesting to see Mademoiselle Mars in her last part, and the younger the part the greater the interest in it.

However, my relations with the five or six artists who acted the *Mariage sous Louis XV.* were excellent throughout ; and they had asked me to write them another play.

One day I went to tell them that the new play, *Les Demoiselles de Saint-Cyr*, was ready. It was written for the same cast, with the exception of Menjaud, himself an excellent artist, who in the interval had retired. The others were Firmin, Plessis, and Anaïs ; Brindeau and Régnier had not been in the *Mariage sous Louis XV.*

Everything went on smoothly. I was amazed ; for it was the first time that such a thing had happened. I was used to continual discussions with the Théâtre Français and I missed them ; it seemed as if I was on good terms with every one. Alas ! Surely I had declined very much in their estimation. It is true that on that point I soon climbed to a height I had never attained before. *Le Testament de César* * was responsible for that.

Either through ill will or through the ignorance of the producer, what would have taken me less than a month at the Théâtre Historique, absorbed the time of seventy rehearsals. Ah, dear reader, you will not be as cruel as Dido. You will not oblige me to renew my sufferings in relating them.

Monsieur Seveste was then the director. Since then he has died ; God rest his soul ! He nearly damned mine.

I was in such a state of exasperation, that as I left I swore never again would I enter these doors ; and for five years I kept my word.

One day I met Régnier, who said to me : " You ought to read a tale by Auguste Lafontaine ; you will find a subject in it for a blood-curdling drama for your Théâtre Historique."

I have great faith in Régnier's judgment. I searched three or four reading-rooms : Auguste Lafontaine romances, which delighted so many at the beginning of the nineteenth century, to-day are almost forgotten. At last I found the romance mentioned by Régnier, the title of which I have completely forgotten.

I did not even finish reading the first volume. Instead of the terrible drama to be found in the third or the fourth, I discovered material for a charming little comedy in the first.

I was too busy at the time with the Théâtre Historique to write a comedy in one act. I called my two young

* This play does not figure in Dumas' collected works.—EDITOR'S NOTE.

friends, Paul Bocage and Octave Feuillet, and describing my idea, I told them to set to work.

Their act completed, they took it to the Théâtre Historique, and at not finding me there, left it with Doligny. Eight days later the theatre closed its doors; and the manuscript of *Romulus* was lost in the wreck which swallowed the one great artistic effort of the last twenty-five years.

A year went by. Fifteen leagues out of Paris I had taken some shooting with my good and very dear friend the Count d'Orsay, four to five miles distant from Melun.

One day, or rather one evening, I left our shooting-box, which was called Mormans, too late to catch the last train from Melun. What can one do in Melun from ten o'clock at night to eight in the morning, when one can't sleep more than three to four hours in one's own bed and not at all in a strange one? I suddenly thought of *Romulus*.

"Why," said I to myself, "here I am with five to six hours on my hands; why not take advantage of it and write *Romulus* ?"

No sooner resolved than executed, to quote from the parody of *La Vestale*. I went out and bought paper and pens at a general store. On the question of writing materials I am quite a monomaniac. I cannot write unless I have the right kind of paper and pen, and, what is more, I use one special paper and pen for my romances, and another special paper and pen for my plays. I found what I wanted, or very nearly so; and I also got a small bottle of ink. The same craze applies to ink as well as to paper and pens; to me it would be quite impossible to use blue ink, even for writing my address.

I piled wood by the corner of the mantelpiece, and after having been provided with a sufficient supply of candles, I sat down to work at about eleven o'clock; and at seven in the morning I was writing the word *end*, that happy word, which to me is only the beginning of the next volume.

I left for Paris by the eight o'clock train. At nine my copyist had arrived. I had not read *Romulus* over again; corrections on one's own writing are badly done as a rule, and in my case I can't make them at all. Therefore I asked for a copy to be ready at the same hour next day.

My copyist made a grimace ; he had twenty-four hours only for copying what I had written in nine. However, he punctually appeared with it.

I read and corrected it ; then I had it copied a second and a third time, after which I sent for Régnier.

" My dear fellow," said I, " do you remember telling me once that I ought to make a blood-curdling drama out of a romance by Auguste Lafontaine ? "

" Yes, I do."

" Well, I have read the book."

" Indeed."

" And I have made a comedy in one act out of it which I believe is very amusing."

" Bravo ! Provided you have made something of it, that is all I want. Where is it ? "

" Here."

" When do you want a reading ? "

" My dear fellow, I read no more at the Comédie Française. I have written a play for you and not for Messieurs the actors of the Republic [we were then under the Republic] ; if you like to act the part, read it yourself, and let it be accepted as coming from a young man who has as yet written nothing."

" Such is your desire ? "

" My earnest desire."

" All right ; but you are prejudiced against the Comédie Française."

" I ? Not at all. I only say that instead of playing comedies, tragedies, and dramas, they play vaudevilles, that's all."

" Then," said Régnier changing the subject, " you give me full power ? "

" Yes, provided my name is not published."

" I give you my word of honour."

" All right, then."

Régnier went ; and I forgot about *Romulus*. Fifteen days later, I received a note from Régnier of two lines :

" The young man who has as yet written nothing has been accepted with acclamation. Rehearsal is arranged for Thursday next.

" Your devoted
" Régnier."

And it is true, the play was announced on the posters ; but an indiscretion was committed. By whom ? I don't know. But if the play had been written by a young man who had as yet done nothing, it would have been acted at once ; being as it was, the work of a man who has written sixty dramas, tragedies, and comedies, it remained for three years on the shelf. It had been written in one night, in October, 1851 ; and was performed on the 15th of January, 1854.

In the meantime, I had written two more comedies : *La Jeunesse de Louis XIV.* and *La Jeunesse de Louis XV.*, both of which had been prohibited by the censor.

This time, I tendered my resignation as playwright to the theatre of the rue de Richelieu, and I left that stage free to play the five-act vaudevilles of M. Scribe and the one-act tragedies of M. Latour Saint-Ybars.

Thus ended my Odyssey. Ulysses wandered for ten years ; I had been journeying for fifteen years longer. It is true I had one advantage over him ; I found no Penelope waiting for me at the end.

THE END.

PRINTED IN GREAT BRITAIN BY WILLIAM CLOWES AND SONS, LIMITED, LONDON AND BECCLES.

www.ingramcontent.com/pod-product-compliance
Lightning Source LLC
Chambersburg PA
CBHW020753250626
47155CB00003B/1044